PRAISE FOR GEORGE PELECANOS'S

THE MARTINI SHOT

"Brisk, hard-boiled....It's well known that George Pelecanos has a terrific ear for street talk, and that his crime novels...sound as credible and unforced as they do cutting-edge....*The Martini Shot* shows that his ear for movie-set argot is just as good....One of Pelecanos's freshest and most original recent works." —Janet Maslin, *New York Times*

"Bracing and witty....An inventive study of deception and fakery—one of Pelecanos's best works, at any length." —Mark Athitakis, *Washington Post*

"Fast, dark, and dangerous....The gritty world Pelecanos knows so well provides ample fodder for the vignettes in this book; the characters are strong and the dialogue is sharp." —Tim Alamenciak, *Toronto Star*

"George Pelecanos is widely considered to be one of the best crime novelists going....His writing is properly hard-boiled, his heroes are attractively flawed, and his villains leave trails of blood from here to yonder. But even at his most gripping... he sets his aims high, bringing a sociologist's concerns to the street-level dramas that play out in his hometown of Washington, D.C., among blacks and whites and immigrants, cops and informants and dealers, working-class stiffs and educators and the unconscionably rich." —Lloyd Sachs, *Chicago Tribune*

"Outstanding." *—Esquire*

"An exemplar of what Pelecanos is best at: twisting plots that play on familiar genre tropes, street-level dialogue, and flashes of startling violence.... *The Martini Shot* feels familiar, like the welcome company of old friends."
—Steven W. Beattie, Globe and Mail

"George Pelecanos is among our most prolific—and compelling—crime novelists, a writer who evokes his hometown of Washington, D.C., much as Dennis Lehane does with Boston or Michael Connelly Los Angeles: as a character in its own right.... Here we see what makes Pelecanos's best writing so resonant: the sense of longing, of miscommunication, the way love does not enlarge us but rather makes us small."
—David L. Ulin, Los Angeles Times

"The undisputed king of D.C. noir. Pelecanos...has been as resourceful and inventive as his heroes, and this collection showcases his versatility." *—Kirkus Reviews*

"Pelecanos knows his terrain intimately and loves it, despite its pockmarks and bullet holes and his characters' bleak fortunes." *—Bethanne Patrick, The Washingtonian*

"Pelecanos is always readable. And when he offers us a glimpse of the choiceless choices of the inner city in places such as Baltimore and Washington, D.C., he can touch greatness." *—Charles Finch, USA Today*

"*The Martini Shot* serves as both an introduction to Pelecanos's dark, unblinking vision and a reason to stay until the night's bitter end....A must-have for newcomers and longtime fans alike." —Joe Hartlaub, BookReporter.com

"The best pieces in this collection do linger in memory...and they showcase an author whose gritty prose style and sympathetic characterization have remained remarkably consistent." —Michael Pucci, *Library Journal*

"Brief and searing tales of loners and losers, drug addicts and snitches, the kind of stories where you can smell the whiff of failure and hear the sigh of dirty pavements, feel the grit of the city Pelecanos writes about so well." —Cameron Woodhead, *Sydney Morning Herald*

"Pelecanos's ability to capture distinct voices—from the banter of a married couple to an ambitious African-American kid whose love of basketball helps him temporarily escape his life—remains strong.... *The Martini Shot* will keep readers turning the pages." —Elizabeth Rabin, *Fredericksburg Free Lance-Star*

The
MARTINI
SHOT

A Novella and Stories

GEORGE PELECANOS

BACK BAY BOOKS

LITTLE, BROWN AND COMPANY

NEW YORK BOSTON LONDON

To Charles C. Mish and Estelle Petrulakis

Copyright © 2015 by Spartan Productions, Inc.

All rights reserved. In accordance with the U.S. Copyright Act of 1976, the scanning, uploading, and electronic sharing of any part of this book without the permission of the publisher constitute unlawful piracy and theft of the author's intellectual property. If you would like to use material from the book (other than for review purposes), prior written permission must be obtained by contacting the publisher at permissions@hbgusa.com. Thank you for your support of the author's rights.

Back Bay Books / Little, Brown and Company
Hachette Book Group
1290 Avenue of the Americas, New York, NY 10104
littlebrown.com

Originally published in hardcover by Little, Brown and Company, January 2015
First Back Bay paperback edition, March 2016

Back Bay Books is an imprint of Little, Brown and Company, a division of Hachette Book Group, Inc. The Back Bay Books name and logo are trademarks of Hachette Book Group, Inc.

The publisher is not responsible for websites (or their content) that are not owned by the publisher.

"When You're Hungry" first appeared in *Unusual Suspects* (Vintage Crime, 1996); "String Music" first appeared in *Murder at the Foul Line* (Mysterious Press, 2006); "The Confidential Informant" first appeared in *D.C. Noir* (Akashic Books, 2006); "The Dead Their Eyes Implore Us" first appeared in *Measures of Poison* (Dennis McMillan Publications, 2002); "Plastic Paddy" first appeared in *Men from Boys* (William Heinemann Ltd., 2003); "Chosen" first appeared in the ebook edition of *The Cut* (Reagan Arthur Books, 2011).

Library of Congress Cataloging-in-Publication Data
Pelecanos, George P.
  [Works. Selections]
  The martini shot : a novella and stories / George Pelecanos. — First edition.
    pages cm
  ISBN 978-0-316-28437-0 (hardcover) / 978-0-316-28438-7 (paperback)
  I. Pelecanos, George P. II. Title.
  PS3566.E354A6 2015
  813'.54—dc23   2014019611

10 9 8 7 6 5 4 3 2 1

RRD-C

Book designed by Marie Mundaca
Printed in the United States of America

CONTENTS

The
MARTINI
SHOT

THE CONFIDENTIAL INFORMANT

I WAS IN the waiting area of the VA hospital emergency room off North Capitol Street, seeing to my father, when Detective Tony Barnes hit me back on my cell. My father had his head down on the crossbar of his walker, and it was going to be a while before someone came and called his name. I walked the phone outside and lit myself a smoke.

"What's goin on, Verdon?" said Barnes.

"Need to talk to you about Rico Jennings."

"Go ahead."

"Not on the phone." I wasn't about to give Barnes no information without feeling some of his cash money in my hand.

"When can I see you?"

"My pops took ill. I'm still dealin with that, so…make it nine. You know where."

Barnes cut the line. I smoked my cigarette down to the filter and went back inside.

My father was moaning when I took a seat beside him.

Goddamn this and goddamn that, saying it under his breath. We'd been out here for a few hours. A girl with a high ass moving inside purple drawstring pants took our information when we came in, and later a Korean nurse got my father's vitals in what she called the triage room, asking questions about his history and was there blood in his stools and stuff like that. But we had not seen a doctor yet.

Most of the men in the waiting room were in their fifties and above. A couple had walkers and many had canes; one dude had an oxygen tank beside him with a clear hose running up under his nose. Every single one of them was wearing some kinda lid. It was cold out, but it was a style thing, too.

Everyone looked uncomfortable, and no one working in the hospital seemed to be in a hurry to do something about it. The security guards gave you a good eye-fuck when you came through the doors, which kinda told you straight off what the experience was going to be like inside. I tried to go down to the cafeteria to get something to eat, but nothing they had was appealing, and some of it looked damn near dirty. I been in white people's hospitals, like Sibley, on the high side of town, and I know they don't treat those people the way they was treating these veterans. I'm saying, this shit here was a damn disgrace.

But they did take my father eventually.

A white nurse named Matthew, redheaded dude with Pop-eye forearms, hooked him up to one of those heart machines, then found a vein in my father's arm and took three vials of blood. Pops had complained about being "woozy" that morning. He gets fearful since his stroke, which paralyzed him on one side. His mind is okay, but he can't go nowhere without his walker, not even to the bathroom.

I looked at him lying there in the bed, his wide shoulders and the hardness of his hands. Even at sixty, even after his stroke, he is stronger than me. I know I will never feel like his equal. What with him being a Vietnam veteran, and a dude who had a reputation for taking no man's shit in the street. And me...well, me being me.

"The doctor's going to have a look at your blood, Leon," said Matthew. I guess he didn't know that in our neighborhood my father would be called "Mr. Leon" or "Mr. Coates" by someone younger than him. As Matthew walked away, he began to sing a church hymn.

My father rolled his eyes.

"Bet you'd rather have that Korean girl taking care of you, Pops," I said, with a conspiring smile.

"That gal's from the Philippines," said my father, sourly. Always correcting me and shit.

"Whateva."

My father complained about everything for the next hour. I listened to him, and the junkie veteran in the next stall over who was begging for something to take away his pain, and the gags of another dude who was getting a stomach tube forced down his throat. Then an Indian doctor, name of Singh, pulled the curtain back and walked into our stall. He told my father that there was nothing in his blood or on the EKG to indicate that there was cause for alarm.

"So all this *bull*shit was for nothin?" said my father, like he was disappointed he wasn't sick.

"Go home and get some rest," said Dr. Singh, in a cheerful way. He smelled like one them restaurants they got, but he was all right.

Matthew returned, got my father back into his street clothes, and filled out the discharge forms.

"The Lord loves you, Leon," said Matthew, before he went off to attend to someone else.

"Get me out this motherfucker," said my father. I fetched a wheelchair from where they had them by the front desk.

I drove my father's Buick to his house, on the 700 block of Quebec Street, not too far from the hospital, in Park View. It took a while to get him up the steps of his row house. By the time he stepped onto the brick-and-concrete porch, he was gasping for breath. He didn't go out much anymore, and this was why.

Inside, my mother, Martina Coates, got him situated in his own wheelchair, positioned in front of his television set, where he sits most of his waking hours. She waits on him all day and sleeps lightly at night in case he falls out of his bed. She gives him showers and even washes his ass. My mother is a church woman who believes that her reward will come in heaven. It's 'cause of her that I'm still allowed to live in my father's house.

The television was real loud, the way he likes to play it since his stroke. He watches them old games on that replay channel on ESPN.

"Franco Harris!" I shouted, pointing at the screen. "Boy was *beast.*"

My father didn't even turn his head. I would have watched some of that old Steelers game with him if he had asked me to, but he didn't, so I went upstairs to my room.

It is my older brother's room as well. James's bed is on the opposite wall, and his basketball and football trophies, from when he was a kid all the way through high school, are still on his dresser. He made good after Howard Law, real good, matter of fact. He lives over there in Crestwood, west of 16th, with his pretty redbone wife and their two light-skinned kids. He doesn't come around this neighborhood all that much, though it ain't but fifteen minutes away. He wouldn't have drove my father over to the VA hospital, either, or waited around in that place all day. He would have said he was too busy, that he couldn't get out "the firm" that day. Still, my father brags on James to all his friends. He got no cause to brag on me.

I changed into some warm shit, and put my smokes and matches into my coat. I left my cell in my bedroom, as it needed to be charged. When I got downstairs, my mother asked me where I was going.

"I got a little side thing I'm workin on," I said, loud enough for my father to hear.

My father kinda snorted and chuckled under his breath. He might as well had gone ahead and said, "Bullshit," but he didn't need to. I wanted to tell him more, but that would be wrong. If my thing was to be uncovered, I wouldn't want nobody coming back on my parents.

I zipped my coat and left out the house.

*   *   *

It had begun to snow some. Flurries swirled in the cones of light coming down from the streetlamps. I walked down to Giant Liquors on Georgia and bought a pint of Popov, and hit the vodka as I walked back up Quebec. I crossed Warder Street, and kept on toward Park Place. The houses got a little nicer here as the view improved. Across Park were the grounds of the Soldiers' Home, bordered by a black iron, spear-topped fence. It was dark out, and the clouds were blocking any kind of moonlight, but I knew what was over there by heart. I had cane-pole fished that lake many times as kid, and chased them geese they had in there, too. Now they had three rows of barbed wire strung out over them spear-tops, to keep out the kids, and the young men who liked to lay their girlfriends out straight on that soft grass.

Me and Sondra used to hop that fence some evenings, the summer before I dropped out of Roosevelt High. I'd bring some weed, a bottle of screw-top wine, and my Sony Walkman cassette player, and we'd go down to the other side of that lake and chill. I'd let her listen to the headphones while I hit my smoke. I had made mix-tapes off my records, stuff she was into, like Bobby Brown and Tone Lōc. I'd tell her about the cars I was gonna be driving, and the custom suits I'd be wearing, soon as I got a good job. How I didn't need no high school diploma to get those things or to prove how smart I was. She looked at me like she believed it. Sondra had some pretty brown eyes.

She married a personal injury lawyer with a storefront of-fice up in Shepherd Park. They live in a house in PG County, in one of those communities got gates. I seen her once, when she came back to the neighborhood to visit her moms, who still stays down on Luray. She was bum-rushing her kids into the house, like they might get sick if they breathed this Park View air. She saw me walking down the street and turned her head away, trying to act like she didn't recognize me. It didn't cut me. She can rewrite history in her mind if she wants to, but her fancy husband ain't never gonna have what I did, 'cause I had that pussy when it was new.

I stepped into the alley that runs north-south between Princeton and Quebec. My watch, a looks-like-a-Rolex I bought on the street for ten dollars, read 9:05. Detective Barnes was late. I unscrewed the top of the Popov and had a pull. It burned nice. I tapped it again and lit myself a smoke.

"Psst. Hey, yo."

I looked up over my shoulder, where the sound was. A boy leaned on the lip of one of those second-floor, wood-back porches that ran out to the alley. Behind him was a door with curtains on the window. A bicycle tire was showing beside the boy. Kids be putting their bikes up on porches around here so they don't get stole.

"What you want?" I said.

"Nothin you got," said the boy. He looked to be about twelve, tall and skinny, with braided hair under a black skully.

"Then get your narrow ass back inside your house."

"You the one loiterin."

"I'm mindin my own, is what I'm doing. Ain't you got no homework or nothin?"

"I did it at study hall."

"Where you go, MacFarland Middle?"

"Yeah."

"I went there, too."

"So?"

I almost smiled. He had a smart mouth on him, but he had heart.

"What you doin out here?" said the kid.

"Waitin on someone," I said.

Just then Detective Barnes's unmarked drove by slow. He saw me but kept on rolling. I knew he'd stop, up aways on the street.

"Awright, little man," I said, pitching my cigarette aside and slipping my pint into my jacket pocket. I could feel the kid's eyes on me as I walked out the alley.

I slid into the backseat of Barnes's unmarked, a midnight-blue Crown Vic. I kinda laid down on the bench, my head against the door, below the window line so no one on the outside could see me. It's how I do when I'm rolling with Barnes.

He turned right on Park Place and headed south. I didn't need to look out the window to know where he was going. He drives down to Michigan Avenue, heads east past the Children's Hospital, then continues on past North Capitol and then Catholic U, into Brookland and beyond. Eventually he turns around and comes back the same way.

"Stayin warm, Verdon?"

"Tryin to."

Barnes, a broad-shouldered dude with a handsome face, had a deep voice. He favored Hugo Boss suits and cashmere overcoats. Like many police, he wore a thick mustache.

"So," I said. "Rico Jennings."

"Nothin on my end," said Barnes, with a shrug. "You?"

I didn't answer him. It was a dance we did. His eyes went to the rearview and met mine. He held out a twenty over the seat, and I took it.

"I think y'all are headed down the wrong road," I said.

"How so?"

"Heard you been roustin corner boys on Morton and canvassing down there in the Eights."

"I'd say that's a pretty good start, given Rico's history."

"Wasn't no drug thing, though."

"Kid was in it. He had juvenile priors for possession and distribution."

"Why they call 'em priors? That was before the boy got on the straight. Look, I went to grade school with his mother. I been knowin Rico since he was a kid."

"*What* do you know?"

"Rico was playin hard for a while, but he grew out of it. He got into some big brother thing at my mother's church, and he turned his back on his past. I mean, that boy was in the AP program up at Roosevelt. Advanced placement, you know, where they got adults, teachers and shit, walkin with you every step of the way. He was on the way to college."

"So why'd someone put three in his chest?"

"What I heard was, it was over a girl."

I was giving him a little bit of the truth. When the whole truth came out, later on, he wouldn't suspect that I had known more.

Barnes swung a U-turn, which rocked me some. We were on the way back to Park View.

"Keep going," said Barnes.

"Tryin to tell you, Rico had a weakness for the ladies."

"Who doesn't."

"It was worse than that. Girl's privates made Rico stumble. Word is, he'd been steady-tossin this young thing, turned out to be the property of some other boy. Rico knew it, but he couldn't stay away. That's why he got dropped."

"By who?"

"Huh?"

"You got a name on the hitter?"

"Nah." Blood came to my ears and made them hot. It happened when I got stressed.

"How about the name of the girlfriend."

I shook my head. "I'd talk to Rico's mother, I was you. You'd think she'd know somethin 'bout the girls her son was running with, right?"

"You'd think," said Barnes.

"All I'm sayin is, I'd start with her."

"Thanks for the tip."

"I'm just sayin."

Barnes sighed. "Look, I've already talked to the mother. I've talked to Rico's neighbors and friends. We've been through his bedroom as well. We didn't find any love notes or even so much as a picture of a girl."

I had the photo of his girlfriend. Me and Rico's aunt, Leticia, had gone up into the boy's bedroom at that wake they had, while his mother was downstairs crying and stuff with her church friends in the living room. I found a picture of the girl, name of Flora Lewis, in the dresser drawer, under his socks and underwear. It was one of them mall photos the girls like to get done, then give to their boyfriends. Flora was sitting on a cube, with columns around her and shit, against a background, looked like laser beams shooting across a blue sky. Flora had tight jeans on and a shirt with thin straps, and she had let one of the straps kinda fall down off her shoulder to let the tops of her little titties show. The girls all trying to look like sluts now, you ask me. On the back of the photo was a note in her handwriting, said, "How U like me like this? xxoo, Flora." Leticia recognized Flora from around the way, even without the name printed on the back.

"Casings at the scene were from a nine," said Barnes, bringing me out of my thoughts. "We ran the markings through IBIS and there's no match."

"What about a witness?"

"You kiddin? There wasn't one, even if there was one."

"Always someone knows somethin," I said, as I felt the car slow and come to a stop.

"Yeah, well." Barnes pushed the trans arm up into Park. "I caught a double in Columbia Heights this morning. So I sure would like to clean this Jennings thing up."

"You *know* I be out there askin around," I said. "But it gets expensive, tryin to make conversation in bars, buyin beers and stuff to loosen them lips…"

Barnes passed another twenty over the seat without a word. I took it. The bill was damp for some reason, and limp like a dead thing. I put it in the pocket of my coat.

"I'm gonna be askin around," I said, like he hadn't heard me the first time.

"I know you will, Verdon. You're a good CI. The best I ever had."

I didn't know if he meant it or not, but it made me feel kinda guilty, backdooring him the way I was planning to do. But I had to look out for my own self for a change. The killer would be got, that was the important thing. And I would be flush.

"How your sons, Detective?"

"They're good. Looking forward to playing Pop Warner again."

"Hmph," I said.

He was divorced, like most homicide police. Still, I knew he loved his kids.

That was all. It felt like it was time to go.

"I'll get up with you later, hear?"

Barnes said, "Right."

I rose up off the bench, kinda looked around some, and got out the Crown Vic. I took a pull out the Popov bottle as I headed for my father's house. I walked down the block, my head hung low.

Up in my room, I found my film canister under the T-shirts in my dresser. I shook some weed out into a wide paper, rolled a joint tight as a cigarette, and slipped it into my pack of Newports. The vodka had lifted me some, and I was ready to get up further.

I glanced in the mirror over my dresser. One of my front teeth was missing from when some dude down by the Black Hole—said he didn't like the way I looked—had knocked it out. There was gray in my patch and in my hair. My eyes looked bleached. Even under my bulky coat, it was plain I had lost weight. I looked like one of them defectives you pity or ridicule on the street. But shit, there wasn't a thing I could do about it tonight.

I went by my mother's room, careful to step soft. She was in there, in bed by now, watching but not watching television on her thirteen-inch color, letting it keep her company, keeping the sound down low so she could hear my father if he called out to her from the first floor.

Down in the living room, the television still played loud, a black-and-white film of the Liston-Clay fight, which my father had spoke of often. He was missing the fight now. His chin was resting on his chest, and his useless hand was kinda curled up like a claw in his lap. The light from the television grayed his face. His eyelids weren't shut all the way, and the whites showed. Aside from his chest, which was moving some, he looked like he was dead.

Time will just fuck you up.

I can remember this one evening with my father, back around '74. He had been home from the war for a while and was working for the Government Printing Office at the time. We were over there on the baseball field, on Princeton, near Park View Elementary. I musta been around six or seven. My father's shadow was long and straight, and the sun was throwing a warm gold color on the green of the field. He was still in his work clothes, with his sleeves rolled up to his elbows. His natural was full and his chest filled the fabric of his shirt. He was tossing me this small football, one of them K2s he had bought me, and telling me to run toward him after I caught it, to see if I could break his tackle. He wasn't gonna tackle me for real; he just wanted me to get a feel for the game. But I wouldn't run to him. I guess I didn't want to get hurt, was what it was. He got aggravated with me eventually, lost his patience and said it was time to get on home. I believe he quit on me that day. At least, that's the way it seems to me now.

I wanted to go over to his wheelchair, not hug him or nothing that dramatic, but maybe give him a pat on his shoulder. But if he woke up he would ask me what was wrong, why was I touching him, all that. So I didn't go near him. I had to meet with Leticia about this thing we was doing, anyway. I stepped light on the clear plastic runner my mother had on the carpet and closed the door quiet on my way out the house.

On the way to Leticia's, I cupped a match against the snow and fired up the joint. I drew on it deep and held it in my lungs. I hit it regular as I walked south.

My head was beginning to smile as I neared the house Leticia stayed in, over on Otis Place. I wet my fingers in the snow and squeezed the ember of the joint to put it out. I wanted to save some for Le-tee. We were gonna celebrate.

The girl, Flora, had witnessed the murder of Rico Jennings. I knew this because we, Leticia and me that is, had found her and made her tell what she knew. Well, Leticia had. She can be a scary woman when she wants to be. She broke hard on Flora, got up in her face and bumped her in an alley. Flora cried and talked. She had been out walking with Rico that night, back up on Otis, round the elementary, when this boy, Marquise

Roberts, rolled up on them in a black Caprice. Marquise and his squad got out the car and surrounded Rico, shoved him some and shit like that. Flora said it seemed like that was all they was gonna do. Then Marquise drew an automatic and put three in Rico, one while Rico was on his feet and two more while Marquise was standing over him. Flora said Marquise was smiling as he pulled the trigger.

"Ain't no doubt now, is it," said Marquise, turning to Flora. "You mine."

Marquise and them got back in their car and rode off, and Flora ran home. Rico was dead, she explained. Wouldn't do him no good if she stayed at the scene.

Flora said that she would never talk to the police. Leticia told her she'd never have to, that as Rico's aunt, she just needed to know.

Now we had a killer and a wit. I could have gone right to Detective Barnes, but I knew about that anonymous tip line in the District, the Crime Solvers thing. We decided that Leticia would call and get that number assigned to her, the way they do, and she would eventually collect the one thousand dollar reward, which we'd split. Flora would go into witness security, where they'd move her to Far Northeast or something like that. So she wouldn't get hurt or be too far from her family, and Leticia and me would get five hundred each. It wasn't much, but it was more than I'd ever had in my pocket at one time. More important to me was that someday, when Marquise was put away and his boys fell, like they always do, I could go to my mother and father and tell them that I, Verdon Coates, had solved a homicide. And it would be worth the wait, just to see the look of pride on my father's face.

I got to the row house on Otis where Leticia stayed at. It was on the 600 block, those low-slung old places they got painted gray. She lived on the first floor.

Inside the common hallway, I came to her door. I knocked and took off my knit cap and shook the snow off it, waiting for her to come. The door opened, but only a crack. It stopped as the chain of the slide bolt went taut. Leticia looked at me over the chain. I could see dirt tracks on the part of her face that showed, from where she'd been crying. She was a hard-looking woman, always had been, even when she was young. I'd never seen her so shook.

"Ain't you gonna let me in?"

"No."

"What's wrong with you, girl?"

"I don't want to see you and you ain't comin in."

"I got some nice smoke, Leticia."

"Leave outta here, Verdon."

I listened to the bass of a rap thing, coming from another apartment. Behind it, a woman and a man were having an argument.

"What happened?" I said. "Why you been cryin?"

"Marquise came," said Leticia. "Marquise made me cry."

My stomach dropped some. I tried not to let it show on my face.

"That's right," said Leticia. "Flora musta told him about our conversation. Wasn't hard for him to find Rico's aunt."

"He threaten you?"

"He never did, direct. Matter of fact, that boy was smilin the whole time he spoke to me." Leticia's lip trembled. "We came to an understandin, Verdon."

"What he say?"

"He said that Flora was mistaken. That she wasn't there the night Rico was killed, and she would swear to it in court. And that if I thought different, I was mistaken, too."

"You sayin that you're mistaken, Leticia?"

"That's right. I been mistaken about this whole thing."

"Leticia—"

"I ain't tryin to get myself killed for five hundred dollars, Verdon."

"Neither am I."

"Then you better go somewhere for a while."

"Why would I do that?"

Leticia said nothing.

"You give me up, Leticia?"

Leticia cut her eyes away from mine. "Flora," she said, almost a whisper. "She told him 'bout some skinny, older-lookin dude who was standin in the alley the day I took her for bad."

"You gave me *up*?"

Leticia shook her head slowly and pushed the door shut. It closed with a soft click.

I didn't pound on the door or nothin like that. I stood there stupidly for some time, listening to the rumble of the bass and the argument still going between the woman and man. Then I walked out the building.

The snow was coming down heavy. I couldn't go home, so I walked toward the Avenue instead.

*   *   *

I had finished the rest of my vodka and dropped the bottle to the curb by the time I got down to Georgia. A Third District cruiser was parked on the corner, with two officers inside it, drinking coffee from paper cups. It was late, and with the snow and the cold there wasn't too many people out. The Spring Laundromat, used to be a Roy Rogers or sumshit like it, was packed with men and women, just standing around, getting out of the weather. I could see their outlines behind that nicotine-stained glass, most of them barely moving under those dim lights.

This time of night, many of the shops had closed. I was hungry, but Morgan's Seafood was shut down, and Hunger Stopper, had those good fish sandwiches, was dark inside. What I needed was a drink of liquor, but Giant had locked its doors. I could have gone to the titty bar between Newton and Otis, but I had been roughed up in there too many times.

I crossed over to the west side of Georgia and walked south. I passed a midget in a green suede coat who stood where he always did, under the awning of the Dollar General. I had worked there for a couple of days, stocking shit on shelves.

The businesses along here were like a roll call of my personal failures. The Murray's meat and produce, the car wash, the Checks Cashed joint, they had given me a chance. In all these places, I had lasted just a short while.

I neared the GA market, down by Irving. A couple of young men came toward me, buried inside the hoods of their North Face coats, hard of face, then smiling as they got a look at me.

"Hey, slim," said one of the young men. "Where you get that vicious coat at? *Baby* Gap?" Him and his friend laughed.

I didn't say nothing back. I got this South Pole coat I bought off a dude, didn't want it no more. I wasn't about to rock a North Face. Boys put a gun in your grill for those coats down here.

I walked on.

The market was crowded inside. I stepped around some dudes and saw a man I knew, Robert Taylor, back by where they keep the wine. He was lifting a bottle of it off the shelf. He was in the middle of his thirties, but he looked fifty-five.

"Robo," I said.

"Verdon."

We did a shoulder-to-shoulder thing and patted backs. I had been knowing him since grade school. Like me, he had seen better days. He looked kinda under it now. He held up a bottle of fortified, turned it so I could see the label, like them waiters do in high-class restaurants.

"I sure could use a taste," said Robert. "Only, I'm a little light this evening."

"I got you, Robo."

"Look, I'll hit you back on payday."

"We're good."

I picked up a bottle of Night Train for myself and moved toward the front of the market. Robert grabbed the sleeve of my coat and held it tight. His eyes, most time full of play, were serious.

"Verdon."

"What?"

"I been here a couple of hours, staying dry and shit. Lotta activity in here tonight. You just standin around, you be hearin things."

"Say what you heard."

"Some boys was in here earlier, lookin for you."

I felt that thing in my stomach.

"Three young men," said Robert. "One of 'em had them silver things on his teeth. They was describin you, your build and shit, and that hat you always be wearin."

He meant my knit cap, with the Bullets logo, had the two hands for the double *l*'s, going up for the rebound. I had been wearing it all winter long. I had been wearing it the day we talked to Flora in the alley.

"Anyone tell them who I was?"

Robert nodded sadly. "I can't lie. Some Bama did say your name."

"Shit."

"I ain't say *nothin* to those boys, Verdon."

"C'mon, man. Let's get outta here."

We went up the counter. I used the damp twenty Barnes had handed me to pay for the two bottles of wine and a fresh pack of cigarettes. While the squarehead behind the Plexiglas was bagging my shit and making my change, I picked up a scratched-out lottery ticket and pencil off the scarred counter, turned the ticket over, and wrote around the blank edges. What I wrote was: *Marquise Roberts killed Rico Jennings.* And: *Flora Lewis was there.*

I slipped the ticket into the pocket of my jeans and got my change. Me and Robert Taylor walked out the shop.

Out on the snow-covered sidewalk I handed Robert his bottle of fortified. I knew he'd be heading west into Columbia Heights, where he stays with an ugly-looking woman and her kids.

"Thank you, Verdon."

"Ain't no thing."

"What you think? Skins gonna do it next year?"

"They got Coach Gibbs. They get a couple receivers with hands, they gonna be all right."

"No doubt." Robert lifted his chin. "You be safe, hear?"

He went on his way. I crossed Georgia Avenue, quickstepping out the way of a Ford that was fishtailing in the street. I thought about getting rid of my Bullets cap, in case Marquise and them came up on me, but I was fond of it, and I could not let it go.

I unscrewed the top off the Night Train as I went along, taking a deep pull and feeling it warm my chest. Heading up Otis, I saw ragged silver dollars drifting down through the light of the streetlamps. The snow capped the roofs of parked cars and it had gathered on the branches of the trees. No one was out. I stopped to light the rest of my joint. I got it going and hit it as I walked up the hill.

I planned to go home in a while, through the alley door, when I thought it was safe. But for now, I needed to work on my head. Let my high come like a friend and tell me what to do.

I stood on the east side of Park Place, my hand on the fence bordering the Soldiers' Home, staring into the dark. I had smoked all my reefer and drunk my wine. It was quiet, nothing but the hiss of snow. And "Get Up Everybody," that old Salt-N-Pepa joint, playing in my head. Sondra liked that one. She'd dance to it, with my headphones on, over by that lake they got. With the geese running around it, in the summertime.

"Sondra," I whispered. And then I chuckled some, and said, "I am high."

I turned and walked back to the road, tripping a little as I stepped off the curb. As I got onto Quebec, I saw a car coming down Park Place, sliding a little, rolling too fast. It was a dark color, and it had them Chevy headlights with the rectangle fog lamps on the sides. I patted my pockets, knowing all the while that I didn't have my cell.

I ducked into the alley off Quebec. I looked up at that rear porch with the bicycle tire leaning up on it, where that boy stayed. I saw a light behind the porch door's window. I scooped up snow, packed a ball of it tight, and threw it up at that window. I waited. The boy parted the curtains and put his face up on the glass, his hands cupped around his eyes so he could see.

"Little man!" I yelled, standing by the porch. "Help me out!"

He cold-eyed me and stepped back. I knew he recognized me. But I guess he had seen me go toward the police unmarked, and he had made me for a snitch. In his young mind, it was the worst thing a man could be. Behind the window all went dark. As it did, headlights swept the alley, and a car came in with the light. The car was black, and it was a Caprice.

I turned and bucked.

I ran my ass off down that alley, my old Timbs struggling for purchase in the snow. As I ran, I pulled on trashcans, knocking them over so they would block the path of the Caprice. I didn't look back. I heard the boys in the car, yelling at me and shit, and I heard them curse as they had to slow down. Soon I was out of the alley, on Princeton Place, running free.

I went down Princeton, cut right on Warder, hung another right on Otis. There was an alley down there, back behind the ball field, shaped like a T. It would be hard for them to navigate back in there. They couldn't surprise me or nothing like that.

I walked into the alley. Straight off, a couple of dogs began to bark. Folks kept 'em, shepherd mixes and rottweilers with heads big as cattle, for security. Most of them was inside, on account of the weather, but not all. There were some who stayed out all the time, and they were loud. Once they got going, they would bark themselves crazy. They were letting Marquise know where I was.

I saw the Caprice drive real slow down Otis, its headlights off, and I felt my ears grow hot. I got down in a crouch, pressed myself against a chain-link fence behind someone's row house. My stomach flipped all the way, and I had one of them throw-up burps. Stuff came up, and I swallowed it down.

I didn't care if it was safe or not; I needed to get my ass home. Couldn't nobody hurt me there. In my bed, the same bed where I always slept, near my brother, James. With my mother and father down the hall.

I listened to a boy calling out my name. Then another boy, from somewhere else, did the same. I could hear the laughter in their voices. I shivered some and bit down on my lip.

Use the alphabet, you get lost. That's what my father told me when I was a kid. Otis, Princeton, Quebec...I was three streets away.

I turned at the T of the alley and walked down the slope. The dogs were out of their minds, growling and barking, and I went past them and kept my eyes straight ahead. At the bottom of the alley, I saw a boy in a thick coat, hoodie up. He was waiting on me.

I turned around and ran back from where I came. Even with the sounds of the dogs, I could hear myself panting, trying to get my breath. I rounded the T and made it back to Otis, where I cut and headed for the baseball field. I could cross that and be on Princeton. When I got there, I'd be one block closer to my home.

I stepped up onto the field. I walked regular, tryin to calm myself down. I didn't hear a car or anything else. Just the snow crunching beneath my feet.

And then a young man stepped up onto the edge of the field. He wore a bulky coat without a cap or a hood. His hand was inside the coat, and his smile was not the smile of a friend. There were silver caps on his front teeth.

I turned my back on him. Pee ran hot down my thigh. My knees were trembling, but I made my legs move.

The night flashed. I felt a sting, like a bee sting, high on my back.

I stumbled but kept my feet. I looked down at my blood,

dotted in the snow. I walked a couple of steps and closed my eyes.

When I opened them, the field was green. It was covered in gold, like it gets around here in summer, round early evening. A Gamble and Huff thing was coming from the open windows of a car. My father stood before me, his natural full, his chest filling the fabric of his shirt. His sleeves were rolled up to his elbows. His arms were outstretched.

I wasn't afraid or sorry. I'd done right. I had the lottery ticket in my pocket. Detective Barnes, or someone like him, would find it in the morning. When they found *me*.

But first I had to speak to my father. I walked to where he stood, waiting. And I knew exactly what I was going to say: I ain't the low-ass bum you think I am. I been workin with the police for a long, long time. Matter of fact, I just solved a homicide.

I'm a confidential informant, Pop. Look at me.

CHOSEN

EVANGELOS "VAN" LUCAS was behind the wheel of a Land Cruiser, his wife, Eleni, beside him. They were driving home from a Sunday barbecue in Upper Northwest hosted by a business associate of Van's. Most of the guests were people Van and Eleni had not met before. There had been polite conversation, food eaten off paper plates, and a bit of afternoon drinking.

"You know that lady I was speaking with by the food table for a long time?" said Van. "With the sweatshirt falling off her shoulder?"

"The *Flashdance* woman. She was nice."

"She was all right. But why'd you have to go and tell her about our kids?"

"She asked to see photographs," said Eleni. "Once I pull those out, there are questions. It's easier just to tell people."

"But see, then I had to continue the conversation with her."

"You didn't look like you minded."

28

"Please. She wasn't my type. That lady was all angles and bones. It would be like doing a skeleton."

"How would you know what that's like?"

"My point is, I'm into a woman who *looks* like a woman. A woman with curves. Like you."

"I think there's a compliment in there."

"And you're smart."

"Thanks loads."

"Not, like, mousy smart. Don't get me wrong; I like a smart woman. But I also like a nice round ass and a beautiful rack. Which, thank you, Jesus, you happen to have. Matter of fact, you've got the whole female package."

"You're about to make me blush."

"But that woman, she just bothered me."

"I noticed."

"Not like that. She wanted to talk about our kids, how wonderful it must be to have a rainbow family, how I was doing God's work, all that bullshit. What a *good man* I am. Like, just because I adopted a bunch of kids, that makes me good."

"As you were trying to look down her sweatshirt."

"Exactly." Van looked over at Eleni. "You saw me?"

"From across the room."

"She's too skinny for me."

"You like a nice round ass and a beautiful rack."

"Don't forget smart," said Van.

"I know," said Eleni. "The whole female package."

They were coming out of the city, going up Alaska Avenue near the District line. Soon they would cross into Maryland and arrive at the close-in neighborhood where the Lucas family made their home. Van and Eleni were in their early thirties. They had four children, ages seven, six, two, and one. All but the oldest had been adopted. It seemed to have happened very fast.

Van Lucas was a big man of Greek descent with the kind of open, honest facial expressions that could be read with ease. The Reagan generation baffled him, and he did not feel he was a part of it. His black curly hair was unfashionably long at a time when the hard-chargers kept theirs short and spiked. He wore a heavy black beard when most went clean shaven and some reached for androgynous. He had the beginnings of a gut inching over the belt line of his Levi's. His appearance suggested casual good nature and a lack of vanity. He was as advertised.

Eleni reached across the buckets and squeezed Van's right hand, which rested on the console between them.

"You *are* good," she said.

"Ah," said Van, "knock it off, Eleni."

He felt electricity when she touched him like that. They'd been together many years and it had never subsided. For a moment he thought he might get lucky that night. But it was false optimism. There was little spontaneous lovemaking between them these days, what with all the commotion around their house. What with all those kids.

When he was single, he had never looked forward to a family. He had no daydreams of watching his children play sports, reading to them at night, helping them with their homework, or kissing the tops of their heads before they left the house. Van Lucas didn't have a great need for fatherhood, and he didn't think he would be particularly good at it. But when it happened, he took to it. It was chaotic at times, but it was manageable. He liked being a father, and he loved his kids. Later, he would look back on that time of his life and think: It was easy when they were young.

Within a year of their wedding, Eleni gave birth to a girl they named Irene. "It means 'peace,'" said Van, selling the name to Eleni. The baby was born after a very difficult pregnancy during which Eleni was required to lie in bed for most of her third trimester. Even with this precaution, Irene arrived prematurely and her survival was in doubt for the first week of her life. But she did fine and progressed without complications. Eleni's doctor suggested that a subsequent pregnancy would be just as problematic, if not worse, and that Irene should be looked upon as a single blessing and not the first of many blessings to come. Or something like that. Eleni got the convoluted message: Do not tempt fate and try to have another child.

Van was fine with having only one child, but Eleni was not. When Irene got to walking a year later, Eleni decided that a child was not "whole" without a companion. Van said, "We could get a dog," and Eleni said, "I was thinking along the lines of something on two legs," to which Van replied, "A monkey, then." She didn't smile, so he knew she was serious. He also knew where this was going. Eleni wanted to adopt.

On the subject of adoption, Van suspected he was in the camp of many other men who were not quite sure. Will I truly love a child who did not come from me? Would I be as good a father to an adopted child? Do I want a kid who doesn't at least look a little like me? He kept these questions to himself for the most part. But they were there.

The one objection a man could legitimately raise was the cost, but Van couldn't belch about money with a straight face or a clear conscience. He had the dough. A high school friend, Ted Leibovitz, an ambitious renovation man turned builder, had invited Van into his venture when both were right out of college, and they had bought properties in the U Street corridor at fire-sale prices while the Metro was being built, the street was torn up, building windows were boarded, and businesses were failing. The sale of these properties at a profit a few years later had funded bigger projects, commercial and residential, in soon-to-be-hot Shaw, Logan, and Columbia Heights. Ted had an eye for seeing the possibilities in rundown areas, while Van's talent was in sensing when to sell at the top. Van, despite no visible signs of type-A drive, was making a small fortune as a relatively young man. He was liquid and he had real estate. He couldn't cry poor to Eleni.

"What are you going to do with all of our money?" she said. "Buy things? You're not about that."

She was right. He was not a clotheshorse or into labels. His work truck, a two-toned Chevy Silverado, was his only vehicle.

Eleni was similarly uninterested in material things. She had inherited a deep reserve of compassion from her parents, who had preached and practiced Christian charity throughout her childhood. Hell, Van had met her at one of those Christmas Day dinner–soup kitchen things, to which he had been dragged by a community activist he had been courting for zoning favors. The moment he saw Eleni, her hair under a scarf, an apron not even close to concealing her figure, he fell in love with her. Looks aside, it was the fact that she was there in that church basement on a cold Christmas morning, trying to reach out to people who had next to nothing, when she could have been sitting comfortably by a fire, sipping tea and opening gifts. Her obvious kindness was what closed the deal for him.

"You could do some good," she said. "Think about the difference you'd make in some kid's life."

"While he's stealing my silverware."

"Van, come on."

He threw up his meaty hands in a gesture she recognized as near-surrender. "I don't know."

They were seated at the kitchen table of their bungalow. Irene was in her high chair, aiming Cheerios in the general direction of her mouth. Eleni reached across the table and took one of his hands. He felt the current pass through him.

"You know what your name means?" said Eleni.

"Evangelos? It means 'big stud.'"

"No, but nice try."

"So tell me."

"It means 'evangelist.' Someone who spreads the gospel. Or, if you want to take it a little further, someone who does good."

"So you're sayin *what?*"

"Somewhere in your past your ancestors probably adopted kids, too, I bet."

"When men were men and sheep were nervous."

"Huh?"

"You're talking about ancient times. When guys wore metal skirts. The meaning of my name is supposed to make me go out and adopt a kid?"

"Honey, let's do this," said Eleni. "We have the money and the opportunity. To, you know, have a reason for being here. Don't you ever think about why we're here?"

"Not really," said Van. "I'm not that deep."

She came around the table and sat on his lap and kissed him on the lips. His sudden erection was like a crowbar underneath her bottom.

"You're right," she said. "You're not that deep."

"I'm not doing any of the legwork," he said. "I got a business to run."

"I'll take care of the details."

"I want a son," he said, rather petulantly.

Eleni said, "Me, too."

Through the recommendation of friends in their neighborhood, Eleni made an appointment with an attorney, Bill O'Leary, who specialized in adoptions. Van and Eleni met O'Leary and his assistant, a junior attorney named Donna Monroe, at O'Leary's downscale office in Silver Spring. O'Leary seemed both distracted and intent on securing them as clients, while Monroe appeared to be more interested in exploring their motivations and needs. Eleni sensed that the lively eyed Monroe was the conscience of the outfit.

After O'Leary had explained the financial aspects of the adoption, in which he pushed for a flat fee rather than itemized billing, they got into the logistics of paperwork, home visits, and matters of timing.

"I've heard this process can take years," said Eleni.

"If you want a baby that looks like you," said Monroe.

"You mean a white baby," said Van.

"There is typically a long waiting period for white adoptees," said O'Leary. "Russia, Eastern Europe. In general you're talking about children from orphanages who are three, four years old."

Van didn't need to be bait-and-switched by O'Leary. He had heard some stories about those kids. He didn't have the fortitude or the altruism of the people who were willing to take on those kinds of problems. He wanted a family, not a project. He felt that you could mold a baby easier than you could a child who had been socialized, or unsocialized, in his or her formative years.

"No," said Van. "I'm not interested in that scenario. I wouldn't want a, you know, handicapped kid, either."

Van shrugged off Eleni's reproachful look and shifted his weight in his chair. There was a brief silence as the lawyers digested his remark.

"Would you adopt an African American infant?" said Monroe, looking into Van's eyes.

Van hesitated. He felt that he was now a customer in the Baby Store, a situation he'd hoped to avoid. And what did you say to the black woman sitting across the table from you? "I'd rather not adopt a black child"?

"You mean, what *color* baby do I want?" he said. "Is that what you're asking?"

"This will be easier if we speak freely," said Monroe.

"We want whoever needs to be adopted," said Eleni.

Van looked at Eleni. In that moment he knew he would love her forever.

"Right," said Van.

"Then let's get started," said Monroe.

"I'll have my assistant run the contracts," said O'Leary, standing excitedly, displaying his tall, birdlike frame. "You do want the flat fee, don't you?"

Van nodded absently.

That is how it began.

They'd been warned that the adoption process was complicated, but for them it was not. The home visits were perfunctory and quick, and they soon "identified" a baby boy after looking at an array of photographs spread like playing cards on a table. Van said to Eleni, "This is kinda weird. When you choose one, you're rejecting the others, in a way. You know what I mean? What happens to *them?*" Eleni agreed that it was mildly troubling but was steadfast in her belief that they should concentrate on the positive impact they would have on one person's life rather than bemoaning the fact that they couldn't help them all. As she was telling him this, her eyes were on the table, and she touched her index finger to the photograph of a black baby who, consciously or not, was staring into the camera, right *at* them, it seemed, with a startled expression.

"Him," said Eleni.

Van said, "Okay."

Van suggested they name the baby Dimitrius, in keeping with his intention of giving their children traditional Greek names. Van was third generation and about as Greek as a Turkish bath, but Eleni did not resist, much.

"Dimitrius is not a traditional African American name."

"Okay, we'll call him *Le*Dimitrius."

"Stop it. I just think we ought to consider what it will mean for him to carry a name like that."

"It'll toughen him up. Y'know, the bullies used to call me Chevy Van." Van balled his fists and held them up. "Until I introduced them to Thunder and Lightning."

"You were never a fighter."

"I know it. But that's the story I'm gonna tell Dimitrius."

Soon after this conversation, Dimitrius came to them. He was a quiet, pleasant baby, and his sister, Irene, took to him right away. She insisted on pushing his stroller and always sat beside him on the family room couch, where his parents frequently propped him up with pillows. He was her breathing doll. He was loved.

A couple of years passed. They were comfortable as a family and Van was still making significant money. They adopted Shilo, a large dog of indeterminate breed, from the Humane Society at Georgia Avenue and Geranium. The house seemed to grow smaller, louder, and hairier.

When Irene was about to enter kindergarten and Dimitrius was in his last year of preschool, Eleni Lucas got a call from Donna Monroe, now a partner in the O'Leary firm, telling her that another baby had become available. He was a black infant who had been due to be adopted by a white couple who changed their minds at the last minute.

Because they were happy, because they were now convinced that this adoption thing worked, Eleni and Van had already talked about bringing another child into the family.

And there was another reason, unspoken to Eleni, which made Van ready to pull the next trigger: Dimitrius was not quite the boy he had imagined he would one day have. He was not particularly coordinated or athletic, and he shied away from any roughhousing or physical contact with his dad. Van loved him, but Van wanted a *boy*-boy for a son.

And so, a few hours after Donna Monroe's phone call, Van and Eleni studied the photograph of the boy Van had decided would be called Leonidas.

"He's beautiful," said Eleni.

"Yeah, what's wrong with him?" said Van. "What I mean is, why did the first couple reject him?"

"Too dark," said Monroe, who now operated without O'Leary in the room and was free to say whatever she pleased. "They initially saw the photos of him when he came into the world, and he was lighter skinned then. They do get darker after the first few weeks. I'm guessing these folks wanted a more Caucasian-looking black baby."

"Their loss," said Eleni, something she would say to herself many times over the years as she looked at her boy with deep love and wonder.

"I'm just curious," said Van. "I know there's a school of thought with some social workers that says that black babies should go to black parents."

"I'm a graduate of that school," said Monroe. "All things equal, I'll try to place a black baby with a black couple first, every time."

"So why'd you call us?" said Van.

"You've been in here with your kids a few times," said

Monroe. "I see that it's working, and you're not trying too hard. You don't do that over-earnest thing, trying to be all multicultural. I get those types, you know, 'Look at me, I adopted a black kid.' You all just act like a family. You're not dressing your boy in kente cloth or anything ridiculous like that."

"We don't celebrate Kwanza, either," said Van.

"Neither do I," said Monroe. "That's a holiday for Hallmark, not for me. Truth is, in this case, I feel like it would be a good fit. Dimitrius should have a black sibling. It would be good for both of them to have a brother to lean on if they get to where they're having identity issues. What would you name this baby, by the way?"

"Leonidas," said Van. "It means 'lion.'"

"Hmph," said Monroe.

"My husband is trying to keep it Greek," said Eleni.

"So are you ready?" said Monroe.

"Is this the part where Bill O'Leary bursts in with the contracts?"

"He saw y'all pull into the parking lot," said Monroe with a small smile, "and he saw his next Mercedes."

"Let's do it," said Eleni.

Leonidas Lucas, wrapped in a blue fleece blanket, wearing a tiny wife beater, was put in Van's arms a few days later in the offices of O'Leary and Monroe. The boy was five weeks old, cooing, looking up into Van's eyes, and Van's thought at that moment was as it would always be when he saw Leonidas: This is my son.

"May I?" said Eleni, who had yet to hold the child.

"Looks like you're gonna have to pry him out of your man's arms," said Monroe.

Van handed him to Eleni.

"He's a keeper," said Van, rocking back on his heels, his face flushed.

"Y'all better get home," said Monroe. "The snow is coming down hard."

They looked out the office window. Indeed, the flurries that had been swirling all morning had turned to heavy flakes.

"He's going to be cold," said Eleni.

"I bought a little something for him," said Monroe, producing a Hecht's bag holding a new outfit. "Congratulations, you two."

Van bear-hugged Monroe before leaving with his wife and son.

They drove through the snow in Van's Silverado, Leonidas secured in a car seat between them, the truck weighted down by sandbags in the bed. Van and Eleni giggled all the way home. Irene and Dimitrius, being watched by a neighbor, were waiting for them at the door.

"Say hello to Leonidas," said Van, snow in his hair and beard, carrying the infant football-style into the house. "Your new brother."

Leonidas was an early walker and it seemed that he would be athletic. He laughed huskily and charmed everyone he met, and he did not cry when the doctors stuck him with needles. Van would never admit it, but Leonidas was his favorite. Van nicknamed him Cool Breeze because it felt that way to him whenever Leonidas toddled into a room.

Dimitrius did not seem to notice or mind that his father was overly focused on Leonidas. Irene and Dimitrius by now had become a unit. They played in their bedrooms, separately or together, and did not spend a great amount of time paying attention to their parents or their new baby brother. As for Leonidas, his eyes followed Van and Eleni as they moved about the room. When he could not see them, he smiled at the sound of their voices. Even Shilo was smitten, and he growled when anyone outside the immediate family approached Leonidas.

Despite the pressure of the new addition, Van and Eleni were getting along fine. They made love a couple of times a week, ate in restaurants without debating if they should, and went out on the occasional movie date. Because they wanted little in the way of material possessions, they felt they lacked nothing. In fact, Van was still doing quite well despite his seeming lack of interest in making money. They had the family they wanted. They hadn't planned any of this and they felt lucky.

Then, when Leonidas was a year old, they got a call from Donna Monroe. Another baby was available. That night, Van and Eleni discussed it over a bottle of red. They didn't *need* another child. Was this a bridge too far? Why tempt the gods?

"Why'd she call us?" said Van.

"I think she likes you."

"Or her partner got a look at my financials." Van shook his head. "This house is already too small."

"We can move."

"I like it here."

"You're a builder. We'll make the house bigger."

"I dunno," said Van.

"There's a reason Donna called us. Someone whispered in her ear and told her to." She reached for his hand. "Aren't you curious?"

The next day they went to the law office. Van remarked that the furnishings were more lavishly appointed than the last time they had visited, but Donna Monroe ignored him as they walked down the hall to an office that Van now called "the closing area." Monroe was seven months pregnant and she lowered herself carefully into a chair as they found seats. Her belly swelled beneath her maternity outfit. She pushed a photograph across the table, and Van and Eleni bent forward to have a look.

"You don't have anything against white babies, do you?" said Monroe.

"We're color-blind," said Van.

"Why us?" said Eleni. "There's gotta be a line out the door for a white infant like this one."

"Actually, not at the moment," said Monroe. "The couple who had identified him claimed that he came available too quickly. They weren't *ready*. I guess they needed to get the nursery set picked out and delivered first. Or have the artist paint the mural in his room before he could sleep there. What they want is a doll, not a child. No lie."

"But there must be other couples."

"None on our list who are uncommitted to other kids. None currently who have completed their home studies. Course, I could put him in foster care for a month or so. But I don't like to do that."

"I should say not," said Eleni, looking at the photo, falling in love.

"Aw, Jesus Christ," said Van.

"He *is* handsome," said Monroe.

"Van," said Eleni.

They named him Spero and brought him home the next day. Upon entering their house, Eleni took a photograph. When it was developed, it showed Spero still in the car seat, Irene and Dimitrius off to the side, Leonidas with his arm around his new baby brother, Van down on one knee, broadly smiling, and Shilo sniffing at the new arrival in the foreground. Behind them, through the double glass doors of the family room, there was a thick wall of clouds, and though it was midday, a light appeared to wink in the gray sky. Van said it was the camera flash reflected in the glass. Eleni claimed it was a star. She would not tell him what she truly believed: that the light was a kind of eye. That there was something out there, watching them and watching over them, this family of six.

Van blew out the back of the house and raised the roof, and their Sears bungalow replica became something taller, deeper, and architecturally unidentifiable. The days became compressed by activity. Time went quickly and there was laughter in their home and raised voices and sometimes tears, but it was good and they were thankful for all they had. As the years passed, the children grew taller and Van grew heavier. Eleni's face became pleasantly lined and she noticed the beginnings of turkey neck beneath her chin. Shilo passed and was replaced by a large tan mixed breed they named Cheyenne.

Aside from the usual fights, vandalism, and mild behavior problems at school, all of the children's lives had been free of serious trouble when they were young. Dimitrius was a skateboarder and video gamer. Leo, as he was known outside his home, played multiple community sports, as did Spero. Irene was into dance, gymnastics, and horseback riding. In Van's and Eleni's eyes, the boys did not seem to have a problem with their adopted status. But they may have been blinded by love. The truth was, they simply felt that these were their children, not their adopted children, and so it was easy for them to deny that in the minds of their sons there could be more complicated feelings swirling in the mix.

In high school, Irene, black haired like her father and lush of figure like her mom, found the influence of her peers stronger than that of her parents, and she began to use pot, alcohol, and speed. She had sex with boys rather indiscriminately. She also kept up her grades and scored high on her SATs. Her crowd was punk in look only, interested in drugs, not music, and did not have the positive, community-activist bent for which the D.C. punk scene was known.

Dimitrius still idolized Irene and trailed in her wake, and because he was black, an outsider in a group of self-proclaimed outsiders, he felt he had to prove himself and did so by being a harder user than his peers. Like any addict, he lied constantly. He stole money and jewelry from his mother, and his grades dropped to failure across the board. His parents set him up with a shrink, but Dimitrius bailed on the appointments until finally, unreasonable and illogical, he announced his intention to drop out of high school and leave home. Van and Eleni pleaded with him to obtain his diploma. They told him that they were there for him. They told him they loved him and had faith in him, and he replied that he didn't care.

Irene, just as eager to get away from home, was no help. She was accepted to the University of Washington in Seattle and took off after her high school graduation. Dimitrius got his GED and soon followed Irene, promising his parents that he would enroll in Seattle's community college. They reluctantly agreed, put him on a plane, and staked him in an apartment out there; soon after he was gone they began to lose touch with him, and eventually there was no communication at all. Van flew to Seattle, looking for his son, but the apartment they had rented for Dimitrius was vacant, and the landlord had been given no forwarding address. Irene, now in her sophomore year, claimed to have no knowledge of her brother's whereabouts, but Van suspected that she was covering for Dimitrius. He drove and walked around Seattle for several days and nights, looking for Dimitrius among the city's numerous homeless kids, many of whom were drug abusers. He hired a local private detective to continue the search and then, angry and anguished, he flew back to D.C.

In their home the night of his return, Van and Eleni discussed the situation. Eleni was not happy with the turn of events, but she was less emotional than Van and told him they needed to concentrate on the children who still lived with them. She noted truthfully that the house was more settled since Irene and Dimitrius had left, and probably a better atmosphere for Leonidas and Spero, and Van had to agree.

"But it shouldn't have happened like this," said Van.

"Irene's always gone her own way," said Eleni. "Her independence is going to serve her well as an adult."

"I'm not worried about Irene. It's Dimitrius. He's lost."

"We'll find him."

A week later, the detective, Paul Garner, phoned Van.

"I located your son," said Garner. "He's staying in a warehouse with a bunch of kids near the university. Living hand to mouth, but he's under a roof."

"Living how?"

"You want it unvarnished?"

"Of course."

"The drug of choice out here for a certain kind of kid is meth. I went to that area near U of W first because that's where a lot of the users are concentrated. Showed around the photograph you gave me, and when I put some cash on top of it I got the information I needed."

"How do you know he's using?"

"Because I live here. He had the complexion and the look. His teeth are brown. He had the rank smell they get from all that perspiration."

"Did you talk to him?"

"Yes."

"Well, what did he say?"

"He said that he was fine. He doesn't want detox and he doesn't want to come home. Most of 'em think the same way: They're fine. I told him that his father had hired me to find him."

"And?"

"Mr. Lucas—"

"Tell me."

Garner cleared his throat. "He said he didn't have a father."

"God," said Van uselessly.

"Sorry. I really am. Y'know, after I divorced his mother, my son cut off contact with me, too. If it's any consolation…"

Van felt as if he had been punched in the face. He heard little of the rest of Garner's story, but he got the address of the warehouse before bringing the conversation to a close. He then phoned Irene, who promised to look in on her kid brother and see to it that he had food and, if needed, a place to stay. Van had the nagging feeling from Irene's cool tone that she was relatively unconcerned about Dimitrius's degeneration, or at best felt that Van's worries were overblown.

"He'll be all right, Dad. You've got to let him come through this himself."

In bed that night, Van and Eleni held each other and talked quietly, though Leonidas and Spero were long asleep in their room. Eleni had cried a little earlier in the evening, but in ways of logic she was stronger than Van, and also an optimist. She felt it was on her to reassure her husband that the family would be whole again someday.

"Dimitrius will come home," said Eleni.

"When?" said Van.

"Soon."

Dimitrius did not come home. During the next several years they spoke to him a few times over the phone, only when he needed cash. After a lecture, and against his better judgment, Van would wire the money. And then nothing, no further contact until the next similar call. They no longer knew where Dimitrius was. As for Irene, she entered law school and stopped coming home, even for holidays. They rarely spoke to her, either. That left them with their two younger sons. Van vowed to get it right with them.

Leonidas's and Spero's high school years went smoothly. After witnessing the stress their older siblings had inflicted on their parents, they had no desire to rebel in any significant way. Irene's and Dimitrius's absence actually allowed them to flourish.

Neither of them was academically gifted, but both were strong and athletic. They were liked and respected by their classmates for the most part, and were rarely kidded about being salt-and-pepper brothers. For their peers it was not much of an issue. That kind of baggage was carried, mostly, by the generations that came before them.

Leonidas was a handsome man-child, fast on his feet, tall, dark skinned, broad shouldered, and soft-spoken, with an electrifying smile. He had a social conscience like his mother. Spero had black hair, pale skin, and hazel eyes, and at a glance could easily be mistaken for the biological product of Van and Eleni. He was quiet, and a bit brooding and intense, which served him well with girls. Leonidas played wide receiver and point guard for their Montgomery County high school. Spero, quick and wiry, wrestled varsity at one nineteen as a freshman and one forty in his senior year, when he was honorable mention All-Met, winning Mount Madness in his weight class and placing at the seriously loaded Beast of the East tournament in Delaware. There were partial scholarship offers, but Spero had other plans.

Leonidas entered the University of Maryland after his graduation from high school with the intention of becoming a teacher and coach. When Spero graduated, a year after Leonidas, he enrolled at Montgomery College, attended two semesters, then stated his intention to enlist in the Marine Corps. Because there was a new war in Iraq, this did not please his parents. Van, whose father was a WWII veteran, was not a pacifist, and in fact believed that there were necessary wars, but he was strongly against this one and argued passionately with his son about the wisdom of entering the service. Eleni tried quiet persuasion, but neither she nor her husband could change Spero's mind. Van blamed Spero's wrestling coach, a thick-browed ex-marine with a Cro-Magnon build who had a combination father/Rasputin-type relationship with his athletes, for influencing his son's decision.

"He jacked up Spero with that bullshit for four years," said Van.

Eleni, who rarely spoke ill of anyone, agreed.

While Leonidas neared completion of his degree and prepared to apply for teaching positions, Spero, now a marine with the Second Battalion, First Regiment and having served in Iraq for a year, was moving toward the Anbar province, where he would be participating in an offensive on insurgent forces in a place called Fallujah. In his letters and e-mails, Spero did not tell his parents of the fierce nature of the battle or the casualties incurred on both sides.

That year, only Leonidas would be around for the Lucas family Christmas. Irene could not make it as usual, and Dimitrius was in the wind. It was a troubling time on many fronts.

Van's business was beginning to falter due in part to the economy but mainly because of the acute alcoholism of his partner, now on his third marriage. The Lucas money was safe, as Van had always been conservative with his investments, but he faced the prospect of an unwelcome career adjustment in his middle age. More disturbing, he considered his track record as a parent to be spotty at best. He still wondered on what had gone wrong with Dimitrius, remained puzzled by Irene's cold nature, and worried considerably about Spero's safety. He began to complain of headaches and memory loss. He sometimes vomited without the usual warning sign of nausea. In sleep, his dreams were filled with snakes.

Over the holidays, Van said to Eleni, "Funny, this time of year I usually gain weight. I got on the scale today and I've lost ten pounds. But I've been eatin like an animal."

"It's stress," said Eleni.

A week later, having experienced periods of low-level fever, he went to the family physician, Dr. Nassarian, for some blood work. Nassarian called the next day and told Van that he had seen something he didn't like, that it was probably nothing to be too concerned about but that he should have it checked. Nassarian was sending him to a specialist to do another workup and some tests.

"What kind of specialist?" said Van.

"An oncologist up in Wheaton," said the doctor, and Van's heart naturally dropped.

There was more blood taken, and an MRI, which led to a follow-up visit with the oncologist, Dr. Veronica Sorenson, in her office overlooking the Westfield Shopping Center, which

Van still called Wheaton Plaza. He had played there as a boy, flirted with girls, acted tough around greasers, taunted security guards, and been nailed in the old Monkey Wards for shoplifting, back when the center was an open-air mall.

"You have an intracranial tumor, Mr. Lucas," said Dr. Sorenson.

"A brain tumor."

"Yes."

"Cancer," he said, almost stuttering on the word.

She tented her hands before her and looked directly into his eyes. She was an attractive brunette in her late thirties with a direct, professional manner that was not cold in the least. Dr. Sorenson had photographs of her children set up on her desk. He idly wondered if she believed in God.

"Let me show you," she said.

Dr. Sorenson turned off the lights in the office and allowed him to examine his scans displayed on her light board.

"It's called a GBM," she said, pointing to the image of the growth. "There. It appears in the form of a lesion."

"What's a GBM?"

"Glioblastoma multiforme. We'll need to do a stereotactic biopsy to confirm, of course."

"You wouldn't be telling me this today if you didn't know."

"Unfortunately, I'm almost completely certain that this is what we're looking at."

"Certain of what, Doctor? What's my prognosis?"

"I wish I could be more positive. This is a most aggressive cancer. The survival rate is very low."

He looked down at his hand and saw that he was twisting

his wedding band around on his ring finger. "How long would a guy with this thing...how long? Ballpark."

"I recommend that you opt for treatment. We'll perform cranial surgery to remove the bulk of the tumor, then radiotherapy and chemotherapy."

"How long, Doctor?"

"Months," said Dr. Sorenson.

Van, always known as an easygoing, take-it-as-it-comes guy, played his role well. He refused treatment and decided to live his life as lucidly and with as much dignity as possible until its conclusion. Even in his private moments with Eleni, when they weren't putting business matters in order, he spoke positively about the time they'd shared together and their good fortune at having found each other, and he didn't break down when he told Irene and Spero by phone and, most challenging, Leonidas face-to-face. His mind was filled with bitterness, confusion, and anger at his Christ, in whom he had never lost faith, but he was determined to keep up a solid front for his wife and kids. Mostly, like any rational human being, he was frightened of death.

He lasted just over two months. His final days were spent in his bed at home, as he wished. He had lost his parents long ago, but he had many friends, and they came to call. Donna Monroe, now a middle-aged divorcée with kids in college, stopped by, and when Van saw her he told Eleni to hide his wallet, and Donna scolded him and laughed. Irene flew in at one point and he was surprised at her appearance. She had gained weight, and her hair was completely gray. In his presence she checked her BlackBerry often. Though he loved her, he felt little affection for her, but he had no guilt in that regard. She flew back to San Francisco and her law firm after a day. Leonidas visited daily. Spero called often and stayed in e-mail contact with Eleni. His tour was almost up but not quite, and he was trying with futility to get leave and come home.

An in-home hospice nurse was on duty, but Eleni kept her out of the room except to administer and regulate the morphine. Eleni talked to Van as he slept. She slipped Popsicles into his mouth and wet his lips with a washcloth when he could no longer drink. On the last night of his life he looked up at her, sitting beside him.

"I'm a failure," he said hoarsely.

"What do you mean?"

"Where are my children?"

"Leonidas is on his way." She squeezed his hand. "You're no failure. Don't ever think that. You did nothing but good. You're a good man."

He drifted in and out of morphine dreams. Leonidas came into the room. He hugged his mother roughly and went to the bedside, where he knelt on the hardwood floor and kissed his father's hand.

"The best day of my life was the day that lawyer put you in my arms," said Van, and Leonidas lowered his head as hot tears ran down his face.

"I love you, Pop."

Van's cracked lips twitched up into a smile. "Cool Breeze," he whispered.

Those were the last words he spoke. He died the next morning, just before dawn.

* * *

Years passed. Eleni adopted a second dog, called him Yuma, and walked him and Cheyenne twice a day. The outings took a long time, as she stopped to talk to many neighbors on her route and sometimes sat up on their porches and shared tea and, in the evenings, glasses of wine. Deep into her forties she had gotten looks on the street, but now in her sixties she seemed invisible to men. She was still a handsome woman, but she was old.

Eleni no longer had a need for sex, but she was often lonely and would not have minded the companionship of a man. Her attitude was, if it happened, fine. She had her neighborhood friends, her church, her garden, her dogs. And her children.

Her two younger sons called her almost daily. They visited a couple of times a week, mostly at dinnertime, because they liked her cooking and because they knew she loved to feed them.

Leo was a high school teacher in the D.C. public system. Spero did investigative work for a defense attorney down by the courts. When she looked at her sons, she saw Van, and she thought: We did well.

Ours was a life well spent.

STRING MUSIC

Washington, D.C., 2001

TONIO HARRIS

DOWN AROUND MY WAY, when I'm not in school or lookin out for my moms and little sister, I like to run ball. Pickup games mostly. That's not the only kind of basketball I do. I been playin organized all my life, the Jelleff league and Urban Coalition, too. Matter of fact, I'm playin for my school team right now, in what used to be called the Interhigh. It's no boast to say that I can hold my own in most any kind of game. But pickup is where I really get amped.

In organized ball, they expect you to pass a whole bunch, take the percentage shot. Not too much showboatin, nothin like that. In pickup, we ref our own games, and most of the hackin and pushin and stuff, except for the flagrant, it gets allowed. I can deal with that. But in pickup, see, you can pretty much freestyle, try everything out you been practicing on your own. Like those Kobe and Vince moves. What I'm sayin is, out here on the asphalt, you can really show your shit.

Where I come from, you've got to understand, most of the time it's rough. I don't have to describe it if you know the area of D.C. I'm talkin about: the Fourth District, down around Park View, in Northwest. I got problems at home, I got problems at school, I got problems walkin down the street. I prob'ly got problems with my future, you want the plain truth. When I'm runnin ball, though, I don't think on those problems at all. It's like all the chains are off, you understand what I'm sayin? Maybe you grew up somewheres else, and if you did, it'd be hard for you to see. But I'm just tryin to describe it, is all.

Here's an example: earlier today I got into this beef with this boy James Wallace. We was runnin ball over on the playground where I go to school, Roosevelt High, on 13th Street, just a little bit north of my neighborhood. There's never any chains left on those outdoor buckets, but the rims up at Roosevelt are straight, and the backboards are forgiving. That's like my home court. Those buckets they got, I been playin them since I was kid, and I can shoot the eyes out of those motherfuckers most any day of the week.

We had a four-on-four thing goin on, a pretty good one, too. It was the second game we had played. Wallace and his boys, after we beat 'em the first game, they went over to Wallace's car, a black Maxima with a spoiler and pretty rims, and fired up a blunt. They were gettin their heads up and listenin to the new Nas comin out the speakers from the open doors of the car. I don't like Nas's new shit much as I did *Illmatic,* but it sounded pretty good.

Wallace and them, they with a dealer in my neighborhood, so they always got good herb, too. I got no problem with that. I might even have hit some of that hydro with 'em if they'd asked. But they didn't ask.

Anyway, they came back pink-eyed, lookin all cooked and shit, debatin over which was better, Phillies or White Owls. We started the second game. Me and mines went up by three or four buckets pretty quick. Right about then I knew we was gonna win this one like we won the first, 'cause I had just caught a little fire.

Wallace decided to cover me. He had switched off with this other dude, Antuane, but Antuane couldn't run with me, not one bit. So Wallace switched, and right away he was all chest-out, talkin shit about how "now we gonna see" and all that. Whateva. I was on my inside game that day and I knew it. I mean, I was crossin motherfuckers *out,* just driving the paint at will. And Wallace, he was slow on me by like, half a step. I had stopped passin to the other fellas at that point, 'cause it was just too easy to take it in on him. I mean, he was givin it to me, so why not?

Bout the third time I drove the lane and kissed one in, Wallace bumped me while I was walkin back up to the foul line to take the check. Then he said somethin about my sneaks, somethin that made his boys laugh. He was crackin on me, is all, tryin to shake me up. I got a nice pair of Jordans, the Penny style, and I keep 'em clean with Fantastik and shit, but they're from, like, last year. And James Wallace is always wearin whatever's new, the Seventeens or whatever it is they got sittin up front at the Foot Locker, just came in. Plus Wallace didn't like me all that much. He had money from his druggin, I mean to tell you that boy had *everything*, but he had dropped out of school back in the tenth grade, and I had stayed put. My moms always says that guys like Wallace resent guys like me who have hung in. Add that to the fact that he never did have my game. I think he was a little jealous of me, you want the truth.

I do know he was frustrated that day. I knew it, and I guess I shouldn't have done what I did. I should've passed off to one of my boys, but you know how it is. When you're proud about somethin you got to show it, 'specially down here. And I was on. I took the check from him and drove to the bucket, just blew right past him as easy as I'd been doin all afternoon. That's when Wallace called me a bitch right in front of everybody there.

There's a way to deal with this kinda shit. You learn it over time. I go six-two and I got some shoulders on me, so it wasn't like I feared Wallace physically or nothin like that. I can go with my hands, too. But in this world we got out here, you don't want to be getting in any kinda beefs, not if you can help it. At the same time, you can't show no fear; you get a rep for weakness like that, it's like bein a bird with a busted wing, sumshit like that. The other thing you can't do, though, you can't let that kind of comment pass. Someone tries to take you for bad like that, you got to respond. It's complicated, I know, but there it is.

"I ain't heard what you said," I said, all ice cool and shit, seein if he would go ahead and repeat it, lookin to measure just how far he wanted to push it. Also, I was tryin to buy a little time.

"Said you's a bitch," said Wallace, lickin his lips and smilin like he was a bitch his *own* self. He'd made a couple steps toward me and now he wasn't all that far away from my face.

I smiled back, halfway friendly. "You know I ain't no faggot," I said. "Shit, James, it hurts me to fart."

A couple of the fellas started laughin then and pretty soon all of 'em was laughin, I'd heard that line on one of my uncle's old-time comedy albums once, that old Signifyin Monkey shit or maybe Pryor. But I guess these fellas hadn't heard it, and they laughed like a motherfucker when I said it. Wallace laughed, too. Maybe it was the hydro they'd smoked. Whatever it was, I had broken that shit down, turned it right back on him, you see what I'm sayin? While they was still laughin, I said, "C'mon, check it up top, James, let's play."

I didn't play so proud after that. I passed off and only took a coupla shots myself the rest of the game. I think I even missed one on purpose toward the end. I ain't stupid. We still won, but not by much; I saw to it that it wasn't so one-sided, like it had been before.

When it was over, Wallace wanted to play another game, but the sun was dropping and I said I had to get on home. I needed to pick up my sister at aftercare, and my moms likes both of us to be inside our apartment when she gets home from work. Course, I didn't tell any of the fellas that. It wasn't somethin they needed to know.

Wallace was goin back my way, I knew, but he didn't offer

to give me a ride. He just looked at me dead-eyed and smiled a little before him and his boys walked back to the Maxima, parked along the curb. My stomach flipped some, I got to admit, seein that flatline thing in his peeps. I knew from that empty look that it wasn't over between us, but what could I do?

I picked up my ball and headed over to Georgia Avenue. Walked south toward my mother's place as the first shadows of night were crawling onto the streets.

SERGEANT PETERS

It's five a.m. I'm sitting in my cruiser up near the station house, sipping a coffee. My first one of the night. Rolling my head around on these tired shoulders of mine. You get these aches when you're behind the wheel of a car, six hours at a stretch. I oughta buy one of those things the African cabbies all sit on, looks like a rack of wooden balls. You know, for your back. I been doin this for twenty-two years now, so I guess whatever damage I've done to my spine and all, it's too late.

I work midnights in the Fourth District. Four-D starts at the Maryland line and runs south to Harvard Street and Georgia. The western border is Rock Creek Park and the eastern line is North Capitol Street. It's what the news people call a "high-crime district." For a year or two I tried working the Third, keeping the streets safe for rich white people basically, but I got bored. I guess I'm one of those adrenaline junkies they're always talking about on those cop shows on

TV, the shows got female cops who look more beautiful than any female cop I've ever seen. I guess that's what it is. It's not like I've ever examined myself or anything like that. My wife and I don't talk about it, that's for damn sure. A ton of cop marriages don't make it; I suppose mine has survived 'cause I never bring any of this shit home with me. Not that she knows about, anyway.

My shift runs from the stroke of twelve till dawn, though I usually get into the station early so I can nab the cruiser I like. I prefer the Crown Victoria. It's roomier, and once you flood the gas into the cylinders, it really moves. Also, I like to ride alone.

Last night, Friday, wasn't much different than any other. It's summer; more people are outside, trying to stay out of their un-air-conditioned places as long as possible, so this time of year we put extra cars out on the streets. Also, like I reminded some of the younger guys at the station last night, this was the week welfare checks got mailed out, something they needed to know. Welfare checks mean more drunks, more domestic disturbances, more violence. One of the young cops I said it to, he said, "Thank you, Sergeant Dad," but he didn't do it in a bad way. I know those young guys appreciate it when I mention shit like that.

Soon as I drove south I saw that the Avenue, Georgia Avenue that is, was hot with activity. All those Jap tech bikes the young kids like to ride, curbed outside the all-night Wing n' Things. People spilling out of bars, hanging outside the Korean beer markets, scratching game cards, talking trash, ignoring the crackheads hitting them up for spare change.

Drunks lying in the doorways of the closed-down shops, their heads resting against the riot gates. Kids, a lot of kids, standing on corners, grouped around tricked-out cars, rap music and that go-go crap coming from the open windows. The farther south you go, the worse all of this gets.

The bottom of the barrel is that area between Quebec Street and Irving. The newspapers lump it all in with a section of town called Petworth, but I'm talking about Park View. Poverty, drug activity, crime. They got that Section 8 housing back in there, the Park Morton complex. What we used to call "the projects" back when you could say it. Government assisted hellholes. Gangs like the Park Morton Crew. Open-air drug markets, I'm talking about blatant transactions right out there on Georgia Avenue. Drugs are Park View's industry; the dealers are the biggest employers in this part of town.

The dealers get the whole neighborhood involved. They recruit kids to be lookouts for 'em. Give these kids beepers and cells to warn them off when the five-O comes around. Entry-level positions. Some of the parents, when there *are* parents, participate, too. Let these drug dealers duck into their apartments when there's heat. Teach their kids not to talk to The Man. So you got kids being raised in a culture that says the drug dealers are the good guys and the cops are bad. I'm not lying. It's exactly how it is.

The trend now is to sell marijuana. Coke, crack, and heroin, you can still get it, but the new thing is to deal pot. Here's why: up until recently, in the District, possession or distribution of marijuana up to ten pounds—*ten pounds*—was a misdemeanor. They've changed that law, but still, kid gets popped for selling grass, he knows he's gonna do no time. Even on a distribution beef, black juries won't send a black kid into the prison system for a marijuana charge, that's a proven fact. Prosecutors know this, so they usually no-paper the case. That means most of the time they don't even go to court with it. I'm not bullshitting. Makes you wonder why they even bother having drug laws to begin with. They legalize the stuff, they're gonna take the bottom right out the market, and the violent crimes in this city would go down to, like, nothing. Don't get me started. I know it sounds strange, a cop saying this. But you'd be surprised how many of us feel that way.

Okay, I got off the subject. I was talking about my night.

Early on I got a domestic call, over on Oris Place. When I got there, two cruisers were on the scene, four young guys, two of them with flashlights. A rookie named Buzzy talked to a woman at the front door of her row house, then came back and told me that the object of the complaint was behind the place, in the alley. I walked around back alone and into the alley, and right off I recognized the man standing inside the fence of his tiny, brown-grass yard. Harry Lang, sixty-some years old. I'd been to this address a few times in the past ten years.

I said, "Hello, Harry," Harry said, "Officer," and I said, "Wait right here, okay?" Then I went through the open gate. Harry's wife was on her back porch, flanked by her two sons, big strapping guys, all of them standing under a triangle of harsh white light coming from a naked bulb. Mrs. Lang's face and body language told me that the situation had resolved itself. Generally, once we arrive, domestic conflicts tend to calm down on their own.

Mrs. Lang said that Harry had been verbally abusive that night, demanding money from her, even though he'd just got paid. I asked her if Harry had struck her, and her response was negative. But she had a job, too, she worked just as hard as him, why should she support his lifestyle and let him speak to her like that…I was listening and not listening, if you know what I mean. I made my sincere face and nodded every few seconds or so.

I asked her if she wanted me to lock Harry up, and of course she said no. I asked what she did want, and she said she didn't want to see him "for the rest of the night." I told her I thought I could arrange that, and started back to have a talk with Harry. The porch light went off behind me as I hit the bottom of the wooden stairs. Dogs had begun to bark in the neighboring yards.

Harry was short and low-slung, a black black man, nearly featureless in the dark. He wore a porkpie hat and his clothes were pressed and clean. He kept his eyes down as I spoke to him over the barks of the dogs. His reaction time was very slow when I asked for a response. I could see right away that he was on a nod.

Harry had been a controlled heroin junkie for the last thirty years. During that time, he'd always held a job, lived in this same house, and been there, in one condition or another, for his kids. I'd wager he went to church on Sundays, too. But a junkie was what he was. Heroin was a slow ride down. Some folks could control it to some degree and never hit the bottom.

I asked Harry if he could find a place to sleep that night

other than his house, and he told me that he "supposed" he could. I told him I didn't want to see him again any time soon, and he said, "It's mutual." I chuckled at that, giving him some of his pride back, which didn't cost me a thing. He walked down the alley, stopping once to cup his hands around a match as he put fire to a cigarette.

I drove back over to Georgia. A guy flagged me down just to talk. They see my car number and they know it's me. Sergeant Peters, the old white cop. You get a history with these people. Some of these kids, I know their parents. I've busted 'em from time to time. Busted their grandparents, too. Shows you how long I've been doing this.

Down around Morton I saw Tonio Harris, a neighborhood kid walking alone toward the Black Hole. Tonio was wearing those work boots and the baggy pants low, like all the other kids, although he's not like most of them. I took his mother in for drugs a long time ago, back when that Love Boat stuff was popular and making everyone crazy. His father, the one who impregnated his mother I mean, he's doing a stretch for manslaughter, his third fall. Tonio's mother's clean now, at least I think she is; anyway, she's done a fairly good job with him. By that I mean he's got no juvenile priors, from what I know. A minor miracle down here, you ask me.

I rolled down my window. "Hey, Tonio, how's it going?" I slowed down to a crawl, took in the sweetish smell of reefer in the air. Tonio was still walking, not looking at me, but he mumbled something about "I'm maintainin," or some shit like that. "You take care of yourself in there," I said, meaning in the Hole, "and get yourself home right after." He didn't respond verbally, just made a half-assed kind of acknowledgment with his chin.

I cruised around for the next couple of hours. Turned my spot on kids hanging in the shadows, told them to break it up and move along. Asked a guy in Columbia Heights why his little boy was out on the stoop, dribbling a basketball, at one in the morning. Raised my voice at a boy, a lookout for a dealer, who was sitting on top of a trash can, told him to get his ass on home. Most of the time, this is my night. We're just letting the critters know we're out here.

At around two I called in a few cruisers to handle the closing of the Black Hole. You never know what's going to happen at the end of the night there, what kind of beefs got born inside the club, who looked at who a little too hard for one second too long. Hard to believe that an ex-cop from Prince George's County runs the place. That a cop would put all this trouble on us, bring it into our district. He's got D.C. cops moonlighting as bouncers in there, too, working the metal detectors at the door. I talked with one, a young white cop, earlier in the night. I noticed the brightness in his eyes and the sweat beaded across his forehead. He was scared, like I gave a shit. Asked us as a favor to show some kind of presence at closing time. Called me "Sarge." Okay. I didn't answer him. I got no sympathy for the cops who work those go-go joints, especially not since Officer Brian Gibson was shot dead outside the Ibex Club a few years back. But if something goes down around the place, it's on me. So I do my job.

I called in a few cruisers and set up a couple of traffic barriers on Georgia, one at Lamont and one at Park. We diverted the cars like that, kept the kids from congregating on the street. It worked. Nothing too bad was happening that I could see. I was standing outside my cruiser, talking to another cop, Eric Young, who was having a smoke. That's when I saw Tonio Harris running east on Morton, heading for the housing complex. A late-model black import was behind him, and there were a couple of YBMs with their heads out the open windows, yelling shit out, laughing at the Harris kid, like that.

"You all right here?" I said to Young.

"Fine, Sarge," he said.

My cruiser was idling. I slid under the wheel and pulled down on the tree.

TONIO HARRIS

Just around midnight, when I was fixin to go out, my moms walked into my room. I was sittin on the edge of my bed, lacing up my Timbs, listening to PGC comin from the box, Flexx doin his shout-outs and then movin right into the new Nelly, which is vicious. The music was so loud that I didn't hear my mother walk in, but when I looked up there she was, one arm crossed over the other like she does when she's tryin to be hard, staring me down.

"Whassup, Mama?"

"What's up with *you?*"

I shrugged. "Back Yard is playin tonight. Was thinkin I'd head over to the Hole."

"Did you ask me if you could?"

"Do I *have* to?" I used that tone she hated, knew right away I'd made a mistake.

"You're living in my house, aren't you?"

"Uh-huh."

"You payin rent now?"

"No, ma'am."

"Talkin about, *do I have to.*"

"Can I go?"

Mama uncrossed her arms. "Thought you said you'd be studyin up for that test this weekend."

"I will. Gonna do it tomorrow morning, first thing. Just wanted to go out and hear a little music tonight, is all."

I saw her eyes go soft on me then. "You gonna study for that exam, you hear?"

"I promise I will."

"Go on, then. Come right back after the show."

"Yes, ma'am."

I noticed as she was walkin out the door her shoulders were getting stooped some. Bad posture and a hard life. She wasn't but thirty-six years old.

I spent a few more minutes listening to the radio and checking myself in the mirror. Pattin my natural and shit. I got a nice modified cut, not too short, not blown-out or nothin like that. For a while now the fellas been wearin braids, tryin to look like the Answer. But I don't think it would look right on me. And I know what the girls like. They look at me, they like what they see. I can tell.

Moms has been ridin me about my college entrance exam.

I fucked up the first one I took. I went out and got high on some fierce chronic the night before it, and my head was filled up with cobwebs the next morning when I sat down in the school cafeteria to take that test. I'm gonna take it again, though, and do better next time.

I'm not one of those guys who's got, what do you call that, illusions about my future. No NBA dreams, nothin like that. I'm not good enough or tall enough, I know it. I'm sixth man on my high school team, that ought to tell you somethin right there. My Uncle Gaylen, he's been real good to me, and straight-up with me, too. Told me to have fun with ball and all that, but not to depend on it. To stick with the books. I know I fucked up that test, but next time I'm gonna do better, you can believe that.

I was thinkin, though, I could get me a partial scholarship playin for one of those small schools in Virginia or Maryland, William and Mary or maybe Goucher up in Baltimore. Hold up—Goucher's for women only, I think. Maybe I'm wrong. Have to ask my guidance counselor, soon as I can find one. Ha-ha.

The other thing I should do, for real, is find me a part-time job. I'm tired of havin no money in my pockets. My mother works up at the Dollar Store in the Silver Spring mall, and she told me she could hook me up there. But I don't wanna work with my mother. And I don't want to be workin at no *Mac*-Donald's or sumshit like that. Have the neighborhood slangers come in and make fun of me and shit, standin there in my minimum wage uniform. But I do need some money. I'd like to buy me a nice car soon. I'm not talkin about some hooptie, neither.

I did have an interview for this restaurant downtown, busin tables. White boy who interviewed kept sayin shit like, "Do you think you can make it into work on time?" and do you think this and do you think that? Might as well gone ahead and called me a nigger right to my face. The more he talked, the more attitude I gave him with my eyes. After all that, he smiled and sat up straight, like he was gonna make some big announcement, and said he was gonna give me a try. I told him I changed my mind and walked right out of there. Uncle Gaylen said I should've taken that job and showed him he was wrong. But I couldn't. I can't stand how white people talk to you sometimes. Like they're just there to make their own selves feel better. I hired a Negro today, and like that.

I *am* gonna take that test over, though.

I changed my shirt and went out through the living room. My sister was watchin the 106 and Park videos on TV, her mouth around a straw, sippin on one of those big sodas. She's startin to get some titties on her. Some of the slick young niggas in the neighborhood been commentin on it, too. Late for her to be awake, but it was Friday night. She didn't look up as I passed. I yelled good-bye to my moms and heard her say my name from the kitchen. I knew she was back up in there 'cause I smelled the smoke comin off her cigarette. There was a ten-dollar bill sittin in a bowl by the door. I folded it up and slipped it inside my jeans. My mother had left it there for me. I'm tellin you, she is cool people.

Outside the complex, I stepped across this little road and the dark courtyard real quick. We been livin here a long time, and I know most everyone by sight. But in this place here, that don't mean shit.

The Black Hole had a line goin outside the door when I got there. I went through the metal detector and let a white rent-a-cop pat me down while I said hey to a friend going into the hall. I could feel the bass from way out in the lobby.

The hall was crowded and the place was bumpin. I could smell sweat in the damp air, Also chronic, and it was nice. Back Yard was doin "Freestyle," off *Hood Related,* that double CD they got. I kind of made my way toward the stage, careful not to bump nobody, nodding to the ones I did. I knew a lot of young brothers there. Some of 'em run in gangs, some not. I try to know a little bit of everybody, you see what I'm sayin? Spread your friends out in case you run into some trouble. I was smilin at some of the girls, too.

Up near the front I got into the groove. Someone passed me somethin that smelled good, and I hit it. Back Yard was turnin that shit out. I been knowin their music for like ten years now. They had the whole joint up there that night: I'm talkin about a horn section and everything else. I must have been up there close to the stage for about, I don't know, an hour, sumshit like that, just dancing. It seemed like all of us was movin together. On "Do That Stuff," they went into this extended drum thing, shout-outs for the hoodies and the crews; I was sweatin clean through my shirt, right about then.

I had to pee like a motherfucker, but I didn't want to use the bathroom in that place. All the hard motherfuckers be congregatin in there, too. That's where trouble can start, just 'cause you gave someone the wrong kinda look.

When the set broke I started to talkin to this girl who'd been dancin near me, smilin my way. I'd seen her around. Matter of fact, I ran ball sometimes with her older brother. So we had somethin to talk about straight off. She had that Brandy thing goin on with her hair, and a nice smile.

While we was talkin, someone bumped me from behind. I turned around and it was Antuane, that kid who ran with James Wallace. Wallace was with him, and so were a coupla Wallace's boys. I nodded at Antuane, tryin to communicate to him, like, "Ain't no thing, you bumpin me like that." But Wallace stepped in and said somethin to me. I couldn't even really hear it with all the crowd noise, but I could see by his face that he was tryin to step *to* me. I mean, he was right up in my face.

We stared at each other for a few. I shoulda just walked away, right, but I couldn't let him punk me out like that in front of the girl.

Wallace's hand shot up. Looked like a bird flutterin out of nowhere or somethin. Maybe he was just makin a point with that hand, like some do. But it rattled me, I guess, and I reacted. Didn't even think about it, though I should've. My palms went to his chest and I shoved him back. He stumbled. I saw his eyes flare with anger, but there was that other thing, too, worse than me puttin my hands on him: I had stripped him of his pride.

There was some yellin then from his boys. I just turned and bucked. I saw the bouncers started to move, talkin into their headsets and shit, but I didn't wait. I bucked. I was out on the street pretty quick, runnin toward my place. I didn't know what else to do.

I heard Wallace and them behind me, comin out the Hole. They said my name. I didn't look back. I ran to Morton and turned right. Heard car doors opening and slammin shut. The engine of the car turnin over. Then the cry of tires on the street and Wallace's boys laughin, yellin shit out. I kept runnin toward Park Morton. My heart felt like it was snappin on a rubber string.

There were some younguns out in the complex. They were sittin up on top of a low brick wall like they do, and they watched me run by. It's always dark here, ain't never no good kinda light. They got some dim yellow bulbs back in the stairwells, where the old-school types drink gin and shoot craps. They was back up in there, too, hunched down in the shadows. There was some kind of fog or haze out that night, too, it was kind of rollin around by that old playground equipment, all rusted and shit, they got in the courtyard. I was runnin through there, tryin to get to my place.

I had to cross the little road in the back of the complex to get to my mother's apartment. I stepped into it and that's when I saw the black Maxima swing around the corner. Coupla Wallace's boys jumped out while the car was still moving. I stopped runnin. They knew where I lived. If they didn't, all they had to do was ask one of those younguns on the wall. I wasn't gonna bring none of this home to my moms.

Wallace was out of the driver's side quick, walkin toward me. He was smilin and my stomach shifted. Antuane had walked back by the playground. I knew where he was goin. Wallace and them keep a gun, a nine with a fifteen-round mag, buried in a shoe box back there.

"Junior," said Wallace, "you done fucked up big." He was still smilin.

I didn't move. My knees were shakin some. I figured this was it. I was thinkin about my mother and tryin not to cry. Thinkin about how if I did cry, that's all anyone would re-member about me. That I went out like a bitch before I died. Funny me thinkin about stupid shit like that while I was waitin for Antuane to come back with that gun.

I saw Antuane's figure walkin back out through that fog.

And then I saw the spotlight movin across the courtyard, and where it came from. An MPD Crown Vic was comin up the street, kinda slow. The driver turned on the overheads, throwing colors all around. Antuane backpedaled and then he was gone.

The cruiser stopped and the driver's door opened. The white cop I'd seen earlier in the night got out. Sergeant Peters. My moms had told me his name. Told me he was all right.

Peters was puttin on his hat as he stepped out. He had pulled his nightstick and his other hand just brushed the Glock on his right hip. Like he was just lettin us all know he had it.

"Evening, gentlemen," he said, easy like. "We got a problem here?"

"Nope," said Wallace, kinda in a white-boy's voice, still smiling.

"Somethin funny?" said Peters.

Wallace didn't say nothin. Peters looked at me and then back at Wallace.

"You all together?" said Peters.

"We just out here havin a conversation," said Wallace.

Sergeant Peters gave Wallace a look then, like he was disgusted with him, and then he sighed.

"You," said Peters, turnin to me. I was prayin he wasn't gonna say my name, like me and him was friends and shit.

"Yeah?" I said, not too friendly but not, like, impolite.

"You live around here?" He *knew* I did.

I said, "Uh-huh."

"Get on home."

I turned around and walked. Slow but not too slow. I heard the white cop talkin to Wallace and the others, and the crackle of his radio comin from the car. Red and blue was strobin across the bricks of the complex. Under my breath I was sayin, thanks God.

In my apartment, everyone was asleep. I turned off the TV set and covered my sister, who was lyin on the couch. Then I went back to my room and turned the box on so I could listen to my music low. I sat on the edge of the bed. My hand was shaking. I put it together with my other hand and laced my fingers tight.

SERGEANT PETERS

After the Park Morton incident, I answered a domestic call over on 1st and Kennedy. A young gentleman, built like a fullback, had beat up his girl pretty bad. Her face was already swelling when I arrived, and there was blood and spittle bubbling on the side of her mouth. The first cops on the scene had cuffed the perp and had him bent over the hood of their cruiser. At this point the girlfriend, she was screaming at the cops. Some of the neighborhood types, hanging outside of a windowless bar on Kennedy, had begun screaming at the cops, too. I figured they were drunk and high on who-knew-what, so I radioed in for a few more cars.

We made a couple of additional arrests. Like they say in the TV news, the situation had escalated. Not a full-blown riot, but trouble nonetheless. Someone yelled out at me, called me a "cracker-ass motherfucker." I didn't even blink. The county cops don't take an ounce of that kinda shit, but we take it every night. Sticks and stones, like that. Then someone started whistling the theme from the old *Andy Griffith Show,* you know, the one where he played a small-town sheriff, and everyone started to laugh. Least they didn't call me Barney Fife. The thing was, when the residents start with the comedy, you know it's over, that things have gotten under control. So I didn't mind. Actually, the guy who was whistling, he was pretty good.

When that was over with, I pulled a car over on 5th and Princeton, back by the Old Soldiers' Home. It matched the description of a shooter's car from earlier in the night. I waited for backup, standing behind the left rear quarter panel of the car, my holster unsnapped, the light from my Mag pointed at the rear window.

When my backup came, we searched the car and frisked the four YBMs. They had those little tree deodorizers hangin from the rearview, and one of those plastic, king-crown deodorizers sitting on the back panel, too. A crown. Like they're royalty, right? God, sometimes these people make me laugh. Anyhow, they were clean with no live warrants, and we let them go.

I drove around, and it was quiet. Between three a.m. and dawn, the city gets real still. Beautiful in a way, even for down here.

The last thing I did, I helped some Spanish guy who was trying to get back into his place in Petworth. Said his key didn't work, and it didn't. Someone, his landlord or his woman, had changed the locks on him, I figured. Liquor-stench was pouring out of him. Also, he smelled like he hadn't taken a shower for days. When I left him he was standing on the sidewalk, sort of rocking back and forth, staring at the front of the row house, like if he looked at it long enough the door was gonna open on its own.

So now I'm parked here near the station, sipping coffee. It's my ritual, like. The sky is beginning to lighten. This here is my favorite time of night.

I'm thinking that on my next shift, or the one after, I'll swing by and see Tonio Harris's mother. I haven't talked to her in years, anyway. See how she's been doing. Suggest to her, without acting like I'm telling her what to do, that maybe she ought to have her son lie low some. Stay in the next few week-end nights. Let that beef he's got with those others, whatever it is, die down. Course, I know those kinds of beefs don't go away. I'll make her aware of it, just the same.

The Harris kid, he's lucky he's got someone like his mother lookin after him. I drive back in there at the housing complex, and I see those young kids sitting on that wall at two in the morning, looking at me with hate in their eyes, and all I can think of is, where are the parents? Yeah, I know, there's a new curfew in effect for minors. Some joke. Like we've got the manpower and facilities to enforce it. Like we're supposed to raise these kids, too.

Anyway, it's not my job to think too hard about that. I'm just lettin these people know that we're out here, watching them. I mean, what else can you do?

My back hurts. I got to get me one of those things you sit on, with the wood balls. Like those African cab drivers do.

TONIO HARRIS

This morning I studied some in my room until my eyes got sleepy. It was hard to keep my mind on the book 'cause I was playin some Ludacris on the box, and it was fuckin with my concentration. That joint was tight.

I figured I was done for the day, and there wasn't no one around to tell me different. My mother was at work at the Dollar Store, and my sister was over at a friend's. I put my sneaks on and grabbed my ball, headed up to Roosevelt.

I walked up Georgia, dribblin the sidewalk when I could, usin my left and keeping my right behind my back, like my coach told me to do. I cut down Upshur and walked up 13th, past my school to the court. The court is on the small side and its backboards are square, with bumper stickers and shit stuck on 'em. It's beside a tennis court and all of it is fenced in. There's a baseball field behind it; birds always be sittin on that field.

There was a four-on-four full-court thing happenin when I got there. I called next with another guy, Dimitrius Johnson, who I knew could play. I could see who was gonna win this game, cause the one team had this boy named Peter Hawk who could do it all. We'd pick up two off the losers' squad. I watched the game, and after a minute I'd already had those two picked out.

The game started kind of slow. I was feelin out my players and those on the other side. Someone had set up a box court-side, and they had that live Roots thing playin. It was one of those pretty days with the sun out and high clouds, the kind that look like pillows, and the weather and that upbeat music comin from the box set the tone. I felt loose and good.

Me and Hawk was coverin each other. He was one of those who could go left or right, dribble or shoot with either hand. He took me to the hole once or twice. Then I noticed he always eye-faked in the opposite direction he was gonna go before he made his move. So it gave me the advantage, knowin which side he was gonna jump to, and I gained position on him like that.

I couldn't shut Hawk down, not all the way, but I forced him to change his game. I made a couple of nice assists on of-fense and drained one my own self from way downtown. One of Hawk's players tried to claim a charge, doin that Reggie Miller punk shit, his arms windmillin as he went back. That shit don't go in pickup, and even his own people didn't back him. My team went up by one.

We stopped the game for a minute or so, so one of mines could tie up his sneaks. I was lookin across the ball field at the seagulls and crows, catchin my wind. That's when I saw James Wallace's black Maxima, cruisin slow down Allison, that street that runs alongside the court.

We put the ball back into play. Hawk drove right by me, hit a runner. I fumbled a pass goin back upcourt, and on the turnover they scored again. The Maxima was going south on 13th, just barely moving along. I saw Wallace in the driver's seat, his window down, lookin my way with that smile of his and his dead-ass eyes.

"You playin, Tone?" asked Dimitrius, the kid on my team.

I guess I had lost my concentration and it showed. "I'm playin," I said. "Let's ball."

Dimitrius bricked his next shot. Hawk got the bound and brought the ball up. I watched him do that eye-fake thing again and I stole the ball off him in the lane before he could make his move. I went bucket-to-bucket with it and leaped. I jammed the motherfucker and swung on the rim, comin down and doin one of those Patrick Ewing silent growls at Hawk and the rest of them before shootin downcourt to get back on D. I was all fired up. I felt like we could turn the shit around.

Hawk hit his next shot, a jumper from the top of the key. Dimitrius brought it down, and I motioned for him to dish me the pill. He led me just right. In my side sight I saw a black car rollin down Allison, but I didn't stop to check it out. I drove off a pick, pulled up in front of Hawk, made a head move and watched him bite. Then I went up. I was way out there, but I could tell from how the ball rolled off my fingers that it was gonna go. Ain't no chains on those rims, but I could see the links dance as that rock dropped through. I'm sayin that I could see them dance in my mind.

We was runnin now. The game was full-on and it was fierce. I grabbed one off the rim and made an outlet pass, then beat the defenders myself on the break. I saw a black car movin slow on 13th, but I didn't even think about it. I was higher than a motherfucker then; my feet and the court and the ball were all one thing. I felt like I could drain it from anywhere, and Hawk, I could see it in his eyes, he knew it, too.

I took the ball and dribbled it up. I knew what I was gonna do, knew exactly where I was gonna go with it, knew wasn't nobody out there could stop me. I wasn't thinkin about Wallace or the stoop of my mom's shoulders or which nigga was gonna be lookin to fuck my baby sister, and I wasn't thinkin on no job or college test or my future or nothin like that.

I was concentratin on droppin that pill through the hole. Watching myself doin it before I did. Out here in the sunshine, every dark thing far away. Runnin ball like I do. Thinkin that if I kept runnin, that black Maxima and everything else, it would just go away.

WHEN YOU'RE HUNGRY

THE WOMAN IN the aisle seat to the right of John Moreno tapped him on the shoulder. Moreno swallowed the last of his Skol pilsner to wash down the food in his mouth. He laid his fork across the segmented plastic plate in front of him on a fold-down tray.

"Yes?" he said, taking her in fully for the first time. She was attractive, though one had to look for it, past the thick black eyebrows and the too-wide mouth painted a pale peach color that did her complexion no favors.

"I don't mean to be rude," she said, in heavily accented English. "But you've been making a lot of noise with your food. Is everything all right?"

Moreno grinned, more to himself than to her. "Yes, I'm fine. You have to excuse me. I rushed out of the house this morning without breakfast, and then this flight was delayed. I suppose I didn't realize how hungry I was."

"No bother," she said, smiling now, waving the manicured

fingers of her long brown hand. "I'm not complaining. I'm a doctor, and I thought that something might be wrong."

"Nothing that some food couldn't take care of." They looked each other over. Then he said, "You're a doctor in what city?"

"A pediatrician," she said. "In Salvador. Are you going to Bahia?"

Moreno shook his head. "Recife."

So they would not meet again. Just as well. Moreno preferred to pay for his companionship while under contract.

"Recife is lovely," the woman said, breathing out with a kind of relief, the suspense between them now broken. "Are you on a holiday?"

"Yes," he said. "A holiday."

"Illiana," she said, extending her hand across the armrest.

"John Moreno." He shook her hand, and took pleasure in the touch.

The stewardess came, a round woman with rigid red hair, and took their plates. Moreno locked the tray in place. He retrieved his guidebook from the knapsack under the seat, and read. Brazil is a land of great natural beauty, and a country unparalleled in its ideal of racial democracy....

Moreno flipped past the rhetoric of the guidebook, went directly to the meat: currency, food and drink, and body language. Not that Brazil would pose any sort of problem for him; in his fifteen-odd years in the business, there were very few places in the world where he had not quickly adapted. This adaptability made him one of the most marketable independents in the field. And it was why, one week earlier, on the first Tuesday of September, he had been called to the downtown Miami office of Mr. Carlos Garcia, vice-president of claims, United Casualty and Life.

Garcia was a trim man with closely cropped, tightly curled hair. He wore a wide-lapelled suit of charcoal gray, a somber color for Miami, and a gray and maroon tie with an orderly geometric design. A phone sat on his desk, along with a blank notepad, upon which rested a silver Cross pen.

Moreno sat in a leather chair with chrome arms across from Garcia's desk. Garcia's secretary served coffee, and after a few sips and the necessary exchange of pleasantries, Moreno asked Garcia to describe the business at hand.

Garcia told him about Guzman, a man in his fifties who had made and lost some boom-years money in South Florida real estate. Guzman had taken his pleasure boat out of Key Largo one day in the summer of 1992. Two days later, his wife reported him missing, and a week after that the remains of his boat were found, along with a body, two miles out to sea. Guzman and his vessel had been the victims of an unexplained explosion on board.

"Any crew?" asked Moreno.

"Just Guzman."

"A positive identification on the body?"

"Well. The body was badly burned. Horribly burned. And most of what was left went to the fish."

"How about his teeth?"

"Guzman wore dentures." Garcia smiled wanly. "Interesting, no?"

The death benefits of Guzman's term policy, a $2 million

payoff, went to the widow. United's attorneys fought it to a point, but the effort from the outset was perfunctory. The company absorbed the loss.

Then, a year later, a neighbor of the Guzmans was vacationing in Recife, a city and resort on the northeast coast of Brazil, and spotted who she thought was Guzman. She saw this man twice in one week, on the same beach. By the time she returned to the States, she had convinced herself that she had in fact seen Guzman. She went to the widow with her suspicions, who seemed strangely unconcerned. Then she went to the police.

"And the police kicked it to you," Moreno said.

"They don't have the jurisdiction, or the time. We have a man on the force who keeps us informed in situations like this."

"So the widow wasn't too shook up by the news."

"No," Garcia said. "But that doesn't prove or even indicate any kind of complicity. We see many different kinds of emotions in this business upon the death of a spouse. The most common emotion that we see is relief."

Moreno folded one leg over the other and tented his hands in his lap. "What have you done so far?"

"We sent a man down to Brazil, an investigator named Roberto Silva."

"And?"

"Silva became very drunk one night. He left his apartment in Recife to buy a pack of cigarettes, stepped into an open elevator shaft, and fell eight stories to his death. He was found the next morning with a broken neck."

"Accidents happen."

Garcia spread his hands. "Silva was a good operative. I sent him because he had a history of success. But I knew that he had a very bad problem with alcohol. I had seen him fall down myself, on more than one occasion. This time, he simply fell a very long way."

Moreno stared through the window at the Miami skyline. After a while he said, "This looks to be a fairly simple case. There is a man in a particular area of Recife who either is or is not Guzman. I will bring you this man's fingerprints. It should take no more than two weeks."

"What do you require?"

"I get four hundred a day, plus expenses."

"Your terms are reasonable," Garcia said.

"There's more," Moreno said, holding up his hand. "My expenses are unlimited, and not to be questioned. I fly first-class and require an apartment with a live-in maid to cook and to clean my clothes. And, I get two and one half percent of the amount recovered."

"That's fifty thousand dollars."

"Correct," Moreno said, standing out of his seat. "I'll need a half-dozen wallet-sized photographs of Guzman, taken as close to his death date as possible. You can send them along with my contract and travel arrangements to my home address."

John Moreno shook Garcia's hand and walked away from the desk.

Garcia said to Moreno's back, "It used to be 'Juan,' didn't it? Funny how the simple change of a name can open so many doors in this country."

"I can leave for Brazil at any time," Moreno said. "You know where to reach me."

Moreno opened Mr. Garcia's door and walked from the office. The next morning, a package was messengered to John Moreno's home.

And now Moreno's plane neared the Brasília airport. He closed the guidebook he had been reading, and turned to Illiana.

"I have a question for you, Doctor," Moreno said. "A friend married a first-generation American of Brazilian descent. Their children, both of them, were born with blue-black spots above their buttocks."

Illiana smiled. "Brazil is a land whose people come from many colors," she said, sounding very much like the voice of the guidebook. "Black, white, brown, and many colors in between. Those spots that you saw"—and here Illiana winked—"it was simply the nigger in them."

So much for the ideal of racial democracy, Moreno thought, as the plane began its descent.

Moreno caught a ride from the airport with a man named Eduardo, who divided his time as an importer/exporter between Brasília and Miami. They had struck up a conversation as they waited in line to use the plane's lavatory during the flight. They were met at the airport by someone named Val, whom Eduardo introduced as his attorney, a title that Moreno doubted, as Val was a giggly and rather silly young man. Still, he accepted a lift in Val's VW Santana, and after a seventy-mile-per-hour ride through the flat, treeless landscape that was Brasília, Moreno was dropped at the Hotel Dos Nachos, a place Eduardo had described with enthusiasm as "two and a half stars."

The lobby of the Hotel Dos Nachos contained several potted plants and four high-backed chairs occupied by two taxicab drivers, an aging tout in a shiny gray suit, and a bearded man smoking a meerschaum pipe. A drunken businessman accompanied by a mulatto hooker in a red leather skirt entered the lobby and walked up the stairs while Moreno negotiated the room rate. The hotel bellman stood sleeping against the wall. Moreno carried his own bags through the elevator doors.

Moreno opened the windows of his small brown room and stuck his head out. Below, in an empty lot, a man sat beneath a Pepsi-Cola billboard with his face buried in his hands, a manged dog asleep at his feet. Moreno closed the window to a crack, stripped to his shorts, did four sets of fifty push-ups, showered, and went to bed.

The next morning he caught an early flight to Recife. At the airport, he hailed a taxi. Several foul-smelling children begged Moreno for change as he sat in the passenger seat of the cab, waiting for the driver to stow his bags. Moreno stared straight ahead as the children reached in his window, rubbing their thumbs and forefingers together in front of his face. Before the cab pulled away, one of the children, a dark boy with matted blond hair, cursed under his breath, and dropped one American penny in Moreno's lap.

Moreno had the cab driver pass through Boa Viagem, Recife's resort center, to get his bearings. When Moreno had a general idea of the layout, the driver dropped him at his *apartamento* in the nine hundred block of Rua Setubal, one street back from the beach. A uniformed guard stood behind the glassed-in gatehouse at the ten-story condominium; Moreno tipped him straight off, and carried his own bags through the patio of hibiscus and standing palm to the small lift.

Moreno's *apartamento* was on the ninth floor, a serviceable arrangement of one large living and dining room, two bedrooms, two baths, a dimly lit kitchen, and a windowless sleeper porch on the west wall where the clothes were hung to dry in the afternoon sun. The east wall consisted of sliding glass doors that opened to a concrete balcony finished in green tile. The balcony gave to an unobstructed view of the beach and the aquamarine and emerald swells of the south Atlantic, and to the north and south the palm-lined beach road, Avenida Boa Viagem. The sliding glass doors were kept open at all times: a tropical breeze blew constantly through the *apartamento*, and the breeze ensured the absence of bugs.

For the first few days, Moreno stayed close to his condominium, spending his mornings at the beach working on his local's tan, watching impromptu games of soccer, and practicing his Portuguese on the vendors selling oysters, nuts, and straw hats. At one o'clock, his maid, a pleasant but silent woman named Sonya, prepared him huge lunches: black beans and rice, salad, mashed potatoes, and pork roasted and seasoned with *tiempero,* a popular spice. In the evenings, Moreno would visit a no-name, roofless café, where a photograph of Madonna was taped over the bar. He would sit beneath a coconut palm and eat a wonderfully prepared filet of fish, washed down with a cold Brahma beer, sometimes with a shot of aguardente, the national rotgut that tasted of rail tequila but had a nice warm kick. After dinner he would stop at the Kiosk, a kind of bakery and convenience market, and buy a bottle of Brazilian Cabernet, have a glass or two of that on the balcony of his *apartamento* before going off to bed. The crow of a nearby rooster woke him every morning through his open window at dawn.

Sometimes Moreno passed the time leaning on the tile rim of his balcony, looking down on the activity in the street below. There were high walls of brick and cinder block around all the neighboring condominiums and estates, and it seemed as if these walls were in a constant state of repair or decay. Occasionally, an old white mare, unaccompanied by cart or harness, would clomp down the street, stopping to graze on the patches of grass that sprouted along the edges of the sidewalk. And directly below his balcony, through the leaves of the black curaçao tree that grew in front of his building, Moreno saw children crawl into the great canvas Dumpster that sat by the curb and root through the garbage in search of something to eat.

Moreno watched these children with a curious but detached eye. He had known poverty himself, but he had no sympathy for those who chose to remain within its grasp. If one was hungry, one worked. To be sure, there were different degrees of dignity in what one did to get by. But there was always work.

As the son of migrant workers raised in various Tex-Mex border towns, Juan Moreno had vowed early on to escape the shackles of his lowly, inherited status. He left his parents at sixteen to work for a man in Austin so that he could attend the region's best high school. By sticking to his schedule of classes during the day and studying and working diligently at night, he was able, with the help of government loans, to gain entrance to a moderately prestigious university in New England, where he quickly learned the value of lineage and presentation. He changed his name to John.

Already fluent in Spanish, John Moreno got degrees in both French and criminology. After graduation, he moved south, briefly joining the Dade County sheriff's office. Never one for violence and not particularly interested in carrying or using a firearm, Moreno took a job for a relatively well-known firm specializing in international retrievals. Two years later, having made the necessary connections and something of a reputation for himself, he struck out on his own.

John Moreno liked his work. Most of all, whenever his plane left the runway and he settled into his first-class seat, he felt a kind of elusion, as if he were leaving the dust and squalor of his early years a thousand miles behind. Each new destination was another permanent move, one step farther away.

> The Brazilians are a touching people. Often men will hug for minutes on end, and women will walk arm in arm in the street.

Moreno put down his guidebook on the morning of the fourth day, did his four sets of fifty push-ups, showered, and changed into a swimsuit. He packed his knapsack with some American dollars, ten dollars' worth of Brazilian cruzeiros, his long-lensed Canon AE-1, and the Guzman photographs, and left the *apartamento*.

Moreno was a lean man, a shade under six feet, with wavy black hair and a thick black mustache. His vaguely Latin appearance passed for both South American and southern Mediterranean, and with his newly enriched tan, he attracted no attention as he moved along the Avenida Boa Viagem toward the center of the resort, the area where Guzman had been spotted. The beach crowd grew denser: women in thong bathing suits and men in their Speedos, vendors, hustlers, and shills.

Moreno claimed a striped folding chair near the beach wall, signaled a man behind a cooler, who brought him a tall Antarctica beer served in a Styrofoam thermos. He finished that one and had two more, drinking very slowly to pass away the afternoon. He was not watching for Guzman. Instead he watched the crowd and the few men who sat alone and unmoving on its periphery. By the end of the day, he had chosen two of those men: a brown Rasta with sun-bleached dreadlocks who sat by the vendors but did not appear to have goods to sell, and an old man with the leathery, angular face of an Indian who had not moved from his seat at the edge of the market across the street.

As the sun dropped behind the condominiums and the beach draped into shadow, Moreno walked over to the Rasta on the wall and handed him a photograph of Guzman. The Rasta smiled a mouthful of stained teeth and rubbed two fingers together. Moreno gave him ten American dollars, holding out another ten immediately and quickly replacing it in his own pocket. He touched the photograph, then pointed to the striped folding chair near the wall to let the Rasta know where he could find him. The Rasta nodded, then smiled again, making a V with his fingers and touching his lips, blowing out with an exaggerated exhale.

"*Fumo?*" the Rasta said.

"*Não fumo,*" Moreno said, jabbing his finger at the photograph once more before he left.

Moreno crossed the road and found the old man at the edge of the market. He replayed the same proposition with the man. The man never looked at Moreno, though he accepted the ten and slid it and the photograph into the breast pocket of his eggplant-colored shirt. In the dying afternoon light, Moreno could not read a thing in the man's black pupils.

As Moreno turned to cross the street, the old man said in Portuguese, "You will return?"

Moreno said, "*Amanhã,*" and walked away.

On the way back to his place, Moreno stopped at a food stand—little more than a screened-in shack on the beach road—and drank a cold Brahma beer. Afterward, he walked back along the beach, now lit by streetlamps in the dusk. A girl of less than twenty with a lovely mouth smiled as she passed his way, her hair fanning out in the wind. Moreno felt a brief pulse in his breastbone, remembering just then that he had not been with a woman for a very long time.

*   *   *

It was this forgotten need for a woman, Moreno decided, as he watched his maid, Sonya, prepare breakfast the next morning in her surf shorts and T-shirt, that had thrown off his rhythms in Brazil. He would have to remedy that, while of course expending as little energy as possible in the hunt. First things first, which was to check on his informants in the center of Boa Viagem.

He was there within the hour, seated on his striped folding chair, on a day when the sun came through high, rapidly moving clouds. His men were there, too: the Rasta on the wall and the old man at the edge of the market. Moreno had an active swim in the warm Atlantic early in the afternoon, going out beyond the reef, then returned to his seat and ordered a beer. By the time the vendor served it, the old man with the Indian features was moving across the sand toward Moreno's chair.

"*Boa tarde,*" Moreno said, squinting up in the sun.

The old man pointed across the road, toward an outdoor café that led to an enclosed bar and restaurant. A middle-aged man and a young woman were walking across the patio toward the open glass doors of the bar.

"*Bom,*" Moreno said, handing the old man the promised ten from his knapsack. He left one hundred and twenty thousand cruzeiros beneath the full bottle of beer, gestured to the old man to sit and drink it, put his knapsack over his shoulder, and took the stone steps from the beach up to the street. The old man sat in the striped folding chair without a word.

Moreno crossed the street with caution, looking back to catch a glimpse of the brown Rasta sitting on the wall. The

Rasta stared unsmiling at Moreno, knowing he had lost. Moreno was secretly glad it had been the old man, who had reminded him of his own father. Moreno had not thought of his long-dead father or even seen him in his dreams for some time.

Moreno entered the restaurant. There were few patrons, and all of them, including the middle-aged man and this woman, sat at a long mahogany bar. Moreno took a chair near an open window. He leaned his elbow on the ledge of the window and drummed his fingers against the wood to the florid music coming from the restaurant. The bartender, a stocky man with a great belly that plunged over the belt of his trousers, came from behind the bar and walked toward Moreno's table.

"Cervejas," Moreno said, holding up three fingers pressed together to signify a tall one. The bartender stopped in his tracks, turned, and headed back behind the bar.

Moreno drank his beer slowly, studying the couple seated at the bar. He considered taking some photographs, seeing that this could be done easily, but he decided that it was not necessary, as he was certain now that he had found Guzman. The man had ordered his second drink, a Teacher's rocks, in English, drinking his first hurriedly and without apparent pleasure. He was tanned and seemed fit, with a full head of silvery hair and the natural girth of age. The woman was in her twenties, quite beautiful in a lush way, with the stone perfect but bloodless look of a photograph in a magazine. She wore a bathing suit top, two triangles of red cloth really, with a brightly dyed sarong wrapped around her waist. Occasionally the man would nod in response to something she had said; on those occasions, the two of them did not look in each other's eyes.

Eventually, the other patrons finished their drinks and left, and for a while it was just the stocky bartender, the man and his woman, and Moreno. A very tall, lanky young man with long, curly hair walked into the bar and with wide strides went directly to the man and whispered in his ear. The man finished his drink in one gulp, tossed bills on the bar, and got off his stool. He, the woman, and the young man walked from the establishment without even a glance in Moreno's direction. Moreno knew he had been made but in a practical sense did not care. He opened his knapsack, rose from his seat, and headed for the bar.

Moreno stopped in the area where the party had been seated and ordered another beer. As the bartender turned his back to reach into the cooler, Moreno grabbed some bar napkins, wrapped them around the base of Guzman's empty glass, and began to place the glass in his knapsack.

A hand grabbed Moreno's wrist.

The hand gripped him firmly. Moreno smelled perspiration, partly masked by a rather obvious men's cologne. He turned his head. It was the lanky young man, who had reentered the bar.

"You shouldn't do that," the young man said in accented English. "My friend João here might think you are trying to steal his glass."

Moreno placed the glass back on the bar. The young man spoke rapidly in Portuguese, and João the bartender took the glass and ran it over the brush in the soap sink. Then João served Moreno the beer that he had ordered, along with a clean glass. Moreno took a sip. The young man did not look more than twenty. His skin and his hard, bright eyes were the color of coffee beans. Moreno put down his glass.

"You've been following my boss," the young man said.

"Really," Moreno said.

"Yes, really." The young man grinned. "Your Rastaman friend, the one you showed the pictures to. He don't like you so good no more."

Moreno looked out at the road through the open glass doors. "What now?"

"Maybe me and a couple of my friends," the young man said, "now we're going to kick your ass."

Moreno studied the young man's face, went past the theatrical menace, found light play in the dark brown eyes. "I don't think so. There's no buck in it for you that way."

The young man laughed shortly, pointed at Moreno. "That's right!" His expression grew earnest again. "Listen, I tell you what. We've had plenty of excitement today, plenty enough. How about you and me, we sleep on top of things, think it over, see what we're going to do. Okay?"

"Sure," Moreno said.

"I'll pick you up in the morning, we'll go for a ride, away from here, where we can talk. Sound good?"

Moreno wrote his address on a bar napkin. The young man took it and extended his hand.

"Guilherme," he said. "Gil."

"Moreno."

They shook hands, and Gil began to walk away.

"You speak good American," Moreno said.

Gil stopped at the doors, grinned, and held up two fingers. "New York," he said. "Astoria. Two years." And then he was out the door.

Moreno finished his beer, left money on the bar. He walked back to his *apartamento* in the gathering darkness.

Moreno stood drinking coffee on his balcony the next morning, waiting for Gil to arrive. He realized that this involvement with the young man was going to cost him money, but it would speed things along. And he was not surprised that Guzman had been located with such ease. In his experience, those who fled their old lives merely settled for an equally monotonous one in a different place and rarely moved after that. The beachfront hut in Pago Pago becomes as stifling as the center-hall Colonial in Bridgeport.

Gil pulled over to the curb in his blue sedan. He got out and greeted the guard at the gate, a man Moreno had come to know as Sérgio, who buzzed Gil through. Sérgio left the glassed-in guardhouse then and approached Gil on the patio. Sérgio broke suddenly into some sort of cartwheel, and Gil stepped away from his spinning feet, moved around Sérgio fluidly and got him into a headlock. They were doing some sort of local martial art, which Moreno had seen practiced widely by young men on the beach. Sérgio and Gil broke away laughing, Gil giving Sérgio the thumbs-up before looking up toward Moreno's balcony and catching his eye. Moreno shouted that he'd be down in a minute, handing his coffee cup to Sonya. Moreno liked this kid Gil, though he was not sure why.

They drove out of Boa Viagem in Gil's Chevrolet Monza, into downtown Recife, where the breeze stopped and the temperature rose an abrupt ten degrees. Then they were driving along a sewage canal near the docks, and across the canal into a kind of shantytown of tar paper, fallen cinder block, and chicken wire, where Moreno could make out a sampling of the residents: horribly poor families, morning drunks, two-dollar prostitutes, men with murderous eyes, criminals festering inside of children.

"It's pretty bad here now," Gil said, "though not so bad like in Rio. In Rio they cut your hand off just to get your watch. Not even think about it."

"The *Miami Herald* says your government kills street kids in Rio."

Gil chuckled. "You Americans are so righteous."

"Self-righteous," Moreno said.

"Yes, self-righteous. I lived in New York City, remember? I've seen the blacks and the Latins, the things that are kept from them. There are many ways for a government to kill the children it does not want, no?"

"I suppose so."

Gil studied Moreno at the stoplight as the stench of raw sewage rode in on the heat through their open windows. "Moreno, eh? You're some sort of Latino, aren't you?"

"I'm an American."

"Sure, American. Maybe you want to forget." Gil jerked his thumb across the canal, toward the shantytown. "Me, I don't forget. I come from a *favela* just like that, in the south. Still, I don't believe in being poor. There is always a way to get out, if one works. You know?"

Moreno knew now why he liked this kid Gil.

They drove over a bridge that spanned the inlet to the ocean, then took a gradual rise to the old city of Olinda, settled and burned by the Dutch in the fifteenth century. Gil parked on cobblestone near a row of shops and vendors, where Moreno bought a piece of local art carved from wood for his mother. Moreno would send the gift along to her in Nogales, a custom that made him feel generous, despite the fact that he rarely phoned her, and it had been three Christmases since he had seen her last. Afterward, Moreno visited a bleached church, five hundred years old, and was greeted at the door by an old nun dressed completely in white. Moreno left cruzeiros near the simple altar, then absently did his cross. He was not a religious man, but he was a superstitious one, a remnant of his youth spent in Mexico, though he would deny all that.

Gil and Moreno took a table shaded by palms near a grill set on a patio across from the church. They ordered one tall beer and two plastic cups. A boy approached them selling spices, and Gil dismissed him, shouting something as an afterthought to his back. The boy returned with one cigarette, which he lit on the embers of the grill before handing it to Gil. Gil gave the boy some coins and waved him away.

"So," Gil said, "what are we going to talk about today?"

"The name of your boss," Moreno said. 'It's Guzman, isn't it?"

Gil dragged on his cigarette, exhaled slowly. "His name, it's not important. But if you want to call him Guzman, it's okay."

"What do you do for him?"

"I'm his driver, and his interpreter. This is what I do in Recife. I hang around Boa Viagem and I watch for the wealthy tourists having trouble with the money and the language. The Americans, they have the most trouble of all. Then, I make my pitch. Sometimes it works out for me pretty good."

"You learned English in New York?"

"Yeah. A friend brought me over, found me a job as a driver for this limo service he worked for. You know, the guys who stand at the airport, holding signs. I learned the language fast, and real good. The business, too. In one year I showed the man how to cut his costs by 30 percent. The man put me in charge. I even had to fire my friend. Anyway, the man finally offered me half the company to run it all the way. I turned him down, you know? His offer, it was too low. That's when I came back to Brazil."

Moreno watched the palm shadows wave dreamily across Gil's face. "What about Guzman's woman?"

"She's some kinda woman, no?"

"Yes," Moreno said. "When I was a child I spotted a coral snake and thought it was the most beautiful thing I had ever seen. I started to follow it into the brush, when my mother slapped me very hard across the face."

"So now you are careful around pretty things." Gil took some smoke from his cigarette. "It's a good story. But this woman is not a poisonous snake. She is just a woman." Gil shrugged. "Anyway, I don't know her. So she cannot help us."

Moreno said, "Can you get me Guzman's fingerprints?"

"Sure," Gil said. "It's not a problem. But what are you going to get me?"

"Go ahead and call it," Moreno said.

"I was thinking, fifty-fifty, what you get."

Moreno frowned. "For two weeks, you know, I'm only going to make a couple thousand dollars. But I'll tell you what—you get me Guzman's fingerprints, and I'll give you one thousand American."

Gil wrinkled his forehead. "It's not much, you know?"

"For this country, I think that it's a lot."

"And," Gil continued quickly, "you got to consider. You, or the people you work for, maybe they're going to come down and take my boss and his money away. And then Gil, he's going to be out of the job."

Moreno sat back and had a swig of beer and let Gil chew things over. After a while, Gil leaned forward.

"Okay," Gil said. "So let me ask you something. Have you reported back to your people that you think you have spotted this man Guzman?"

"No," Moreno said. "It's not the way I work. Why?"

"I was thinking. Maybe my boss, it's worth a lot of money to him that you don't go home and tell anyone you saw him down here. So I'm going to talk to him, you know? And then I'm going to call you tomorrow morning. Okay?"

Moreno nodded slowly. "Okay."

Gil touched his plastic cup to Moreno's and drank. "I guess now," Gil said, "I work for you, too."

"I guess you do."

"So anything I can get you, Boss?"

Moreno thought about it and smiled. "Yes," he said. "There is one thing."

They drove back down from Olinda into Recife, where the heat and Gil's cologne briefly nauseated Moreno, then on into Boa Viagem, where things were cooler and brighter and the people looked healthy and there were not so many poor. Gil parked the Monza a few miles north of the center, near a playground set directly on the beach.

"There is one," Gil said, pointing to a woman, young and lovely in denim shorts, pushing a child on a swing. "And there is another." This time he pointed to the beach, where a plainer woman, brown and finely figured in her thong bathing suit, shook her blanket out on the sand.

Moreno wiped some sweat from his brow and nodded his chin toward the woman in the bathing suit. "That's the one I want," he said, as the woman bent over to smooth her towel. "And that's the way I want her."

Gil made arrangements with the woman, then dropped Moreno at his *apartamento* on the Rua Setubal. After that he met some friends on the beach for a game of soccer, and when the game was done, he bathed in the ocean. He let the sun dry him, then drove to Guzman's place, an exclusive condominium called Des Viennes on the Avenida Boa Viagem. Gil knew the guard on duty, who buzzed him through.

Ten minutes later, he sat in Guzman's living room overlooking the Atlantic, where today a group of sailboats tacked back and forth while a helicopter from a television station circled overhead. Guzman and Gil sat facing each other in heavily cushioned armchairs, while Guzman's woman sat in an identical armchair but facing out toward the ocean. Guzman's maid served them three aguardentes with fresh lime and sugar over crushed ice. Guzman and Gil touched glasses and drank.

"It's too much sugar and not enough lime," Guzman said to no one in particular.

"No," Gil said. 'I think it's okay."

Guzman set down his drink on a marble table with a marble obelisk centerpiece. "How did it go this morning with the American?"

But Gil was now talking in Portuguese to Guzman's woman, who answered him contemptuously without turning her head. Gil laughed sharply and sipped from his drink.

"She's beautiful," Guzman said. "But I don't think you can afford her."

"She's not my woman," Gil said cheerfully. "And anyway, the beach is very wide." Gil's smile turned down, and he said to Guzman, "Dismiss her. Okay, Boss?"

Guzman put the words together in butchered Portuguese, and the woman got out of her seat and walked glacially from the room.

Guzman stood from his own seat and went to the end of the living room where the balcony began. He had the look of a man who is falling to sleep with the certain knowledge that his dreams will not be good.

"Tell me about the American," Guzman said.

"His name is Moreno," Gil said. "I think we need to talk."

*   *   *

Moreno went down to the condominium patio after dark and waited for the woman on the beach to arrive. A shirtless boy with kinky brown hair walked by pushing a wooden cart, stopped and put his hand though the iron bars. Moreno ignored him, practicing his Portuguese instead with Sérgio, who was on duty that night behind the glass guardhouse. The shirtless boy left without complaint and climbed into the canvas Dumpster that sat by the curb, where he found a few scraps of wet garbage that he could chew and swallow and perhaps keep down. The woman from the beach arrived in a taxi, and Moreno paid the driver and received a wink from Sérgio before he led the woman up to his *apartamento*.

Sonya served a meal of whole roasted chicken, black beans and rice, and salad, with a side of shrimp sautéed in coconut milk and spice. Moreno sent Sonya home with extra cruzeiros, then uncorked the wine, a Brazilian Cabernet, himself. He poured the wine, and before he drank, he asked the woman her name. She touched a finger to a button on her blouse and said, "Cláudia."

Moreno knew the dinner was unnecessary, but it pleased him to sit across the table from a woman and share a meal. Her rather flat, wide features did nothing to excite him, but the memory of her fullness on the beach kept his interest, and she laughed easily and seemed to enjoy the food, especially the chicken, which she cleaned to the bone.

After dinner, Moreno reached across the table and undid the top two buttons of the woman's blouse, and as she took the cue and began to undress, he pointed her to the open glass doors that led to the balcony. He extinguished the lights and stepped out of his trousers as she walked naked across the room to the edge of the doors and stood with her palms pressed against the glass. He came behind her and moistened her with his fingers, then entered her, and kissed her cheek near the edge of her mouth, faintly tasting the grease that lingered from the chicken. The breeze came off the ocean and whipped her hair across his face. He closed his eyes.

Moreno fell to sleep alone that night, hearing from someplace very far away a woman's voice, singing mournfully in Spanish.

Moreno met Gil the following morning at the screened-in food shack on the beach road. They sat at a cable-spool table, splitting a beer near a group of teenagers listening to accordion-drive *ferro* music from a transistor radio. The teenagers were drinking beer. Gil had come straight from the beach, his long curly hair still damp and touching his thin bare shoulders.

"So," Gil said, tapping his index finger once on the wood of the table. "I think I got it all arranged."

"You talked to Guzman?"

"Yes. I don't know if he's going to make a deal. But he has agreed to meet with you and talk."

Moreno looked through the screen at the clouds and, around the clouds, the brilliant blue of the sky. "When and where?"

"Tonight," Gil said. "Around nine o'clock. There's a place

off your street, Setubal, where it meets the commercial district. There are many fruit stands there—"

"I know the place."

"Good. Behind the largest stand is an alley. The alley will take you to a bar that is not marked."

"An alley."

"Don't worry," Gil said, waving his hand. "Some friends of mine will be waiting for you to show you to the bar. I'll bring Guzman, and we will meet you there."

"Why that place?"

"I know the man, very well, who runs the bar. He will make sure that Guzman leaves his fingerprints for you. Just in case he doesn't want to play football."

"Play ball," Moreno said.

"Yes. So either way, we don't lose."

Moreno drank off the rest of his beer, placed the plastic cup on the cable-spool table. "Okay," he said to Gil. "Your plan sounds pretty good."

In the evening, Moreno did four sets of fifty push-ups, showered, and dressed in a black polo shirt tucked into jeans. He left his *apartamento* and took the lift down to the patio, where he waved to a guard he did not recognize before exiting the grounds of his condominium and hitting the street.

He walked north on Setubal at a brisk pace, avoiding the large holes in the sidewalk and sidestepping the stacks of brick and cinder block used to repair the walls surrounding the estates. He passed his no-name café, where a rat crossed his path and dropped into the black slots of a sewer grate. He walked by people who did not meet his eyes and bums who held out their hands but did not speak.

After about a mile, he could see through the darkness to the lights of the commercial district, and then he was near the fruit stands. In the shadows he could see men sitting, quietly talking and laughing. He walked behind the largest of the stands. In the mouth of an alley, a boy stood leaning on a homemade crutch, one leg severely twisted at the shin, the callused toes of that leg pointed down and brushing the concrete. The boy looked up at Moreno and rubbed his fingers together, and Moreno fumbled in his pockets for some change, nervously dropping some bills to the sidewalk. Moreno stooped to pick up the bills, handing them to the boy, then entered the alley. He could hear *ferro* music playing up ahead.

He looked behind him and saw that the crippled boy was following him into the alley. Moreno quickened his step, passing vendors' carts and brick walls whitewashed and covered with graffiti. He saw an arrow painted on a wall, and beneath the arrow the names of some boys, and an anarchy symbol, and to the right of that the words "Sonic Youth." He followed the direction of the arrow, the music growing louder with each step.

Then he was in a wide-open area that was no longer an alley because it had ended with walls on three sides. There were four men waiting for him there.

One of the men was short and very dark and held a machete at his side. The crippled boy was leaning against one of the walls. Moreno said something with a stutter and tried to smile. He did not know if he had said it in Portuguese or

English, or if it mattered, as the *ferro* music playing from the boom box on the cobblestones was very loud.

Moreno felt a wetness on his thigh and knew that this wetness was his own urine. The thing to do was simply to turn and run. But now he realized that one of the men was Sérgio, the guard at his condominium, whom he had not recognized out of his uniform.

Moreno laughed, and then all of the men laughed, including Sérgio, who walked toward Moreno with open arms to greet him.

The Brazilians are a touching people. Often men will hug for minutes on end, and women will walk arm in arm in the street.

Moreno allowed Sérgio to give him the hug. He felt the big muscled arms around him, and caught the stench of cheap wine on Sérgio's breath. Sérgio smiled an unfamiliar smile, and Moreno tried to step back, but Sérgio did not release him. Then the other men were laughing again, the man with the machete and the crippled boy, too. Their laughter rose on the sound of the crazy music blaring in the alley.

Sérgio released Moreno.

A forearm from behind locked across Moreno's neck. There was a hand on the back of his head, pressure, and a violent movement, then a sudden, unbelievable pain, a white pain but without light. For a brief moment, Moreno imagined that he was looking at his own chest from a very odd angle.

If John Moreno could have spoken later on, he could have

told you that the arm that killed him smelled heavily of perspiration and cheap cologne.

Gil knocked on Guzman's door late that night. The maid offered him a drink. He asked for aguardente straight up. She returned with it and served it in the living room, where Gil sat facing Guzman, and then she walked back to the kitchen to wash the dishes before she went to bed.

Guzman had his own drink, a Teacher's over ice, on the marble table in front of him. He ran his fingers slowly through his lion's head of silver hair.

"Where is your woman?" Gil said.

"She took a walk," Guzman said. "Is it over?"

"Yes," Gil said. "It is done."

"All this killing," Guzman said softly.

"You killed a man yourself. The one who took your place on the boat."

"I had him killed. He was just a rummy from the boatyard."

"It's all the same," Gil said. "But maybe you have told yourself that it is not."

Guzman took his scotch and walked to the open glass doors near the balcony, where it was cooler and there was not the smell that was coming off Gil.

"You broke his neck, I take it. Like the other one."

"He has no neck," Gil said. "We cut his head off and threw it in the garbage. The rest of him we cut to pieces."

Guzman closed his eyes. "But they'll come now. Two of their people have disappeared."

"Yes," Gil said. "They'll come. You have maybe a week. Argentina would be good for you, I think. I could get you a new passport, make the arrangements—"

"For a price."

"Of course."

Guzman turned and stared at the lanky young man. Then he said, "I'll get your money."

"You split the two million with your wife, and there have been many others to pay." Gil shrugged. "It costs a lot to become a new man, you know? Anyway, I'll see you later."

Gil headed for the door, and Guzman stopped him.

"I'm curious," Guzman said. "Why did this Moreno die, instead of me?"

"He bid very low," Gil said. "Goodnight, Boss."

Gil walked from the room.

Down on the Avenida Boa Viagem, Gil walked to his Chevrolet Monza and got behind the wheel. Guzman's woman, who was called Elena, was in the passenger's seat, waiting for Gil to arrive. She leaned across the center console and kissed Gil on the lips, holding the kiss for a very long while. It was Gil who finally broke away.

"Did you get the money?" Elena said.

"Yes," Gil said. "I got it." He spoke without emotion. He looked up through the windshield to the yellow light spilling onto Guzman's balcony.

"We are rich," Elena said, forcing herself to smile and pinching Gil's arm.

"There's more up there," Gil said. "You know?"

Elena said, "You scare me a little bit, Gil."

She went into her purse, found a cigarette, and fired the cigarette off the lighter from the dash. After a couple of drags, she passed the cigarette to Gil.

"What was it like?" Elena said.

"What's that?"

"When you killed this one," she said. "When his neck was broken, did it make a sound?"

Gil dragged on the cigarette, squinted against the smoke that rose off the ash.

"You know how it is when you eat a chicken," he said. "You have to break many bones if you want to get the meat. But you don't hear the sound, you know?

"You don't hear it," Gil said, looking up at Guzman's balcony, "when you're hungry."

MISS MARY'S ROOM

I WAS ALWAYS cool with Mrs. Sullivan. I been knowing her son, Pat, since we were in the same kindergarten class. His mom had one of those houses that were open to the kids in the neighborhood, and me, Pat, and some of the other fellas around our way hung out there often. Playing Xbox, going on Facebook to check out the females, shit like that. I spent the night a few times, and when I'd wake up in the morning, a blanket had been put on top of me by Pat's mom. She always asked after my mother, and when she talked about my younger brother, she knew what grade he was in. She was thoughtful like that.

I called her Miss Mary, which is how we do around here to adults when we want to show respect. My name is Tim, but she called me Sleepy, the street name I got on account of my half-mast eyes. I guess I thought of Miss Mary like family. I mean that in a good way, not in the way that I think of family when I think of my own situation at home.

We had free rein in the Sullivan house. I mean, we knew our boundaries, but still. Miss Mary trusted us boys so much that she left her open purse and wallet on the kitchen counter when she visited a neighbor or went for a walk. I know for a fact that none of us ever took a dollar. A couple of times we snagged a little liquor from that rolling cart she had and swiped beers out the refrigerator, but there was certain lines we wouldn't cross. Another one was, none of Pat's friends would ever go in her bedroom.

I remember it, though. From the hall, up on the second floor, I sometimes looked through her open door.

It was small bedroom. It had a double bed, which seemed to take up most of the space. I don't recall seeing no dresser. The wallpaper was busy with some old-timey pattern, looked like those ink tests the shrink gave me that time I set a trash can on fire in our middle school. What I remember most, beside the bed, was a fireplace mantel with no fireplace underneath it. It was just sort of mounted on the wall, framing the wallpaper. On top of the mantel was some kind of candle holder thing, a snow globe, and what looked like a painted rock. Above the candle holder was a crucifix that had been mounted on the wall. Also on the wall, two icons: Madonna and the baby Jesus, and Jesus grown up.

Miss Mary was straight Catholic. One time, from in the hall, I saw her praying the Rosary, holding those beads she had, looking up at the bearded Jesus picture on the wall. I had to look away. Didn't seem right somehow to be looking at her while she was doing that private thing.

This wasn't long after Pat's dad had died of a cancer. I don't even remember him much 'cause I was too young. Around that time, me and Pat were in a talent show together at our elementary. Up on stage, doing that "Jump" joint. Two tiny white boys in bow ties, lip-synching to Kris Kross. The crowd, kids and parents, went off. My mother was there, and one of her meth-tweak boyfriends, too. Man with a ponytail and a skinny behind.

Me and Pat was tight all through elementary, middle school, and high school, until I moved over to the tech high to learn the electrician's trade. We played rec league football and basketball as youngsters, but once we got to high school, neither of us had the grades to qualify for athletics, so we stopped. The way it is where we live, there are smart kids and tough kids, and they get separated early on. The smart kids, they get recognized as such in elementary. They're put in special classes and are protected all the way in magnet and AP programs on their paths to college and beyond. Dudes like me and Pat got identified way back as unmotivated students with behavior problems, and all the kids like us got thrown together in another group. We were put on what they call a different "track" than those nerd kids. Our track was the one that leads to nothing much. Those people at the schools wished it on us, in a way, and it became so.

Our neighborhood could be tough. A mix of colors, immigrant cabbies, on-and-off laborers, fathers who worked with their hands and backs if they were still around. Wasn't like us kids were gonna prove ourselves on the debate team, so what it came down to was, be willing to steal someone in the face or get stole, or be a punk and walk away. We did get tested and sometimes we were outnumbered. Pat had my back most times, and it wasn't easy for him to step up and fight. He did it, but he was on the soft side. That happened to some who didn't have a man around the house. Though, I got to say, it didn't happen to me.

Me and Pat started smoking weed when we were fourteen years old. This boy named Rollo, a dealer with a genuine rep who lived down in the apartments, turned us on to it. Rollo was twenty at the time. I guess I was ready to try marijuana. Ready or no, I wouldn't have turned down Rollo's offer. I didn't want to look like a faggot in his eyes.

As we got older, Rollo began to front us pounds of weed that we would split into ounces and sell off to our friends. In that way, Rollo expanded his business in our neighborhood, and me and Pat got free weed to smoke. It was a good deal for all of us.

Pat really loved being high. He'd get real quiet and happy after firing up. He was a big boy with black hair he kept shaved to the scalp. He had braces on his teeth, but he wasn't pressed by it. Matter of fact, he smiled a lot. Like his mother, Miss Mary, he had green eyes.

The deal between us was, I kept our scale and Baggies at my house, in my bedroom. My mother hardly ever went in my room, and if she had found anything, I don't believe she would have cared. Pat made the calls to kids we knew who were pot-heads, and both of us did what we called the transactions. Any conversations we had on our cell phones, we used codes. Money was Kermit, meaning green; an ounce was an osmosis; marijuana was M.J., for Michael Jordan. We weren't stupid.

We never moved product through the Sullivan house. Pat's place was for relaxing and being up. Miss Mary must have known me and her son was blazed most of the time, because we were always eating stuff from out the pantry and watching TV and laughing at it even when the shit was not funny, and the shows we were watching were like, UFO shows and shit. I think she was all right with it because her son was safe in the house. Having lost her husband and all, I believe she feared losing Pat to the street. So she knew we were smoking weed. What she didn't know was that we were dealing it, and all the complications that come with that.

The police in this county here are all about catching kids in the act of smoking, like it's some kind of high crime. They even got plainclothes Spanish guys, young dudes who look like they could be in high school, busting Latino kids who smoke in the woods. Young black and white police who do the same to their own kind. Meantime, if you are one of those nerd boys, you are pretty much safe, even if you partake in the sacrament yourself. The smart kids, the ones who been protected their whole lives, can go off to college and smoke all the weed they want in their dorm rooms. Shit is damn near legal for them. Just like it was for their parents.

Turns out, the police had been watching Rollo for some time. He had two possession charges on him. The first had been dismissed, but he had a court date coming up on the second and an expensive lawyer to represent him. We found out later from this same lawyer, he had been under suspicion as a known drug dealer by one of them county task forces they had. I'm thinking that some kid who got busted for possession

identified Rollo as his dealer once the police got that kid under the hot lights.

The night the bad thing went down, we were driving
around in Rollo's car, an old Mercury Marquis which has the
same platform as a Ford Crown Victoria and a Lincoln Con-
tinental. What they call the sister car. I didn't mention that
Rollo is black. Means nothing to me, but it's part of the story.
Police see a black dude and a couple of white dudes rolling
around in a Crown Vic look-alike, they see, what do you call
that, *misadventure*, and they are going to pull you over to the
side of the road. That came later.

We had gone down to the Summit apartments, which people around our way called Slum It. Blacks and Spanish lived
there, many females with their single mothers. There was this
one chick I liked to bang whose name was Lucia, and we
stopped by her spot. Lucia had told me her mom was out with
her boyfriend for the night, so it was a perfect setup. We all sat
around in her living room and got smoked up, listening to go-
go and some Latin stuff to make Lucia happy, and then me and
Lucia went to her bedroom and Rollo and Pat stayed where
they was at. Back in the bedroom, Lucia said she was on her
period, so I told her to suck it. After I busted a nut, me and
her went back out to the living room, and I told my boys that
it was time to go. I put a little weed on the coffee table for Lucia, and we left out of there.

Rollo said he needed to make a quick delivery in the building. We got in the elevator, which smelled like fried chicken and
cigarettes, went up a few floors, and followed Rollo down a hallway where he knocked on a door. Behind it someone said, "Who

is it?" and Rollo said, "UPS man," which was the answer they had agreed on. The door opened, and we went inside.

It was just one person in there, a dude named David, who went by Day. He was on the small side, but cocky. Had braids, like most dudes do these days, trying to be Gucci Mane. He was wearing hundred-dollar jeans, Air Force Ones, and a Blac Label T-shirt. It's like a uniform around here.

He said to Rollo, "You got it?"

Rollo said, "You got the Kermit?"

Day said, "I'm good."

And Rollo said, "Then I got it."

We sat around a cable-spool table that had a bong on top of it, matches, an ashtray, and a shoe box top Day used to clean the seeds away from the buds. Day wanted to try the weed. Rollo handed him the Baggie, and Day kind of hefted it in his hand and said, "Feels light."

"You think so?" said Rollo.

Day fired up a piece and poked it through the bowl with a thin rod. He sat back on the couch, holding his breath, and coughed out a stream of smoke. His eyes were already pink.

"Good funk," said Day.

"I know it," said Rollo.

"But light."

"Now you gonna negotiate."

"I could get my scale, you want me to."

"You prolly don't need a scale. With your superpowers and shit, you can just, you know, weigh the bag in your hand."

"I'm sayin."

"It's an ounce. I scaled that shit my *own* self two hours ago."

119

"I don't think so."

"I'm lyin?"

"We got a difference of opinion, is all. Thinkin, we can meet each other halfway."

" 'Nother words, you want a discount."

"This here ain't no O-Z, Rollo. I just want to pay you for what it is."

"Okay," said Rollo, standing from his seat. "I'm a let you set the price."

"Ain't you want to discuss it?"

Rollo, his eyes empty, shook his head.

Day straightened his legs so he could get a hand inside the pocket of his jeans, then pulled out a roll of bills. He began to peel off notes, soundlessly counting with his lips. When he was satisfied, he held the bills that he had separated from the roll out to Rollo. That was when Rollo pulled a nine-millimeter Beretta from out of his dip.

Rollo swung the heater fast and hard. Its barrel connected high on Day's cheek. A worm of blood appeared immediately beneath his eye socket. Day touched the wound, split open wide, with his fingers. Rollo laughed.

"Take the money, Sleepy," said Rollo, snicking back the hammer on the nine. "All a that shit."

I went to Day and grabbed the money from each of his hands. I was excited, I got to admit. I had never robbed no one.

Pat had stood up and backed away. The color had drained out his face.

Rollo picked up the Baggie off the cable-spool table, re-sealed and rolled it, and stuffed it into the pocket of his jeans.

"Now you gonna take that, too," said Day, in a low voice. He was trying not to cry. He looked small on that couch. "You not gonna leave me anything?"

"Leave you with your life," said Rollo. He eased the trigger down and holstered the Beretta behind his back. He pulled his shirttail out to cover it and said, "Let's go."

We were out of that building quick.

On the way to the Marquis, Pat said, "Why'd you do that, Rollo?"

Rollo shrugged and said, "That little muthafucka just aggravate me, man."

"Bad for business," said Pat. He was still real nervous, you could tell. "I'm sayin, if it gets around."

"Day ain't gonna say shit to anybody," said Rollo. "Day's a bitch."

When we got into the downtown area of where we lived, where they got the restaurants, pawn shops, and movie theaters and shit, we saw lights flashing behind us and heard the burst of a siren. We were being pulled over by the law.

Rollo cut the Mercury to the curb and killed the engine. He put the gun under the seat. He handed me the bag of weed, and I laid it up under the dash where he had a small space for it in a cradle of wires.

"They just gonna talk to us," said Rollo. "It'll be all right."

But the police officers in the patrol vehicle didn't get out and approach our car. They sat where they were and waited, and soon many other squad cars, their light bars afire, began to appear from different directions. Several uniformed officers came upon us then, their weapons drawn. They screamed at us and ordered us out of the car, telling us to keep our hands raised, and then we were pushed down on the ground and cuffed with plastic bands.

Day had called 911 on us. I couldn't believe it. You always left the police out your business. I mean, that shit was just not done.

The officers found the weed. They found the gun.

Lying facedown on the street beside me, I heard Pat say, "Mom."

All of us were arrested and spent the night in the county lockup. We were charged with drug possession, unlawful possession of a firearm, and using a firearm in the commission of felony robbery. Me and Pat were eighteen, so we were charged as adults. The felony gun charge carried a five-year mandatory sentence if we were convicted of it. Because of the gun thing, the commissioner set our bails high. Rollo stayed in jail several days until his supplier bailed him out with drug money. My mother got a bond somehow. Pat's mom, Miss Mary, had to put her house up for collateral to get him released.

I was assigned a public defender. When I saw how young he was, and his cheap suit and wrinkled shirt, I knew I was in trouble. Rollo had his expensive lawyer, who he was more and more in debt to by the day. I heard from this fellah I knew that Pat had got some well-known criminal defense attorney in the county, a man Miss Mary knew from her church.

I say "I heard" because I had not spoken to Pat since the night of the arrest. Well, not more than a few words. Once we were released, I had called him on his cell.

"Can't speak to you, Sleepy," said Pat. "My lawyer says we shouldn't be talkin to each other. 'Specially not on a cell. Could be our phones are tapped."

"What are you gonna do?"

"Huh?"

"You ain't give no statement or nothin, did you?"

"Nah, man…"

"Did you?"

Pat said, "I gotta go," and the cell connection went dead. That was our conversation. He sounded scared.

Time passed and nothing happened. That is how these things go. You get charged and then you wait. We didn't even have a trial date. But I couldn't relax. Personally, I felt that I was in a tight spot. I wasn't gonna cut no deal with anybody, cause that meant I had to roll over on my boys. And yet, I didn't trust my rookie lawyer to make a good case for me at a jury trial. I could do prison for a short stay, but I didn't know if I could do the full nickel.

One day, I saw Rollo out on the street, sitting curbside in his idling Marquis. I slid into the shotgun seat and dapped him up. Rollo had that skunky smell on him. He had been getting his head up, but his high had not taken him to a good place. His face said grim.

"What you think, Sleepy?"

I knew he was talking about our chances. "I don't know."

"I need money," said Rollo. "My lawyer's costin me. My man put up my bail and I owe him big, too. What I got to do is, I got to be back in business so I can get in the flow."

"You can't do that now."

"I know it. But I can't get back to doin what I do best if I'm incarcerated."

"Maybe we'll walk. If Day don't show up to testify, they got no case."

"I'm tryin to take care of that. What I'm stressed on is Pat. If he flips on us—"

"Pat's my boy."

"I'm sayin, if he *does* testify against us, to keep his self out of the joint—"

"He wouldn't. He'll stand tall."

"Okay," said Rollo, looking at me full for the first time, his eyes flat and waxed. "I'm bringin it up, is all."

"Pat's straight," I said, but my voice sounded weak, like I didn't believe my own words. Rollo had put a cold seed in my stomach.

Not long after, I was walking through the business district of our neighborhood, when I saw Pat, Miss Mary, and their attorney, a slick-looking dude in pinstripes, sitting in the local coffeehouse at a window-side table. Pat had grown his hair out some, which made him look less hard. He was wearing khaki pants and a blue button-down shirt. He looked like one of those prep school boys the two of us had hated on all our lives. He was smiling. I stood on the street, watching him. It was September, still warm out. But I felt cold.

Later in the evening I tried to phone his cell, but he didn't pick up. He had caller ID, and he knew it was me. It was plain to me that he didn't want to talk to me no more. I got the feeling that, far as he was concerned, we were through.

He was coming home from work, this hardware store they

got downtown, the next time I saw him. This was in November. He was on foot. Since our arrest he had gotten a job, his first. He was wearing a red shirt with the store logo on the front of it under his North Face fleece, and he had his head down, his arms pumping at his sides, the way he had always moved since we was kids. I had gone to the store earlier in the day, looked through the plate glass that fronted it, and seen him in there, talking to a customer. I figured he was on till closing. And I knew the way he'd walk home after he got off, through that alley that cuts down toward his mother's house.

I was sitting beside Rollo, who was under the wheel of his Marquis. In the backseat was JoJo, this man Rollo knew from where he grew up, in the housing units deep in the city. JoJo had been in lockup for a time, but he was home now. Me and Pat had got smoked up with him before, a while back.

When Pat saw Rollo's car in the shadows of the alley, he stopped walking. He didn't back up or nothin like that. But he didn't come forward, neither.

"Fellas," he said, with that easy smile of his. Like he had done no one dirt.

"Waitin on you," I said, leaning out the window. "Let's get our heads up, man."

"I'd like to," said Pat. "But I can't be dropping a positive if they make me pee."

"I got some shit can fix that," I said, meaning this drink I got up the health store that could erase the marijuana in your urine. Pat knew what it was. He had told me about it originally.

"I better not."

"Come on and visit, son," said Rollo, his booming voice coming genially from inside the car.

Pat shook his head, relaxed his shoulders, and walked to the Marquis. He got in the backseat, next to JoJo. Pat recognized him and they pounded fists.

"How you doin, young?" said JoJo.

"Working," said Pat, with a shrug. "You know what that's like."

"Not really," said JoJo, and everyone laughed.

"You been all right?" said Rollo, looking at Pat in the rearview.

"I'm straight," said Pat.

"Nothin to report?" said Rollo.

"My lawyer said I ain't supposed to talk about the case with you guys."

"Uh-huh."

"I'm a listen to my lawyer," said Pat.

"Right," said Rollo. "You *should*. I guess what I'm askin is, though, have you heard anything about our chances? 'Cause none of us have heard shit."

"I don't know any more than y'all do," said Pat, with a shrug.

Looking at him, knowing him as long as I did, I almost believed him.

"Thought you guys had some pieces," said Pat.

"I got some bud will make your dick hard," said JoJo.

"We can't smoke it in my car, though," said Rollo. "I ain't tryin to get pulled over again."

"I heard *that*," said Pat.

"Let's go over to the school," I said.

Rollo pulled down on the transmission arm and gave the Mercury gas. We rolled down the alley with the lights off until we hit the main road.

It was full night. Rollo parked in the lot of a garden-style apartment building. We looked around, saw no one, and got out of the car and crossed the street. We passed under a lamp and then into shadows. Then we went up a grassy hill covered in fallen leaves, and into the woods that bordered the elementary school where me and Pat had gone to kindergarten and beyond.

In the woods it was plenty dark. There was not much of a moon overhead, but our eyes adjusted quick. The branches of the trees were damn near bare. JoJo had freaked a Black 'n Mild with his weed, and he lit it from a Bic and passed it around. It wasn't long before we got up on JoJo's hydro. We started laughing and stuff. Pat got to giggling, like he did when he got blazed.

"Hey, Sleepy," said Pat. "You remember that time, in elementary, when we got up on stage and did that song?"

"Yeah," I said.

"Kris Kross," said Pat, blowing off the embers of the blunt. "What happened to them?"

"They grew up," I said.

"We were wearing bow ties, man," said Pat. "My mom was there, watching us. Yours was, too. Remember?"

"I do." My voice cracked some when I said it. The branches above us were like black arms. Rollo nodded his head, just a little. Pat didn't notice, but I did.

"We were *kids*," said Pat, as if in wonder.

JoJo shot Pat in the back of the head. Pat said "Uh," and fell forward. His blood, like one of them ink drawings, bloomed in the night. There wasn't no gunshot sound. JoJo had one of those suppressors screwed into the barrel of his heater. He was a professional. He owed Rollo a favor, and now his debt was erased. Rollo put another one into Pat's head, and we walked real quiet out the woods.

Days later, at the funeral home, there was police in vans, taking pictures from out in the lot. It was an old scheme of theirs, trying to see if the killer would show up at the viewing for his victim. Me and Rollo had been questioned right away, but they had nothing. What they needed was a weapon or a witness. The gun was gone forever, and we damn sure wasn't gonna talk. So on the murder, they had no case.

It was a big turnout for Pat: kids from our high school, relatives, people from the Sullivans' church. Miss Mary was in the viewing room, standing by Pat's casket. I avoided her at first, but I had to go up there. Pat did not look as bad as I thought he would. They had done a good job on him with makeup and shit. He was wearing a suit.

I stood before Miss Mary, stepped into her arms, and gave her a hug. She looked wasted, her skin the color of putty. Her hair was tangled, and lipstick was uneven on her mouth. She stood back from me and took my hand and squeezed it.

"Sleepy."

"Yes, ma'am."

"Look at me, Sleepy," she said, staring deep into my eyes. "Do you know who did this?"

"No, ma'am," I said. "But I'm gonna find out."

"I want you to promise me something," she said.

"What?"

"I don't want any retribution for this. I don't want another young man to die. I don't want you or your friends to murder someone over my son and go to prison for it. This all…this has to stop."

"Okay."

"Do you promise?"

"Yes."

I couldn't believe it. In spite of all that had gone down, she was thinking of me.

Funny thing is, I don't even know for sure if Pat was gonna flip. It might not have mattered, because Rollo had been right all along about Day. He turned out to be a straight bitch. Day did not show up to testify in court, and the hard felony charges against me and Rollo were dropped. I got probation on the possession and walked out of that courtroom free. Rollo got a little bit of time.

I should be relieved, but I'm not. I can't stop thinking on Miss Mary. She was always real kind to me, and it hurts to picture her now. 'Cause in my head I can see her, sitting on the edge of her bed. Praying the Rosary, up in her room.

I am writing this down now for her. I ran into Rollo once or twice since he been out, and I did not like the look he had in his eyes. In case something happens to me, I want Miss Mary to know that I was involved in this thing. The truth is, I got no deep remorse for what got did to Pat. Pat was in the game, and he knew what time it was. But I'm real sorry for what I took from his mom.

PLASTIC PADDY

"**I HATE ARABS**," said Paddy.

A guy sat facing a good-looking blonde in a booth against the far wall. The guy was minding his own business. He and the girl were splitting a pitcher of draft and smiling at each other across the table. He would say something, or she would, and the other one would laugh. It looked like they were having a nice time. Paddy was staring at the guy like he wanted to kick his ass.

"How you know he's an Arab?" I said.

"Look at him," said Paddy. "Looks like Achmed Z-med, that guy on *T. J. Hooker.*"

"Adrian Zmed," said Scott, the smart guy of our bunch.

"Another Arab," said Paddy. This was five or six years after the Ayatollah, Nuke Iran, and all that crap. Paddy was the only guy I knew who hadn't given that up.

Me and Paddy and Scott were in Kildare's, a pub up in Wheaton we used to drink at pretty regular. Wheaton was our neighborhood, not too far over the D.C. line, but a thousand miles away from the city, if you know what I mean. It was a night like most nights back then: a little drinking, some blow, then more drinking to take the thirst off the blow. Only this night ended up different than the rest.

I'd put the year at 1985, 'cause I can remember the bands and singers that were coming from the juke: Mr. Mister, Paul Young, Foreigner, Wham. Hell, you could flush the whole Top 40 from that decade down the toilet and no one would miss it. Also, Len Bias was lighting it up for Maryland on the TV screen over the bar, so I know it couldn't have been later than '85. Maybe it was early '86. It was around then, anyway.

Paddy was up that night, and not only from the coke. He always seemed angry at something back in those days, but we had chalked up his behavior to his hyper personality. Just "Tool being Tool."

O'Toole, I should say. Up until he was twenty-three, Paddy's name was John Tool. Most everyone who knew him, even his old man before he kicked, called him Tool. It was a nickname you gave to a fraternity brother or something, like Animal Man or Headcase, which was all right around the fellas, but didn't go over too good with the girls. Paddy liked it all right when he was growing up, but when he got to be a man he suddenly felt it didn't suit him. Still, he wanted a handle, something that could make him stand out in a crowd. He wasn't a guy you noticed, either for his character or his appearance. I think that's why he changed his name. That and his women problem. He'd never had much success with the ladies, and he was looking to change his luck.

What he told us was, he'd paid to have one of those family-tree things done, and found that he was all Irish on his mother's side. Turned out that his great-grandfather's name was O'Toole. A lightning-strike coincidence, he said, that Tool and O'Toole were so similar. So he made the legal switch, adding Paddy as his first name. He said he liked the way Paddy O'Toole "scanned."

It was around this time that he went Irish all the way. Started listening to the Chieftains and their kind. Became a Notre Dame fan, got the silver four-leaf clover charm on a silver-plated necklace, and had that T-Bird he drove, the garbage wagon with the Landau roof, painted Kelly green at the body shop where he worked. Then he fixed a "Kiss Me, I'm Irish" sticker on the rear bumper, which totally fucked up what was already a halfway fucked-looking car.

Paddy began to drink more, too. I guess he thought that being a lush would admit him to the club. When he got really torched, he talked about his mother's cooking like it was special or something, and referred to his late father as "Da." His eyes would well with tears then, even though the old man had beat him pretty good when he was a kid. We thought it was all bullshit, and a little off, but we didn't say nothin to him. He wasn't hurting anyone, after all.

We didn't say anything to his face, that is. Scott, the only one of us who had graduated from college, analyzed the situation, as usual. Scott said that Americans who had that Irish identity thing going on were Irish the way Tony Danza was Italian. That most Americans' idea of Ireland was John Ford's Ireland, Technicolor green and Maureen O'Hara red and

Barry Fitzgerald, Popeye-with-a-brogue blarney. And by the way, said Scott, John Ford was born in Maine. I didn't know John Ford from Gerald Ford, but it sounded smart. Also, it sounded like a lecture, the way Scott always sounded since he'd come back home with that degree. Scott could be a little, what do you call that, *pompous* sometimes, but he was all right.

So back to Kildare's. For years we had gone to this other joint around the corner, Garner's, made your clothes smell like Marlboro Lights and steak-and-cheese. But Paddy, who before he went Irish had never moved up off of Miller Lite, said the Guinness there was "too cold," so we changed locales. "Kildare is a county in Ireland," said Paddy, the first time we went in there, like he was telling us something we didn't know, and Scott said, "So is Sligo," meaning the junior high school where all of us had gone. Paddy's mouth kind of slacked open then, like it did when he thought Scott was putting him on. I said, "Dr. Kildare," just to hear my own voice.

Kildare's wasn't anything special. It was your standard fake pub, loaded with promotional posters and mobiles, courtesy of the local liquor distributors. The sign outside said "A Publick House," like you could fool people into thinking Wheaton was London. I don't know, maybe the hometown rednecks bought into it, 'cause the joint was usually full. More likely they didn't care what you called it or what you dressed it up as. It was a place to get drunk. That was all anyone in these parts needed to know.

So the three of us were sitting at a four-top in the center of the room. I was hammering a Bud and Scott had a Michelob, another way he had of wearing his "I went to college" badge.

Paddy was on his third stout, and there was a shot of Jameson set neat next to the mug. I didn't know how he afforded to drink the top-shelf stuff. He made jack shit at the body shop and went through a gram of coke every few days. But he still lived with his mother over on Tenbrook, and it didn't look like he spent any money on clothes. I guess his paycheck went to getting his head up.

"I Want to Know What Love Is" was coming from the jukebox. Lou Gramm was crooning, and I was thinking about my girl. I had met this fine young lady, Lynne, worked an aluminum siding booth up in Wheaton Plaza, who I thought might be the one. She had dark hair and a rack on her like that PR or Cuban chick who played on *Miami Vice*. I wanted to be with her but I was here. It was partly out of habit, and mostly because I knew Paddy would be holding. Also, Paddy had practically begged me to come. He didn't like to drink alone.

"You guys ready to do a bump?" said Paddy.

"Shit, yeah," I said. I mean, what did he think? Hell, it was why I was sitting there.

"I gotta work tomorrow," said Scott.

"What's your point?" said Paddy.

"It's a real job," said Scott. At the time, Scott was putting in hours at a downtown law firm and studying for what he called the "L-sats."

Paddy looked over at the booth where the Arab dude sat, smiled kind of mean, then moved his eyes back to Scott. "Like my job isn't real?"

"All I'm saying is, it's not the kind of job where you can just fall out of bed, stumble into a garage with a headache, and start banging out dings."

"Oh, I get you. Big smart lawyer. What you makin down at that law firm, Scott?"

"Nothing. It's an internship."

"Better get in there refreshed in the morning, then. You wouldn't want to lose a gig like that." Paddy turned his attention to me. "Meet me in the head in a few minutes, Counselor. Okay?"

I had just dropped out of community college for the last time and had gotten this job at a local branch of a big television-and-stereo chain. The company called us "Sales Counselors," like we were shrinks or something. Paddy thought it was a laugh.

"Okay," I said.

"Watch this," said Paddy, and he got out of his seat.

Paddy navigated the space between the floor tables and headed for the booth where the guy was drinking with the blonde. He walked right up to their table and bumped his thigh against it, hard enough to rattle their mugs and spill some of their beer. The guy looked up, not angry, just surprised. Paddy pointed his finger at the guy's face and said, "Pussy." Then Paddy made a beeline to the men's room, which was down a serpentine hall. The doorman, one of three cousins who owned the place, was standing nearby. He saw the whole thing.

"That was smooth," said Scott.

The guy at the booth was staring at us, like, what's up with your buddy? Funny, with his face square on us, he did look like that Achmed Z-med dude. The blonde was busy mopping up the spilled beer with some napkins. I thought of going over to apologize, or shrugging to let them know that we were innocent in whatever had just happened, but I didn't, 'cause it would have been a betrayal of my friend. I just looked away.

"The lucky leprechaun's in rare form tonight," said Scott. "You guys drop me at my parents' place after this, okay?"

"Yeah, sure."

"You want to get busted for something, that's up to you, but I got too much to lose."

"I said we would."

Scott's eyeglasses reflected neon from a Bud Light sign up on the wall. His hair was curly and short, and he was soft-featured and overweight. He had rose-petal lips, like a girl's. Scott was one of those guys, you could tell what he was gonna look like when he got to be an old man, even when we were kids.

I pushed my chair away from the table, got up, and walked toward the head. The doorman was giving me the fisheye, his arms folded across his chest. I didn't look at the Arab guy or the blonde.

I made it through the hall, black-paneled walls lit by a red bulb, and knocked on the locked men's room door. Paddy opened up and I slid in. The room held a toilet, a stand-up urinal, and a sink, all on the same wall. The toilet didn't have a door on it or nothin like that, so if you had to take a shit you did it in front of strangers. There was a casement window by the toilet, always cranked open some to let out the smell. Everything was filthy in here. Paper towels overflowed the plastic trash can by the sink and were crumpled like dirty white carnations on the tiled floor.

"Here you go, Counselor," said Paddy. He held a small amber vial in one hand and a black screw-on top in the other. Inside the top, a small spoon dangled by a chain. He dipped the spoon into the vial and produced a tiny mound of coke that he held to my nose.

I could see that there wasn't hardly any coke left in the vial. I knew if I did one jolt I'd be hungry for it the rest of the night. Even if we could find someplace to cop, I didn't have the dough to buy any more, and I didn't know if Paddy did, either.

I was thinking of this as I pressed a forefinger to one nostril and snorted the mound into the other. A good cool ache came behind my eyes.

Paddy produced another mound, and I did it up the other nostril the same way. He scraped out what was left in the vial and did that himself. He found some more in there somehow and rubbed that on his gums while I ran water from the faucet, wet my fingers, tipped my head back, and let some droplets go down my nose. Then I took a leak in the stand-up head.

"Hurry up," said Paddy. "Everyone's gonna think you're in here suckin my dick."

"No they won't. 'Cause everyone knows you don't have one."

"Axe your mama if I have one."

"Look, you gonna be a good boy out there?"

"I was just fuckin with that guy."

"For what?"

"I don't know."

I tucked myself back in and zipped up my fly. I was already speeding and there was a drip, tasted like medicine, back in my throat. I wished my girl was out there; I could break away with her if she was. But it wouldn't be cool to split now, seeing as Paddy had just got me lit up. And by the time I got to her place, I'd be crashing. I'd hang with Paddy for a while, cop some more someplace, then knock on Lynne's door later on.

We walked out into the hall. "Everytime You Go Away" was playing in the house. I felt tall and funny. Our waitress was going to the girls' room, and I reminded her to wash her hands. She edged by us in the narrow passageway without even giving us a smile.

Good as I felt, I had forgotten about the doorman. My stomach flipped some as I saw him standing by our table. Our bill was on the table, and Scott was kinda slumped in his seat. We went there, and Paddy spread his hands, like, What's going on?

"Pay your tab and get out," said the doorman, pointing at the bill.

"We're not finished drinking," said Paddy.

"You're finished," said the doorman. "Pay your tab and get out."

"What, 'cause of *that* guy?" said Paddy, jerking his head toward the Arab and the blonde. "He was bothering me. Sayin shit, and stuff. I wasn't just gonna let it pass."

"I saw the whole thing," said the doorman. His face was ugly and it was stone. "Pay up and get out. You're not welcome in here anymore."

The doorman was short and wore one of those Woody Allen hats to cover his hair plugs. Basically, he was an insecure guy who liked to act tough. We all knew he couldn't walk it, and he knew we knew, and it just made him more mean. He was not a physical problem, but the Harris brothers, a couple of guys worked nights in the kitchen, were. They had been wrestlers at our old high school, and there was no love lost between them and Paddy.

We dropped some money on the four-top. Scott stood and put some green in, too. A few of the drinkers at the tables and booths were checking us out with anticipation, waiting to see what we would do.

I already knew we weren't going to do a thing. Paddy's face had gone pink and he was just standing there, sway-backed, staring at his shoes. He was a pale-skinned strawberry blond who could have been handsome if his features had been hooked up better. I couldn't say what made him unattractive exactly, but there was something off about his looks. Scott called him an inbred Redford.

The three of us walked out, slow enough to salvage some dignity. But we kept moving, and we didn't give any more lip to the little doorman with the hair plugs. I locked eyes for a moment with the guy in the booth. He didn't smile or anything, and he wasn't gloating about us getting tossed, either. He handled it all right. It was us that came off looking like assholes.

Out in the lot, walking toward Paddy's T-Bird, Scott said, "Say good-bye to Kildare's, boys. We'll never drink in there again."

"No loss," said Paddy. "We'll just drink at Garner's."

"Aye, Garner's," said Scott. "I don't think so, lads. The Guinness is too cold."

"Big college smart-ass, now."

"How green was my valley," said Scott, with a lilt.

"Fuck you," said Paddy.

"Suck *what?*" said Scott.

They went on like that until we dropped Scott at his father's house on Gabel. I didn't get in on the conversation. I was too busy thinking of my next bump.

Paddy left rubber on the street, hard to do with that heavy car, as we drove away from Scott's. He said that he was tired of Scott, how he wasn't the same since coming back from that fancy school, how he only tolerated him 'cause Scott and me went back to elementary, all that.

"I ain't goin drinking with him again," said Paddy.

I didn't comment, thinking that they would kiss and make up and we'd be up at Garner's or someplace like it the next week. But it turned out Paddy was right.

We picked up a six of domestic in Four Corners and cracked a couple of cans straightaway. Both of us had a terrific thirst. Paddy drove down University Boulevard, then cut a left onto Piney Branch Road and took it to New Hampshire Avenue. We listened to a tape Paddy'd made, a balladeer named Christy Moore. He had a nice voice, with those whistles and pipes and shit like that in the background, but it sounded like something my father listened to, Vic Damone with an accent. I really thought Paddy had taken this Mick thing too far.

I saw where he was going as he cut up New Hampshire. They had garden apartments up along there where I'd heard you could cop. It was just above Langley Park—not as dangerous as Langley with the El Salvies and those crazy-assed Jamaicans, but still kinda grim. All varieties of Spanish here and a lot of blacks. Not that I was scared of 'em or nothin like that.

Paddy turned into the parking lot, found a spot, and cut the engine and the lights. We sat there killing the rest of our beers.

"Who we gonna see?" I said.

"Some girl," said Paddy. "This guy I know at work hooked it up."

"You don't know her?"

"It's just a girl. Don't worry, nothing could happen. I called her before I met you guys and she said it was cool. She sounded all right." Paddy grinned. "I bet she's fine, too."

The way he said fine, like "foyne," I knew she was a black girl. Paddy had a thing for black chicks, though I don't think he'd ever had any. Except for that one time, when that girl down at Benny's Rebel Room jacked him off for forty-five bucks.

"What're we getting?" I said.

"An eight ball."

"Shit, Paddy, c'mon." I had, like, sixteen bucks in my wallet, and next to nothing in the bank.

"I got you, man."

So he was dealing. Small-time, but there it was. That's how Paddy always had coke. It was the first time he'd let me know, even if it was in a backdoor way. Because I was still high and feeling bold, it excited me some that he had let me in on his action. Also, I was a little bit scared.

"This your regular connection?"

"Nah, uh-uh, he's out of town. This is a one-time deal."

I looked up at the apartments and the grounds. Some of the balconies were sagging, and fast-food trash was strewn about the lot. "Maybe we oughta wait until your man gets back."

"You wanna get high, don't you?"

"Well, yeah." I was at that stage; I was hungry for more.

Paddy threw his head back to drain his can of beer. He lofted the can over his shoulder. It hit some dead soldiers on the floorboard and made a dull metallic sound. I killed mine and dropped the can between my feet.

We got out of the car and walked across the lot. There were a couple of guys wearing mustaches, sitting in a black late-model Ford parked nearby. Their heads were moving to music; the bass was up so loud I could hear it behind the closed windows of their car. I didn't make eye contact with them or anything. I figured they were doing some blow. Hell, everyone was rocking it back then. They were a little old for it, but it wasn't any business of mine.

We went up a stairwell, one of those open-air jobs with cinder-block walls. Paddy stopped on the second-floor landing. It was dark when it should have been lit. Then I saw the busted-out lightbulb hung in a cage. I wondered if the girl dealing the blow had deliberately broken the light, made it so you couldn't see her apartment too good from the parking lot. Paddy knocked on the door, waited, then knocked again.

In a little while, a girl's voice came forward, muffled over some music that was playing inside the apartment. Paddy put his face close to the door and said his name, and also the name of his coworker at the body shop. The door opened, and Paddy stepped inside. I followed him. The girl stepped back against the wall to let us pass.

The girl was black, on the short side, with all the woman parts in place, including her black girl's onion. She wore Jordache jeans and a jean shirt unbuttoned kinda low. I could see one of her tits hanging in a loose white bra. She caught me checking her out as I squeezed by. She didn't seem to care. It was hard to read anything in her hard, unfriendly face and dark, almond-shaped eyes. I didn't say "hey" to her or smile or anything like it. She took a deep cokehead's drag off the cigarette she was holding and closed the door.

Paddy put out his hand. "C'mon," said the girl, ignoring his gesture. We followed her down a short hall.

The music got louder as we walked. It was rap music, some black guy shouting over hard chords of electric guitar. We entered a living room/dining room arrangement, two small rooms, really, separated by nothing, where all the curtains were drawn tight. The place stunk of cigarettes, and smoke hung in the room.

A light-skinned black dude sat on the couch, dragging on a smoke, jonesing for the nicotine like the girl. On the table before the couch was a mirror holding a largish mound of coke heaped beside a single-edged blade. An ashtray sat beside the mirror and was filled with butts. The dude raised his head as we came into the room and sized us up the way guys do. The way he looked at us, you could tell he wasn't too impressed.

Another black guy, darker skinned with ripped arms, sat at the dining room table. He wore a sleeveless black T-shirt to show off his guns. He was rapping along to the guy shouting from the stereo. There was a large amount of cocaine on the table, along with a scale, a big mirror, some blades, plastic Baggies of various sizes, and Snow Seals. The Snow Seals were real, the pharmaceutical kind, not just paper ripped from magazines and folded to size.

The coke was a mountain. I mean, it was Tony Montana big. I'd never seen so much shit before in my life.

A stainless-steel pistol, a short-nosed revolver, sat on the table. The guy touched the grip, turning it just an inch so that the barrel pointed our way. He looked at us, and his eyes were laughing and bright. As the voice came from the stereo, he kept his gaze on us, and shouted along: "It's *like* that, and that's the way it *is*."

It's real clear, even today, what I was thinking: You just got your life started, and this is how you die. All you want to do is get your head up, nothing more than that. You walk into the wrong apartment, there's guns, and you fucking die.

"You got it?" said Paddy, to the girl. I had to hand it to him. He was acting pretty cool. Knowing Paddy, he was trying to keep himself together to impress her. For a guy who got no play, Paddy was an optimist. He always thought he had a chance.

The girl went and turned down the stereo to almost nothing. The guy at the table kept rapping to the song.

"An eight, right?" said the girl to Paddy.

"That's right, baby."

I was thinking, Nah, don't go there, Paddy. Don't put on that bullshit black-talk of yours, not here. But she didn't even blink. She went down another hall and into a kitchen that was visible through a cutout in the dining room wall. I watched her ratfuck through the freezer.

The guy at the table stopped rapping and said, "Y'all want a taste?"

Paddy smiled friendly and put up his hands. "That's all right," he said. I'd never seen him turn down a blast of coke.

"Ain't like I'm asking you to drink out the same bottle as me."

Paddy chuckled unconvincingly. "It's not that. I just don't want any right now."

"Well, I'm a little surprised, 'cause you look like a pro. Don't you always check out what you're buyin?" The guy glanced at the dude sitting on the couch, then back at us. "C'mon over here and give it a road test."

Paddy shrugged and moved over to the table. I stayed where I was.

The guy at the table dipped a blade into an open Baggie that held some coke. I wondered why he didn't take it off the Everest that was in front of him. He dumped some powder off the blade and tracked out four thick lines on the mirror without giving it any chop. He handed a short tube of plastic, the cut-down barrel of a Bic pen, to Paddy.

When Paddy leaned over the table to do his lines, his four-leaf clover pendant fell out of his shirt and hung suspended between the zippers of his Members Only jacket.

"Irish, huh?" said the guy.

Paddy said, "All the way." He did a line and made a show of rearing his head back to take it all in.

145

"They call me Carlos. What do they call *you?*"

"Paddy."

"No last name?"

"O'Toole."

"Wow. That damn sure *is* Irish." Carlos's voice was almost musical. "Been to the motherland?"

"Not yet."

"Tell the truth, man: that can't be your real name, right?"

"I changed it," said Paddy, real low. The room was quiet, but you could barely hear him. He bent forward and quickly snorted the other line.

"You're like, *fake* Irish, then. That's what you tellin me?"

Paddy cleared his nostrils with a pinch of his fingers. His eyes narrowed some as he straightened his posture. "I'm Irish."

Paddy said it real strong, like he was looking to make something of it.

"*All* the way," said the guy on the couch.

Carlos looked Paddy over real slow. Then Carlos smiled.

"Plastic Paddy," said Carlos. The guy on the couch laughed.

Paddy's face grew pink, like it had gotten at Kildare's. The girl came back through the hall with a Baggie in her hand and stood near the table. The cigarette still burned between her fingers; it was down to the filter now. Paddy turned to me, his face flushed, and held out the tube. I waved the offer away with my hand.

"Take it," said Paddy. He sounded kinda mad.

I was frozen. I didn't want any coke. I was thinking of my parents and my kid sister. I just wanted to get outside.

"What's the matter with your boy?" said Carlos. "Can't he find his tongue?"

"Give it to me," I said to Paddy. The sound of my own voice was a relief. I walked a few steps and took the Bic from Paddy's outstretched hand. I did the lines fast, one right behind the other, and dropped the plastic tube on the table.

"Here you go, ace," said the girl, speaking to Paddy. She handed him a Baggie that I guessed she had gotten from the freezer. I could see grains of rice in there with the coke.

"This from the same batch I just did?" said Paddy.

"Yeah," said Carlos. "It's good, right?"

Good. It wasn't even close. I knew right away that this shit was wrong. A curtain had dropped throughout my body, and everything had gotten pushed down into my bowels. I was speeding without the happiness, and I had to take a dump. This was bullshit coke. They had stepped all over it with baby laxative and who knew what else. Paddy had to be feeling the same way I was. He *knew* he was getting ripped off. It was like the guy was asking, "You don't mind if I fuck you, do you?"

But Paddy didn't complain. He reached into his jeans and pulled out a roll of bills. He handed the bills to the girl, who counted out the money with dead eyes.

"Ain't you gonna weigh it out?" said Carlos, chinning in the direction of the Baggie. "I got a scale right here."

Paddy didn't answer. He rolled the Baggie tight and slipped it in the inside pocket of his Members Only.

"You just gonna eyeball it, *huh?*" said Carlos.

"Let's go," said Paddy. He turned and began to walk. I followed him back down the hall toward the front door. We heard the guy on the couch say, "Plastic Paddy," in the voice of a game-show host, and then all of them laughed. I didn't care because it looked like we were going to get out of there alive. But I know Paddy must have been hurting inside, 'cause they'd ripped something out of him. Also, it was the second time he'd been shamed that night.

We took the stairwell down toward the lot. As we crossed the sidewalk, Paddy said, "Fuckin niggers," and right about then the guys I'd noticed in the Ford came out of nowhere, holding guns on us, shouting at us to lock our hands behind our heads and drop to the asphalt and kiss it. I went down shaking, seeing other men running around in the dark, hearing their adrenalized voices and the screech of tires and the closing of heavy car doors.

As I hit the ground, I lost control of everything and crapped my pants.

You know all those cop shows on TV, where the detectives convince the suspect to talk before the lawyer arrives? It's bullshit, the worst thing you can do. My father always told me that if I ever got jammed up just to keep my mouth shut and wait for the guys in the suits. Also, 'cause he figured I'd get DWI'd someday, he told me to refuse the breath tests and keep my piss inside me. Judging from what happened to Paddy, I don't think he ever had any guidance like that. Plus, they gave him some court-appointed attorney who didn't help his case. My lawyer was a heavy hitter, a friend of my dad's, and he did me right.

Paddy did a few months' detention up at Seven Locks, and I got a community service thing where I had to wear a jumpsuit and pick up trash in Sligo Creek Park. Also, I was required to attend these classes at an old Catholic school on Riggs Road, where some horse-faced guy talked about the evils of alcohol and drugs, one night a week for six weeks. It was me and a bunch of losers, alkies and spentheads who'd flip the teacher the bird behind his back when they weren't drawing sword-and-sorcery artwork in their notebooks or scratching their initials into their desks.

You'd think it was lucky we walked into that bust before something worse happened to us. That I might have looked around me in that rehab class, checked out the company I was keeping, and realized that I needed to turn my life around. But I guess I wasn't that smart.

Soon after those classes ended, I started doing the occasional blast on weekends again, telling myself it was recreational. Then, big surprise, I began to hunt for it during the week. One night I got drunk and wanted it so bad that I went into a rough neighborhood down in Petworth, off Georgia Avenue in D.C., where this guy in a bar had told me I could cop. I bought a half from some hard-looking black dudes and got knocked out with a lead pipe by the same dudes while I was walking back to my car. I woke up at the Washington Hospital Center, my face looking like a duck's. I never did another line. My father said that I had to fall down and hit my head to find out I wasn't normal, and I guess he was right.

Paddy went away after his jail time, to Florida or some shit, and after that I lost contact with him completely. Scott had this theory that Paddy had flipped on Carlos and them and was probably too scared to stay in Maryland. As for Scott, him and me drifted apart.

I saw them both at the twentieth reunion for my high school, held a few years ago at some hotel up in Gaithersburg. Scott was heavy and bald and on his second wife. He mentioned his law firm and something about a new model Lexus he had his eye on. He didn't really need to boast like that, 'cause I could tell from his suit that he had done all right. But I noticed that most of the night he was standing by himself. Nobody from our high school days seemed to recognize him. Scott had money, but he didn't have friends.

I caught glimpses of Paddy during the evening, standing near the cash bar or hanging around the buffet table, where most of the food had been picked clean. His image was fuzzy—I was too vain to wear my glasses to the reunion—but I knew from the way he was standing, swaybacked like he'd always been, that it was him. When I'd try to catch his eye, though, he'd look away.

Our paths crossed in the bathroom later that night. I was taking a leak in the urinal when Paddy walked in. I got a good look at him while I zipped up my fly. He was wearing an ill-fitting suit, and a hat sat crookedly on his head. The hat was one of those plastic derbies, green and covered in cellophane, with shamrocks glued underneath the cellophane. Like something you'd win at a carnival. Paddy's face was puffy and there were gray bags under his unfocused eyes. He leaned against the wall and looked me up and down.

"Paddy," I said. "How you doin?"

"Big store manager," he said, drawing out the words. His lip was curled with contempt.

I figured that someone at the reunion must have told him that I was managing a Radio Shack. But I was doing better than that. I had been promoted to merchandising director, and I was in charge of four stores. Hell, I was knocking down close to forty-two grand a year.

I didn't correct him, though. I just went to the sink and washed my hands. I washed them real good before I left the room.

Paddy had been my bud for a long time, so I felt kinda bad for a couple days after, seeing him like that. He had taken a long fall. Or maybe, I don't know, he'd just kept moving sideways. Anyway, I haven't seen him since, and that suits me fine.

It's not like I'm denying who I was. I do think about those nights with Paddy, and I know we had some laughs. But for the life of me I can't tell you what it was we were laughing about. I mean, I used to love to get my head up. But now I can't remember what was so great about it. Mostly, when I think about it, it seems like it was all a waste of time.

THE DEAD THEIR EYES IMPLORE US

SOMEDAY I'M GONNA write all this down. But I don't write so good in English yet, see? So I'm just gonna think it out loud.

Last night I had a dream.

In my dream, I was a kid, back in the village. My friends and family from the *chorio,* they were there, all of us standing around the square. My father, he had strung a lamb up on a pole. It was making a noise, like a scream, and its eyes were wild and afraid. My father handed me my Italian switch knife, the one he gave me before I came over. I cut into the lamb's throat and opened it up wide. The lamb's warm blood spilled onto my hands.

My mother told me once: every time you dream some-thing, it's got to be a reason.

I'm not no kid anymore. I'm twenty-eight years old. It's early in June, nineteen hundred and thirty-three. The tem-perature got up to 100 degrees today. I read in the *Tribune,* some old people died from the heat.

Let me try to paint a picture, so you can see in your head the way it is for me right now. I got this little one-room place I rent from some old lady. A Murphy bed and a table, an icebox and a stove. I got a radio I bought for a dollar and ninety-nine. I wash my clothes in a tub, and afterward I hang the *roúcha* on a cord I stretched across the room. There's a bunch of clothes, *pantalóni* and one of my work shirts and my *vrakia* and socks, on there now. I'm sitting here at the table in my union suit. I'm smoking a Fatima and drinking a cold bottle of Abner Drury beer. I'm looking at my hands. I got blood underneath my fingernails. I washed real good, but it was hard to get it all.

It's five, five thirty in the morning. Let me go back some, to show how I got to where I am tonight.

What's it been, four years since I came over? The boat ride was a boat ride, so I'll skip that part. I'll start in America.

When I got to Ellis Island, I came straight down to Washington to stay with my cousin Toula and her husband, Aris. Aris had a fruit cart down on Pennsylvania Avenue, around 17th. Toula's father owed my father some *lefta* from back in the village, so it was all set up. She offered me a room until I could get on my feet. Aris wasn't happy about it, but I didn't give a good goddamn what he was happy about. Toula's father should have paid his debt.

Toula and Aris had a place in Chinatown. It wasn't just for Chinese. Italians, Irish, Polacks, and Greeks lived there, too. Everyone was poor except the criminals. The Chinamen controlled the gambling, the whores, and the opium. All the business got done in the back of laundries and in the restaurants. The Chinks didn't bother no one if they didn't get bothered themselves.

Toula's apartment was in a house right on H Street. You had to walk up three floors to get to it. I didn't mind it. The milkman did it every day, and the old Jew who collected the rent managed to do it, too. I figured, so could I.

My room was small, so small you couldn't shut the door all the way when the bed was down. There was only one toilet in the place, and they had put a curtain by it, the kind you hang on a shower. You had to close it around you when you wanted to shit. Like I say, it wasn't a nice place or nothing like it, but it was okay. It was free.

But nothing's free, my father always said. Toula's husband, Aris, made me pay from the first day I moved in. Never had a good word to say to me, never mentioned me to no one for a job. He was a sonofabitch, that one. Dark, with a hook in his nose—looked like he had some Turkish blood in him. I wouldn't be surprised if the *gamoto* was a Turk. I didn't like the way he talked to my cousin, either, 'specially when he drank. And this *malaka* drank every night. I'd sit in my room and listen to him raise his voice at her, and then later I could hear him fucking her on their bed. I couldn't stand it, I'm telling you, and me without a woman myself. I didn't have no job then so I couldn't even buy a whore. I thought I was gonna go nuts.

Then one day I was talking to this guy, Dimitri Karras, lived in the 606 building on H. He told me about a janitor's job opened up at St. Mary's, the church where his son, Panayoti, and most of the neighborhood kids went to Catholic school.

I put some Wildroot tonic in my hair, walked over to the church, and talked to the head nun. I don't know, she musta liked me or something, 'cause I got the job. I had to lie a little about being a handyman. I wasn't no engineer, but I figured, what the hell, the furnace goes out you light it again, god-damn.

My deal was simple. I got a room in the basement and a coupla meals a day. Pennies other than that, but I didn't mind, not then. Hell, it was better than living in some Hoover Hotel. And it got me away from that bastard Aris. Toula cried when I left, so I gave her a hug. I didn't say nothing to Aris.

I worked at St. Mary's about two years. The work was never hard. I knew the kids and most of their fathers: Karras, Angelos, Nicodemus, Recevo, Damiano, Carchedi. I watched the boys grow, I didn't look the nuns in the eyes when I talked to them so they wouldn't get the wrong idea. Once or twice I treated myself to one of the whores over at the Eastern House. Mostly, down in the basement, I played with my *poutso*. I put it out of my mind that I was jerking off in church.

Meanwhile, I tried to make myself better. I took English classes at St. Sophia, the Greek Orthodox church on 8th and L. I bought a blue serge suit at Harry Kaufman's on 7th Street, on sale for eleven dollars and seventy-five. The Jew tailor let me pay for it a little bit at a time. Now when I went to St. Sophia for the Sunday service I wouldn't be ashamed.

I liked to go to church. Not for religion, nothing like that. Sure, I wear a *stavro*, but everyone wears a cross. That's just superstition. I don't love God, but I'm afraid of him. So I went to church just in case, and also to look at the girls. I liked to see 'em all dressed up.

There was this one *koritsi,* not older than sixteen when I first saw her, who was special. I knew just where she was gonna be, with her mother, on the side of the church where the women sat separate from the men. I made sure I got a good view of her on Sundays. Her name was Irene, I asked around. I could tell she was clean. By that I mean she was a virgin. That's the kind of girl you're gonna marry. My plan was to wait till I got some money in my pocket before I talked to her, but not too long so she got snatched up. A girl like that is not gonna stay single forever.

Work and church was for the daytime. At night I went to the coffeehouses down by the Navy Yard in Southeast. One of them was owned by a hardworking guy from the neighborhood, Angelos, lived at the 703 building on 6th. That's the *cafeneion* I went to most. You played cards and dice there if that's what you wanted to do, but mostly you could be yourself. It was all Greeks.

That's where I met Nick Stefanos one night, at the Angelos place. Meeting him is what put another change in my life. Stefanos was a Spartan with an easy way, had a scar on his cheek. You knew he was tough, but he didn't have to prove it. I heard he got the scar running protection for a hooch truck in upstate New York. Heard a cheap *pistola* blew up in his face. It was his business, what happened, none of mine.

We got to talking that night. He was the head busman down at some fancy hotel on 15th and Penn, but he was leaving to open his own place. His friend Costa, another *Spartiati,* worked there and he was gonna leave with him. Stefanos asked me if I wanted to take Costa's place. He said he could set it up. The pay was only a little more than what I was making, a dollar-fifty a week with extras, but a little more was a lot. Hell, I wanted to make better like anyone else. I thanked Nick Stefanos and asked him when I could start.

I started the next week, soon as I got my room where I am now. You had to pay management for your bus uniform, black pants and a white shirt and short black vest, so I didn't make nothing for a while. Some of the waiters tipped the busmen heavy, and some tipped nothing at all. For the ones who tipped nothing, you cleared their tables slower, and last. I caught on quick.

The hotel was pretty fancy, and its dining room, up on the top floor, was fancy, too. The china was real, the crystal sang when you flicked a finger at it, and the silver was heavy. It was hard times, but you'd never know it from the way the tables filled up at night. I figured I'd stay there a coupla years, learn the operation, and go out on my own like Stefanos. That was one smart guy.

The way they had it set up was, Americans had the waiter jobs, and the Greeks and Filipinos bused the tables. The coloreds, they stayed back in the kitchen. Everybody in the restaurant was in the same order that they were out on the street: the whites were up top and the Greeks were in the middle; the *mavri* were at the bottom. Except if someone was your own kind, you didn't make much small talk with the other guys unless it had something to do with work. I didn't have nothing against anyone, not even the coloreds. You didn't talk to them, that's all. That's just the way it was.

The waiters, they thought they were better than the rest of us. But there was this one American, a young guy named John Petersen, who was all right. Petersen had brown eyes and wavy brown hair that he wore kinda long. It was his eyes that you remembered. Smart and serious, but gentle at the same time.

Petersen was different than the other waiters, who wouldn't lift a finger to help you even when they weren't busy. John would pitch in and bus my tables for me when I got in a jam. He'd jump in with the dishes, too, back in the kitchen, when the dining room was running low on silver, and like I say, those were coloreds back there. I even saw him talking with those guys sometimes like they were pals. It was like he came from someplace where that was okay. John was just one of those who made friends easy, I guess. I can't think of no one who didn't like him. Well, there musta been one person, at least. I'm gonna come to that later on.

Me and John went out for a beer one night after work, to a saloon he knew. I wasn't comfortable because it was all Americans and I didn't see no one who looked like me. But John made me feel okay, and after two beers I forgot. He talked to me about the job and the pennies me and the colored guys in the kitchen were making, and how it wasn't right. He talked about some changes that were coming to make it better for us, but he didn't say what they were.

"I'm happy," I said, as I drank off the beer in my mug. "I got a job, what the hell."

"You want to make more money don't you?" he said. "You'd like to have a day off once in a while, wouldn't you?"

"Goddamn right. But I take off a day, I'm not gonna get paid."

"It doesn't have to be like that, friend."

"Yeah, okay."

"Do you know what 'strength in numbers' means?"

I looked around for the bartender 'cause I didn't know what the hell John was talking about and I didn't know what to say.

John put his hand around my arm. "I'm putting together a meeting. I'm hoping some of the busmen and the kitchen guys will make it. Do you think you can come?"

"What we gonna meet for, huh?"

"We're going to talk about those changes I been telling you about. Together, we're going to make a plan."

"I don't want to go to no meeting. I want a day off, I'm just gonna go ask for it, eh?"

"You don't understand." John put his face close to mine. "The workers are being exploited."

"I work and they pay me," I said with a shrug. "That's all I know. Other than that? I don't give a damn nothing." I pulled my arm away, but I smiled when I did it. I didn't want to join no group, but I wanted him to know we were still pals. "C'mon, John, let's drink."

I needed that job. But I felt bad, turning him down about that meeting. You could see it meant something to him, whatever the hell he was talking about, and I liked him. He was the only American in the restaurant who treated me like we were both the same. You know, man to man.

Well, he wasn't the only American who made me feel like a man. There was this woman, name of Laura, a hostess who also made change from the bills. She bought her dresses too small and had hair bleached white, like Jean Harlow. She was about two years and ten pounds away from the end of her looks. Laura wasn't pretty, but her ass could bring tears to your eyes. Also, she had huge tits.

I caught her giving me the eye the first night I worked there. By the third night, she said something to me about my broad chest as I was walking by her. I nodded and smiled, but I kept walking 'cause I was carrying a heavy tray. When I looked back she gave me a wink. She was a real whore, that one. I knew right then I was gonna fuck her. At the end of the night I asked her if she would go to the pictures with me sometime. "I'm free tomorrow," she says. I acted like it was an honor and a big surprise.

I worked every night, so we had to make it a matinee. We took the streetcar down to the Earle, on 13th Street, down below F. I wore my blue serge suit and high-button shoes. I looked like I had a little bit of money, but we still got the fish-eye, walking down the street. A blonde and a Greek with dark skin and a heavy black mustache. I couldn't hide that I wasn't too long off the boat.

The Earle had a stage show before the picture. A guy named William Demarest and some dancers who Laura said were like the Rockettes. What the hell did I know, I was just looking at their legs. After the coming attractions and the short subject, the picture came on: *Gold Diggers of 1933*. The man dancers looked like cocksuckers to me. I liked Westerns better, but it was all right. Fifteen cents for each of us. It was cheaper than taking her to a saloon.

Afterward, we went to her place, an apartment in a row house off H in Northeast. I used the bathroom and saw a Barnard's Shaving Cream and other man things in there, but I didn't ask her nothing about it when I came back out. I found her in the bedroom. She had poured us a couple of rye whiskies and drawn the curtains so it felt like the night. A radio played something she called "jug band"; it sounded like colored music to me. She asked me, did I want to dance. I shrugged and tossed back all the rye in my glass and pulled her to me rough. We moved slow, even though the music was fast.

"Bill?" she said, looking up at me. She had painted her eyes with something and there was a black mark next to one of them where the paint had come off.

"Uh," I said.

"What do they call you where you're from?"

"Vasili."

I kissed her warm lips. She bit mine and drew a little blood. I pushed myself against her to let her know what I had.

"Why, Va-silly," she said. "You are like a horse, aren't you?"

I just kinda nodded and smiled. She stepped back and got out of her dress and her slip, and then undid her brassiere. She did it slow.

"Ella," I said.

"What does that mean?"

"Hurry it up," I said, with a little motion of my hand. Laura laughed.

She pulled the bra off and her tits bounced. They were everything I thought they would be. She came to me and un-buckled my belt, pulling at it clumsy, and her breath was hot on my face. By then, God, I was ready.

I sat her on the edge of the bed, put one of her legs up on my shoulder, and gave it to her. I heard a woman having a baby in the village once, and those were the same kinda sounds that Laura made. There was spit dripping out the side of her mouth as I slammed myself into her over and over again. I'm telling you, her bed took some plaster off the wall that day.

After I blew my load into her, I climbed off. I didn't say nice things to her or nothing like that. She got what she wanted and so did I. Laura smoked a cigarette and watched me get dressed. The whole room smelled like pussy. She didn't look so good to me no more. I couldn't wait to get out of there and breathe fresh air.

We didn't see each other again outside of work. She only stayed at the restaurant a coupla more weeks, and then she disappeared. I guess the man who owned the shaving cream told her it was time to quit.

For a while there, nothing happened and I just kept work-ing hard. John didn't mention no meetings again, though he was just as nice as before. I slept late and bused the tables at night. Life wasn't fun or bad. It was just ordinary. Then that bastard Wesley Schmidt came to work and everything changed.

Schmidt was a tall young guy with a thin moustache, big in the shoulders, big hands. He kept his hair slicked back. His eyes were real blue, like water under ice. He had a row of big, straight teeth. He smiled all the time, but the smile, it didn't make you feel good.

Schmidt got hired as a waiter, but he wasn't any good at it. He got tangled up fast when the place got busy. He served food to the wrong tables all the time, and he spilled plenty of drinks. It didn't seem like he'd ever done that kind of work before.

No one liked him, but he was one of those guys, he didn't know it, or maybe he knew and didn't care. He laughed and told jokes and slapped the busmen on the back like we were his friends. He treated the kitchen guys like dogs when he was tangled up, raising his voice at them when the food didn't come up as fast as he liked it. Then he tried to be nice to them later.

One time he really screamed at Raymond, the head cook on the line, called him a "lazy shine" on this night when the place was packed. When the dining room cleared up, Schmidt walked back into the kitchen and told Raymond in a soft voice that he didn't mean nothing by it, giving him that smile of his and patting his arm. Raymond just nodded real slow. Schmidt told me later, "That's all you got to do, is scold 'em and then talk real sweet to 'em later. That's how they learn. 'Cause they're like children. Right, Bill?" He meant coloreds, I guess. By the way he talked to me, real slow the way you would to a kid, I could tell he thought I was a colored guy, too.

At the end of the night the waiters always sat in the dining room and ate a stew or something that the kitchen had prepared. The busmen, we served it to the waiters. I was running dinner out to one of them and forgot something back in the kitchen. When I went back to get it, I saw Raymond, spitting into a plate of stew. The other colored guys in the kitchen were standing in a circle around Raymond, watching him do it. They all looked over at me when I walked in. It was real quiet and I guess they were waiting to see what I was gonna do.

"Who's that for?" I said. "Eh?"

"Schmidt," said Raymond.

I walked over to where they were. I brought up a bunch of stuff from deep down in my throat and spit real good into that plate. Raymond put a spoon in the stew and stirred it up.

"I better take it out to him," I said, "before it gets cold."

"Don't forget the garnish," said Raymond.

He put a flower of parsley on the plate, turning it a little so it looked nice. I took the stew out and served it to Schmidt. I watched him take the first bite and nod his head like it was good. None of the colored guys said nothing to me about it again.

I got drunk with John Petersen in a saloon a coupla nights after and told him what I'd done. I thought he'd a get a good laugh out of it, but instead he got serious. He put his hand on my arm the way he did when he wanted me to listen.

"Stay out of Schmidt's way," said John.

"Ah," I said, with a wave of my hand. "He gives me any trouble, I'm gonna punch him in the kisser." The beer was making me brave.

"Just stay out of his way."

"I look afraid to you?"

"I'm telling you, Schmidt is no waiter."

"I know it. He's the worst goddamn waiter I ever seen. Maybe you ought to have one of those meetings of yours and see if you can get him thrown out."

"Don't ever mention those meetings again, to anyone," said John, and he squeezed my arm tight. I tried to pull it away from him but he held his grip. "Bill, do you know what a Pinkerton man is?"

"What the hell?"

"Never mind. You just keep to yourself, and don't talk about those meetings, hear?"

I had to look away from his eyes. "Sure, sure."

"Okay, friend." John let go of my arm. "Let's have another beer."

A week later John Petersen didn't show up for work. And a week after that the cops found him floating down river in the Potomac. I read about it in the *Tribune*. It was just a short notice, and it didn't say nothing else.

A cop in a suit came to the restaurant and asked us some questions. A couple of the waiters said that John probably had some bad hooch and fell into the drink. I didn't know what to think. When it got around to the rest of the crew, everyone kinda got quiet, if you know what I mean. Even that bastard Wesley didn't make no jokes. I guess we were all thinking about John in our own way. Me, I wanted to throw up. I'm telling you, thinking about John in that river, it made me sick.

John didn't ever talk about no family and nobody knew nothing about a funeral. After a few days, it seemed like everybody in the restaurant forgot about him. But me, I couldn't forget.

One night I walked into Chinatown. It wasn't far from my new place. There was this kid from St. Mary's, Billy Nicodemus, whose father worked at the city morgue. Nicodemus wasn't no doctor or nothing, he washed off the slabs and cleaned the place, like that. He was known as a hard drinker, maybe because of what he saw every day, and maybe just because he liked the taste. I knew where he liked to drink.

I found him in a no-name restaurant on the Hip Sing side of Chinatown. He was in a booth by himself, drinking something from a teacup. I crossed the room, walking through the cigarette smoke, passing the whores and the skinny Chink gangsters in their too-big suits and the cops who were taking money from the Chinks to look the other way. I stood over Nicodemus and told him who I was. I told him I knew his kid, told him his kid was good. Nicodemus motioned for me to have a seat.

A waiter brought me an empty cup. I poured myself some gin from the teapot on the table. We tapped cups and drank. Nicodemus had straight black hair wetted down and a big mole with hair coming out of it on one of his cheeks. He talked better than I did. We said some things that were about nothing, and then I asked him some questions about John. The gin had loosened his tongue.

"Yeah, I remember him," said Nicodemus, after thinking about it for a short while. He gave me the once-over and leaned forward. "This was your friend?"

"Yes."

"They found a bullet in the back of his head. A twenty-two."

I nodded and turned the teacup in small circles on the table. "The *Tribune* didn't say nothing about that."

"The papers don't always say. The police cover it up while they look for who did it. But that boy didn't drown. He was murdered first, then dropped in the drink."

"You saw him?" I said.

Nicodemus shrugged. "Sure."

"What'd he look like?"

"You really wanna know?"

"Yeah."

"He was all gray and blown up, like a balloon. The gas does that to 'em, when they been in the water."

"What about his eyes?"

"They were open. Pleading."

"Huh?"

"His eyes. It was like they were sayin please."

I needed another drink. I had some more gin.

"You ever heard of a Pinkerton man?" I said.

"Sure," said Nicodemus. "A detective."

"Like the police?"

"No."

"*What*, then?"

"They go to work with other guys and pretend they're one of them. They find out who's stealing. Or they find out who's trying to make trouble for the boss. Like the ones who want to make a strike."

"You mean, like if a guy wants to get the workers together and make things better?"

"Yeah. Have meetings and all that. The guys who want to start a union. Pinkertons look for those guys."

We drank the rest of the gin. We talked about his kid. We

talked about Schmeling and Baer, and the wrestling match that was coming up between Londos and George Zaharias at Griffith Stadium. I got up from my seat, shook Nicodemus's hand, and thanked him for the conversation.

"*Efharisto, patrioti.*"

"*Yasou, Vasili.*"

I walked back to my place and had a beer I didn't need. I was drunk and more confused than I had been before. I kept hearing John's voice, the way he called me "friend." I saw his eyes saying please. I kept thinking, I should have gone to his goddamn meeting, if that was gonna make him happy. I kept thinking I had let him down. While I was thinking, I sharpened the blade of my Italian switch knife on a stone.

The next night, last night, I was serving Wesley Schmidt his dinner after we closed. He was sitting by himself like he always did. I dropped the plate down in front of him.

"You got a minute to talk?" I said.

"Go ahead and talk," he said, putting the spoon to his stew and stirring it around.

"I wanna be a Pinkerton man," I said.

Schmidt stopped stirring his stew and looked up my way. He smiled, showing me his white teeth. Still, his eyes were cold.

"That's nice. But why are you telling me this?"

"I wanna be a Pinkerton, just like you."

Schmidt pushed his stew plate away from him and looked around the dining room to make sure no one could hear us. He studied my face. I guess I was sweating. Hell, I *know* I was. I could feel it dripping on my back.

"You look upset," said Schmidt, his voice real soft, like music. "You look like you could use a friend."

"I just wanna talk."

"Okay. You feel like having a beer, something like that?"

"Sure, I could use a beer."

"I finish eating, I'll go down and get my car. I'll meet you in the alley out back. Don't tell anyone, hear, because then they might want to come along. And we wouldn't have the chance to talk."

"I'm not gonna tell no one. We just drive around, eh? I'm too dirty to go to a saloon."

"That's swell," said Schmidt. "We'll just drive around."

I went out to the alley where Schmidt was parked. Nobody saw me get into his car. It was a blue '31 Dodge coupe with wire wheels, a rumble seat, and a trunk rack. A five-hundred-dollar car if it was dime.

"Pretty," I said, as I got in beside him. There were hand-tailored slipcovers on the seats.

"I like nice things," said Schmidt.

He was wearing his suit jacket, and it had to be 80 degrees. I could see a lump under the jacket. I figured, the bastard is carrying a gun.

We drove up to Colvin's, on 14th Street. Schmidt went in and returned with a bag of loose bottles of beer. There must have been a half-dozen Schlitz in the bag. Him making waiter's pay, and the fancy car and the high-priced beer.

He opened a coupla beers and handed me one. The bottle was ice cold. Hot as the night was, the beer tasted good.

We drove around for a while. We went down to Hains

Point. Schmidt parked the Dodge facing the Washington Channel. Across the channel, the lights from the fish vendors on Maine Avenue threw color on the water. We drank another beer. He gave me one of his tailor-mades and we had a couple smokes. He talked about the Senators and the Yankees, and how Baer had taken Schmeling out with a right in the tenth. Schmidt didn't want to talk about nothing serious yet. He was waiting for the beer to work on me, I knew.

"Goddamn heat," I said. "Let's drive around some, get some air moving."

Schmidt started the coupe. "Where to?"

"I'm gonna show you a whorehouse. Best secret in town."

Schmidt looked me over and laughed. The way you laugh at a clown.

I gave Schmidt some directions. We drove some, away from the park and the monuments to where people lived. We went through a little tunnel and crossed into Southwest. Most of the streetlamps were broke here. The row houses were shabby, and you could see shacks in the alleys and clothes hanging on lines outside the shacks. It was late, long past midnight. There weren't many people out. The ones that were out were coloreds. We were in a place called Bloodfield.

"Pull over there," I said, pointing to a spot along the curb where there wasn't no light. "I wanna show you the place I'm talking about."

Schmidt did it and cut the engine. Across the street were some houses. All except one of them was dark. From the lighted one came fast music, like the colored music Laura had played in her room.

"There it is right there," I said, meaning the house with the light. I was lying through my teeth. I didn't know who lived there and I sure didn't know if that house had whores. I had never been down here before.

Schmidt turned his head to look at the row house. I slipped my switch knife out of my right pocket and laid it flat against my right leg.

When he turned back to face me, he wasn't smiling no more. He had heard about Bloodfield and he knew he was in it. I think he was scared.

"You bring me down to niggertown, for *what?*" he said. "To show me a whorehouse?"

"I thought you're gonna like it."

"Do I look like a man who'd pay to fuck a nigger? *Do* I? You don't know anything about me."

He was showing his true self now. He was nervous as a cat. My nerves were bad, too. I was sweating through my shirt. I could smell my own stink in the car.

"I know plenty," I said.

"Yeah? *What* do you know?"

"Pretty car, pretty suits…top-shelf beer. How you get all this, huh?"

"I earned it."

"As a Pinkerton, eh?"

Schmidt blinked real slow and shook his head. He looked out his window, looking at nothing, wasting time while he decided what he was gonna do. I found the raised button on the pearl handle of my knife. I pushed the button. The blade flicked open and barely made a sound. I held the knife against my leg and turned it so the blade was pointing back.

Sweat rolled down my neck as I looked around. There wasn't nobody out on the street.

Schmidt turned his head. He gripped the steering wheel with his right hand and straightened his arm.

"What do you want?" he said.

"I just wanna know what happened to John."

Schmidt smiled. All those white teeth. I could see him with his mouth open, his lips stretched, those teeth showing. The way an animal looks after you kill it. Him lying on his back on a slab.

"I heard he drowned," said Schmidt.

"You think so, eh?"

"Yeah. I guess he couldn't swim."

"Pretty hard to swim, you got a bullet in your head."

Schmidt's smile turned down. "Can *you* swim, Bill?"

I brought the knife across real fast and buried it into his armpit. I sunk the blade all the way to the handle. He lost his breath and made a short scream. I twisted the knife. His blood came out like someone was pouring it from a jug. It was warm and it splashed onto my hands. I pulled the knife out, and while he was kicking at the floorboards, I stabbed him a coupla more times in the chest. I musta hit his heart or something because all of the sudden there was plenty of blood all over the car. I'm telling you, the seats were slippery with it. He stopped moving. His eyes were open and they were dead.

I didn't get tangled up about it or nothing like that. I wasn't scared. I opened up his suit jacket and saw a steel revolver with wood grips holstered there. It was small caliber. I didn't touch the gun. I took his wallet out of his trousers, pulled the bills out of it, wiped off the wallet with my shirttail, and threw the empty wallet on the ground. I put the money in my shoe. I fit the blade back into the handle of my switch knife and slipped the knife into my pocket. I put all the empty beer bottles together with the full ones in the paper bag and took the bag with me as I got out of the car. I closed the door soft and wiped off the handle and walked down the street.

I didn't see no one for a couple of blocks. I came to a sewer and I put the bag down the hole. The next block, I came to another sewer and I took off my bloody shirt and threw it down the hole of that one. I was wearing an undershirt, didn't have no sleeves. My pants were black, so you couldn't see the blood. I kept walking toward Northwest.

Someone laughed from deep in an alley and I kept on.

Another block or so I came up on a group of *mavri* standing around the steps of a house. They were smoking cigarettes and drinking from bottles of beer. I wasn't gonna run or nothing. I had to go by them to get home. They stopped talking and gave me hard eyes as I got near them. That's when I saw that one of them was the cook, Raymond, from the kitchen. Our eyes kind of came together, but neither one of us said a word or smiled or even made a nod.

One of the coloreds started to come toward me and Raymond stopped him with the flat of his palm. I walked on.

I walked for a couple of hours, I guess. Somewhere in Northwest I dropped my switch knife down another sewer. When I heard it hit the sewer bottom I started to cry. I wasn't crying 'cause I had killed Schmidt. I didn't give a damn nothing about him. I was crying 'cause my father had given me that knife, and now it was gone. I guess I knew I was gonna be in America forever, and I wasn't never going back to Greece. I'd never see my home or my parents again.

When I got back to my place I washed my hands real good. I opened up a bottle of Abner-Drury and put fire to a Fatima and had myself a seat at the table.

This is where I am right now.

Maybe I'm gonna get caught and maybe I'm not. They're gonna find Schmidt in that neighborhood and they're gonna figure a colored guy killed him for his money. The cops, they're gonna turn Bloodfield upside down. If Raymond tells them he saw me, I'm gonna get the chair. If he doesn't, I'm gonna be free. Either way, what the hell, I can't do nothing about it now.

I'll work at the hotel, get some experience and some money, then open my own place, like Nick Stefanos. Maybe if I can find two nickels to rub together, I'm gonna go to church and talk to that girl, Irene, see if she wants to be my wife. I'm not gonna wait too long. She's clean as a whistle, that one.

I've had my eye on her for some time.

THE MARTINI SHOT

I WAS UP in my suite in a residence hotel, where the production housed out-of-town talent and department heads, when I heard a knock on my door. It was late, around two in the morning, but we had wrapped less than an hour earlier, and crew kept different hours than straights. Few of us went to sleep as soon as we got home. We had to have a snack, or a couple of drinks, or some smoke, a little television, sex if we could get it. Anything to make us feel normal at the end of the day. Anything that would make us feel that we led normal lives.

I looked through the peephole. Annette was standing out in the carpeted hall. She'd called me minutes earlier on the house phone and asked if I wanted some company. I was expecting her, but still, I liked to watch her out there, waiting for me to open the door. It made my pulse run. Both of us had been single for a long while, but our relationship was private.

I let Annette in and closed the door.

"Hi," she said, her mouth curved up in a sweet smile. She stepped out of her sandals.

"Hi."

I kissed her soft lips, held her and stroked her bare arms. She was warm to the touch. She wore tailored velour sweats and a cutoff tee, and her copper-and-brown hair was up and back in a soft band. She was in her early forties, a large-featured woman with green eyes. She was curvy, big-breasted, thick in the thighs, and generous in back. She was olive-skinned and exotic, a Mediterranean girl built like a black woman. She was exactly what I like.

"Good day?" she said.

"Fourteen hours. The director shot too much stuff we'll never use. Anyway, we got the pages. You?"

"A little rough." It was all she needed to say. I knew she was under the gun. "I could use a glass of wine."

I opened a bottle of Rodney Strong, a good everyday Merlot that Annette liked, poured it into two short hotel-issue glasses, and took it over to the living room couch, where we had a seat. I lit a couple of candles and programmed my phone to play some tunes through a Bluetooth speaker I took from job to job. The phone and speaker arrangement was my portable stereo. Everything I owned was portable: the push-up stands, my shaving kit, my fold-up Beats, my Swiss Army knife. Everything. I owned a condo in a Mid-Atlantic city, but I lived in hotels.

Annette and I drank wine and talked about our day. We laughed about the bosses, though she was a department head, and technically, I was management, too. Typically, I was on set call-to-wrap, and she popped in at various locations before rehearsal to check out the work of her crew. Then she'd go off to prep the next episode. Seeing her arrive on set wearing one of her many cool, understated outfits was always the highlight of my day. Hats were her trademark. She walked like a cat. She was smart and talented, a true artist. Annette was our art director and she had style.

"You mind if I take this off?" she said, her hands going up under her shirt. "It's too tight."

"I like tight things."

"Stop."

She unfastened her bra, produced it like a magician, and dropped it on the carpet beside the couch.

"Don't forget this." I took liberties and pulled her T-shirt up over her head.

"You too, Buster."

"Don't call me Buster. That's a name for a dog."

"Come on."

I removed my shirt. We embraced and kissed, both of us naked above the waist, skin to skin. I caressed her and squeezed one of her dark nipples, rolled it between my thumb and forefinger until it was a pebble.

Our tongues mingled. I felt a catch in her breath and heard her moan. She gently pushed me away and chuckled.

"Who's this?" she said, nodding at my speaker.

"The new xx," I said, and shrugged sheepishly. "Not very original of me, I know."

"Wine, candles, and make-out music."

"I'm not as creative as you."

"It's perfect."

We kissed some more and had a few laughs. While we talked, I slid my hand beneath her sweats, pushed the crotch of her damp lace panties aside, slipped my longest finger inside her, and stroked her clit. It got warm in the room. She lay back on the couch and arched her back, and I peeled off her pants and thong. Now she was nude. I stripped down to my boxer briefs and crouched over her. I let her pull me free because I knew she liked to. She stroked my pole and took off my briefs, and I got between her and spread her muscular thighs with my knees and rubbed myself against her until she was wet as a waterslide, and then I split her. We fucked for a while, slow and deep, with my feet against the scrolled arm of the couch for leverage. Neither of us allowed ourselves to come. It was too good to end.

"Let's go to my bed," I said. We were pretty sweaty by then.

I brought the candles, the speaker, and my phone. Annette followed with the glasses and the bottle of wine. Entering my bedroom, I switched the music over to an Anthony Hamilton mix and let that ride. Anthony was our favorite, spiritual and secular, authentic and sublime.

My room was large, with a four-poster bed and floor-to-ceiling windows that gave to a view of the street below and the city skyline. Because it was on the top floor of the hotel, and because there were no nearby buildings as high as mine, it was completely private. Moonlight and candlelight are a heady aphrodisiac, and I kept the curtains open at all times.

I pulled her to me. I took her band off, and her hair fell free about her shoulders. I cupped my hand around the back of her neck, and we made out standing beside my bed. It felt good to both of us, pressed together, her body lush, soft, and hot against mine. She was a good kisser; our mouths fit.

She got onto the bed, atop the blankets, and I spread her out. I held her hands and raised them above her, and I kissed her. I kissed her chest and her inner thighs and everywhere. Her pussy was clean, with a five-o'clock shadow and just a hint of smell. I penetrated her with my thumb while I licked and kissed and pressed my tongue into her swollen button. She talked to me and told me what to do. "There," she said, and "Yeah," and she said my name, and then her thighs tensed and shuddered. She spasmed and pushed my head away. I lay back and left her alone to enjoy her last rippling throes. But I only left her for a minute. She was ripe, and I pulled her to the edge of the mattress and stood beside the bed and spread her legs. I fucked her like that, me, looking down and watching myself, thick, plunging into her velvet, standing on the carpet with great purchase, her lying there, her knees bent, taking me in. I turned her face to lick inside her ear and kiss her neck, and then her mouth, and she said, "God," and said it louder, and I controlled it, and she bucked as she came, this time harder than the last.

When her heart had slowed down, I withdrew from her and handed her a short glass. I took mine off the dresser, and both of us drank some wine.

"Now you," she said.

I lay on my back, and Annette put a pillow under my head. She spread my legs as I had done for her before, and got between me and played with my dick. She knocked the head of it against the nipples of her pendulous breasts and hit it on her tongue like a hammer to a bell.

"I love your cock," she said.

"It loves *you*."

"What do you want me to do?"

"Touch my ass."

She tickled my anus as she licked my balls and shaft, and slathered her tongue on my helmet. I laced my fingers through her hair and closed my eyes.

"Go," I said.

I stopped breathing and, like her, invoked a higher power. My orgasm was eye-popping, as I blew a hot load into her mouth. It seemed to last forever, and she took it all.

"Thank you," I said, my hand still in her hair. I must have been twisting it. It was a mess.

"My pleasure."

"Sorry. I know that it was a lot. It felt like a lot."

"You could help me out and empty that thing once in a while."

"I don't care to spill my seed. I like to save it all for you."

She moved up and came beside me, rested her head on my chest. It was quiet now, with just the soul music playing in the room. She blinked slowly and shut her eyes, and I listened and waited for her breathing to slow down. Soon, with each of her inhales, I heard a small click. That was the sound of her in sleep. In the candlelight, I watched her.

I checked my wristwatch. It was nearly four a.m. We had a short turnaround, a nine-o'clock call, which meant I had to be up at eight. Four hours' sleep for both of us, but that was workable, and not unusual. It was late in the shoot, and all of us were running on fumes.

A little while later, I touched her shoulder and said, "Annette." Her eyes fluttered open. I hated to rouse her, but I knew she liked to wake up in her own bed.

"Hey," she said.

"Hey."

She looked up at me without raising her head. The moon had dropped, and its light came full into the room and it was in her eyes.

"That was nice," she said.

"Yes."

"I love you, Vic."

I made no comment. I studied her face, a mix of affection and disappointment, and felt a rush of emotion. When production wrapped we'd go our separate ways. "If it happened on location, it didn't happen." That's what was said in our line of work. Maybe it would be like that with me and Annette, too. She'd move on, and so would I. But I knew that she'd always be deep in my head.

Our driver, a Teamster named Louise, picked us up in a white Ford window van at eight thirty. There were five of us standing on the sidewalk as she pulled to the curb. This episode's director, Alan Lomax, out of L.A.; our DP, a Danish cinematographer, Eigil, now spelled Eagle for marketing purposes; the camera operator, Van "Go" Cummings, from Venice, California; the gaffer, Skylar Branson, a young Texan who ran the electric crew; and me, Victor Ohanian, writer/producer. We got into the van.

As was decorum, the director rode in the shotgun bucket beside Louise, a religious woman with kinky blond hair. Van plugged his iPhone into the auxiliary jack of the stereo and programmed some Laurel Canyon singer/songwriter jive into the system. The deal was, Van commandeered the music in the mornings, Skylar (college radio) had the middle of the day, Eagle (jazz) took the post-lunch DJ spot, and I (all over the place) had the ride home. The director listened to whatever we played and was at our mercy.

Skylar handed me the latest *New Yorker*. When he was finished with magazines and novels, he passed them on to me. He was wearing a Stihl chainsaw ball cap and a trumpeter's triangle below his lower lip. He was improbably young for a department head, and very bright. He also sold marijuana to the crew. His girlfriend, Laura, a wardrobe assistant, was in on it, too. It wasn't as if he needed the money. He was a pothead and felt that he was selling happiness to his friends.

"Thanks, buddy." I slid the magazine into my book bag.

"My pleasure," he said.

There was no hint of pleasure on his face. He was troubled about something. I knew him well enough to see it. But it was his business, and I didn't push it.

Skylar was a good soul. We'd been friends since the first day of production, though I was practically old enough to be his wayward uncle. I had his back, and he had mine.

"You all right?"

"Fine," he said. "I just need to work."

We'd been at it for six months. The shoot was a cop drama for one of the cable networks, based in a southern port city, in a state that offered significant tax credits to film productions. It was a good, long gig. It paid enough to set most of us up for the year. When the money ran out, we'd get on something else. That was what we did.

Our morning ride to the first location was usually low-key. Some read the *USA Today* provided by the hotel; others made phone calls to family. Eagle, Van, and Skylar often discussed the first shot and how it would be lit. Or they discussed their golf game. If any of them or the director had a question about the content or tone of the day's scenes, I tried to answer it. It was business, but not as defined by the straight world. We were playing with many million dollars of studio money, but we dressed as we wanted to, and wore our hair and facial hair as we desired. We thought of ourselves as handsomely compensated rebels. No conventions, no uniforms.

I studied the landscape as we made our way across town. Often, the crew sees more of a city than the locals do, because we have access and security. The low-end neighborhoods, the seedier bars, the rat-and-needle infested alleys, the Mayor's office, police stations, prison and jails, the private mansions, back-of-the-house kitchens, and homeless camps under the freeways. I was the curious type, so that aspect of the job suited me well.

As we neared our destination, we glanced at our call sheets, which detailed our daily shooting schedule. The director was on his cell, talking to his daughter and telling her to have a good day at school. It was early morning in Los Angeles, and she had just woken up.

"Three moves today," said Eagle, in his heavy Scandi accent. It sounded like "moofs." He was tall and lean with long, flowing hair and a beard. He looked like a showered Viking.

"Four scenes," said Van, youthful in his fifties, now on his third marriage. Van was a connoisseur of women and a bit of a philosopher. He sometimes entertained us with his ruminations on romance and the fleeting aspect of life.

"A lot of dialogue in scene thirty-eight," I said. "Two pages, four people at the table. And then the secretary comes in from the BG and drops the file on the table. She's got a line, too. We'll have to cover that."

"Why'd you give her a line?" said Van, playfully.

I'd cast the secretary, a young would-be actress, as a day player after seeing her audition. I was just giving her a break. She'd get an extra eight hundred bucks for that one line, and residuals. Maybe someone would notice her and she'd get more work. Plus, she was hot as balls. Van knew me well.

"Lots of coverage, is all I'm saying."

"It'll be fine," said the director, turning his head to us in the back rows of bench seats, interrupting his call to his kid. Lomax was wearing a black Patagonia vest under a black Marmot shell, Merrell shoes. He was overdressed for the weather, a walking billboard for REI. "I storyboarded it and I know what I need. Two hours, tops."

He was telling us that he was prepared, that the scene wouldn't take long, and that he wouldn't overshoot. But we knew Lomax's MO. He leaned toward artsy, with shots that made no sense in terms of POV, angles and footage we'd never use when it came time to cut. The secretary's arrival, easily accomplished by a walk into frame, would be complicated by his insistence on bringing her in with a dolly shot, which meant laying down track and more lighting, which meant time. We'd get behind, and the rest of the day we'd be playing catch-up, and consequently the last scene or two would suffer. We'd worked with Lomax before. He made the days longer than they had to be, but he was all right.

Louise dropped Eagle off at catering so he could get his usual hearty breakfast, then drove the rest of us to the location. The company trucks were parked on a street in the business district of town, and crew members were milling about, waiting for the AD to call out that we were "in." First up was a scene in a bank (INT: BANK, DOWNTOWN— DAY), where our protagonist would interview some board members about the death of a teller, whose body had been found in the teaser, a scene we had yet to get in the can. We rarely shot in sequence.

Louise told us to have a blessed day as we exited the van. The lead set PA, waiting on the sidewalk, handed me my sides, which were the day's scenes, complete with dialogue, collated into one stapled set of pages. I folded the sides and slipped them into the back pocket of my Levi's, and asked the PA to order me a breakfast burrito and a coffee from catering.

"You got it, sir," he said.

I thanked him and said good morning to crew as I walked down the street toward the bank.

This was my favorite time of the day. To step out of the van in the morning and walk onto a set among a hundred other crew members, all of us gathering in one place to build something together, is a feeling of great anticipation and promise. Costumers; hair and makeup people; props; set dressers; scenic, light, and camera crew; sound recordists—all of these people, in their own way, were artists. Unlike a painting, signed by one person, or a book, with one author's name on its spine, the tail credits on a movie or television show carried hundreds of signatures. I *liked* that. I had no illusions that what I did as a television writer had weight or permanence. But, because of my comrades, I was proud to have my name on that scroll.

Inside the bank, the first AD called for a private rehearsal as the actors arrived on set. Eagle had come in with his breakfast and was shoveling it down. The lead actor, supporting actors, day players, and director stood in a circle and read their lines. I stood nearby with Lillie, the script supervisor out of New York, who was wearing New York black. She was by necessity a hyper, detail-oriented person who had one of the most demanding and important jobs in the production. Lillie watched every take in the monitors for continuity and matching issues; she was a pain in the ass, in a good way.

As the actors rehearsed the lines, I looked for trouble spots. Often the written word seems fine on the page, but when spoken it can lose its luster. Occasionally, what I thought was a great scene didn't work in practice, and I was there to adjust lines. The actor might not like something I'd written, and I had the authority to change the words if I felt the objection was warranted, or stand my ground if it was not. An actor could misinterpret my writing and not do it justice, and an actor could also elevate what I'd done. Sometimes the words or sentences were just too much of a mouthful, or there was a redundancy I had not seen before, and I'd subtract. All of this came out on set.

"Scene," said Lomax, when the actors were done. He then blocked the action, putting the actors through their movements and stops. We were to shoot this one with two cameras, A and B. During the second rehearsal, the B camera assistant laid down the actor's marks with pieces of colored tape. Lomax discussed the various shots with Eagle and Van, Skylar standing close by. Master, medium shot, then the singles, tighter, tighter, tighter, three sizes. Lomax expressed his desire to bring the secretary in with a dolly shot. Van wiggled his eyebrows at Eagle: *I knew it.*

"Crew has the set," said the first AD.

The actors went to their trailers as the crew flooded the set and prepped the first shot. Stand-ins took the marks of the actors so that they could be properly lit. It would be about forty-five minutes before the cameras rolled. My breakfast arrived and I ate it while Brandon, the on-set prop master, set up the cast chairs around the monitors, an arrangement called Video Village. I had my own chair with my name printed on the canvas backing, as well as the name of the series: *Tanner's Team.*

The show was a serialized cop drama. It detailed the exploits of an elite Homicide squad headed by a handsome, middle-aged lieutenant named Jeremiah Tanner, a semi-clairvoyant father figure whose detectives, his children in effect (Tanner's Team), consisted of various attractive youngish men and women, a mix of blacks (but not *too* many blacks), whites, and Hispanics, cast to hit all the demographic buttons. The lead was Brad Slaughter, a former film actor who had briefly flirted with cinema stardom and was now highly compensated for his work on the small screen. His co-lead was Meaghan O'Toole, an actress who had come from the stage originally and had won an Emmy for her work in an HBO original. She played Mackenzie Hart, the "hard-charging" assistant district attorney who prosecuted the criminals the squad arrested. Mainly, to the actress's chagrin, she was written as the love interest for the lieutenant.

As we neared the start of the first shot, the executive producers arrived, and immediately the tenor of the crew changed. People stood straighter and worked faster. There was less joking around and grab-assing than there was when I was in charge of the set. The big guns were in the house.

Bruce Kaplan was the show's creator, head writer, and showrunner. His partner was Ellen Stern. Ellen was not a writer but rather a general of sorts who hired and fired crew, kept the trains running on time, negotiated with the vendors, and brought the show in on budget. They complemented each other and made a good, efficient team. The credits listed five executive producers, but Bruce and Ellen were the only two who actually worked on the day-to-day production. Today they looked very tired, with black circles under their eyes, ill-fitting clothing, and uncombed hair. The hours and craft services were a killer for everyone, and they had the added pressure of bringing the show in on budget and taking the calls of the cable execs.

I had no desire to do or learn Ellen's job, and no ambition to become an EP, so there was little friction between us. I had a decent relationship with both of them, though I was "just" a writer/producer and was kept out of the loop on major decisions. As for Bruce, he was respectful to the writing team but tended to rewrite our scripts in a rather mercenary fashion. I was good with that, for the most part; I knew that there had to be one voice for the show and uniformity from episode to episode. But my ego was such that I felt he cut some of my best stuff at random. On the other hand, he sometimes made my writing better, and unlike other showrunners, who put their name on scripts they reworked, he always gave me sole credit. After a while I learned to beat the game and began to write in Bruce's voice rather than my own. It was another thing I'd given up. I was a long way from my youth, when I'd wandered the stacks of the county libraries and dreamed of someday being a published novelist. I *had* become a writer, in a manner of speaking. But mainly I was a well-paid hack.

I said hello to Bruce and updated him on our progress. "We're just about to shoot."

"You have a laptop?" he said.

"There's one in my trailer."

"I'm gonna need you to do a little rewrite on scene forty-two."

"Hold up." I fished my blue script (the blues) out of my book bag and turned the pages to the scene. It was a restaurant scene (INT. CAFÉ, UPTOWN—DAY) where Tanner and Hart discuss a case in dialogue overripe with lame double entendres. Brad Slaughter was a pro and would read the lines. Meaghan O'Toole would be the problem.

"Meaghan called me first thing this morning," said Bruce.

"She thinks the scene makes her out to be a slut rather than a professional."

"What's her beef, exactly?" I asked, disingenuously.

"I'm guessing it's the part about the in-box."

I pretended to study the lines, but I already knew the trouble spot. In the scene, Mackenzie tells Tanner that she needs the arrest report A-SAP so she can get started on the prosecution of the case.

> TANNER
>
> Where do you want the report?

> MACKENZIE
>
> Just put it in my in-box.

> TANNER
>
> It'll be my pleasure.

"Oh," I said. "*That.* How about if I just have her say, 'Shove it in my box'?"

"Asshole. And what's that bit about what he's gonna have for lunch?"

"*What?* All he says is, 'I'm partial to fish.'"

"And then the action says, *She smiles demurely.*"

"I'll change it, boss."

"Get it done. We're publishing pinks today, and the scene's up this afternoon."

"Right."

"Crazy fucker." Bruce smirked a little and went off

to craft services for a Slim Jim and some peanut butter crackers.

We were ready to shoot. The second second called "last looks," and the hair and makeup crew went in to touch up the actors. Lomax and Lillie were in the first row of chairs, right in front of the monitors. I was in the second row, behind them. The second AC slated the scene on camera by slapping the sticks.

"Camera"

"Speed."

"Action!"

We rolled. I watched the first take to make sure Lomax was getting what we needed. Among the actors, there was one dreaded ham.

"Anything, Victor?" said Lillie, after Lomax had cut it.

"Tell Board Member One to say his lines as I wrote them," I said, referring to a day player who was being far too creative.

"I'll do that," she said, and went in to give him the note.

"He's playing it too defensive, right?" said Lomax, turning to me.

"Well, he did kill the teller," I said. "But we don't want him to telegraph it. It's a reveal for later on."

"He's making a meal out of it."

"Yeah, guy thinks he's Larry fucking Olivier."

"I'll tell him to bring it down," said Lomax.

When Lillie returned to the Village, I told her I was going to my trailer for a little while. She said she'd call me if anything came up.

I saw Annette out on the street, showing Ellen something she had drawn in a sketchbook. Ellen was nodding her head in encouragement while giving Annette some suggestions. Ellen's cell rang and she walked down the block to take the call. I approached Annette, who was wearing brown velvet pants tucked into dark brown, buckled boots, and a tan newsboy cap with tiny mirrors across the bill.

"Hi," she said.

"Hey. What are you up to?"

"Just showing Ellen how I plan to dress the nightclub in one-thirteen." She opened the spiral book and showed me some sketches. "What do you think of these?"

"They're beautiful," I said, looking at her breasts, standing up firm in her scoop-necked shirt.

"Stop it," she said. She had instantly blushed.

I lowered my voice. Crew was walking by us, standing about.

"I can't help it," I said.

"People are looking at us."

"No, they're not. Remember last night?"

"I'm not an amnesiac."

"It was good, wasn't it?"

"Yes."

"I'm hard as a two-by-four right now."

"Victor."

"And thick as a can of Coke."

"*Vic.*"

"Okay, I'll stop. But damn, girl, you were hot."

"*We* were."

"Will I see you later?"

"I'll be around. Where you off to?"

"I've got to rewrite a scene for Number Two." We were supposed to call Meaghan O'Toole "Number One," since she was the lead actress in our show. But we often called her Number Two. As in, doo-doo.

"Good luck."

"Check you later, beautiful."

I watched her walk toward her car.

My trailer was around the corner. I went there and rewrote the scene.

The company moved for the next two scenes to a café uptown. The first featured Meaghan O'Toole and a day player, cast as a confidential informant who was also a possible suspect in a rape/murder case, the B-line of this episode. The second featured O'Toole and Brad Slaughter, meeting that same night to discuss the information conveyed in the previous scene, as well as to go back and forth with the aforementioned double entendres, now softened to accommodate the actress. It was improbable that both scenes would occur in the same café, but for the purposes of logistics and scheduling, I had written them there.

Meaghan arrived on set, regally stepping out of her van, trailed by the hair and makeup crew and their Zucas, storage containers on rollers that they also sat on. The makeup department head, Donna Yost, had phoned me on my cell and given me an update on Meaghan's mood. The hair and makeup trailer was a good source of information for the temperature of the actors on any given day. That morning, Meaghan had been complaining about her trailer, how it was smaller than the producers' trailers and smelled of "sewerage," so I knew her knickers would be up in a twist.

She was in one of three rather dowdy outfits that she insisted upon wearing, which drove the cable execs and the costume department batty. She favored black slacks and vertical-striped shirts worn out to cover her widening bottom, and comfortable, asexual clogs on her feet. Meaghan, black-haired with emerald green eyes, was an attractive individual by most standards. In fact, if one didn't know her, a person might even find her desirable. But we knew her.

In the middle of the first rehearsal, she stopped reading from her sides and waved her hands in a theatrical show of impatience.

"Who *writes* this shit?" she said, musically, with a smile, looking around at the crew for some reaction to her joking tone, as if that excused her insult.

"That would be me," I said, standing nearby.

"I know, darling," she said. "And ordinarily, Victor, I love your words. Of course, I'm no writer, but..." Here she pretended to carefully study the dialogue. "Why in the world is she asking this guy if he likes her shoes?"

"Well, she suspects he's a rapist and a killer. She's trying to determine if he has a shoe fetish. The victim was redressed after her murder. She'd been wearing flats because she'd just come off work. She was a cocktail waitress and she wore comfortable shoes. But when her body was found, she was wearing ankle straps with four-inch heels. *Remember?*"

I was asking if she'd read the entire script, and not just her scenes.

"Of course I remember." Meaghan's eyes went from reason to ice, a change I knew well; it was as if some inner switch had been thrown, like the tilt light on a pinball machine. "But when I ask the CI if he likes my shoes, it makes me out to be some kind of vacuous shopping queen or something. I'm an assistant district attorney, Victor, an *A-D-A*. I'm not a fucking *house*wife."

The day player had reddened a bit, and grips and electric, bored with her antics, had settled in for what they thought might be a long argument. Some even stepped away from the set. When Meaghan's name was on the call sheet, the morale of the crew went down the toilet.

I could have been contentious, but I had to pick my battles, and wasted time on a shoot meant overages and expenses. Keeping my cool was where I earned my money.

"Okay," I said. "What would you like to say, Meaghan?"

"*You're* the writer."

"How about, 'Do you like shoes'?"

"It's rather generic. I mean, *everyone* likes shoes, don't they? But I suppose that would be fine."

I was always defusing bombs and putting out fires with her. When she was off her meds, it was even worse. Mostly, she just made us all tired.

The rehearsal ended, the crew had the set, and a half hour later Meaghan returned from her trailer to do the scene and get into her position. We waited for her to do her mouth exercises, and then we shot it. It took a long while; the day player was nervous in Meaghan's presence, and when we turned around on him he continually flubbed his lines. He grew more nervous as she coached him on the finer points of acting, and then directed him, to the annoyance of Lomax, our actual director. Now we were behind.

The next scene, between Meaghan and Brad, had to be lit day-for-night. The camera crew changed lenses and filters, and the grips laid down the tracks. I watched my friend Skylar directing his lamp operators, rigging gaffers, and rigging electricians as they set up the lights. I could tell that he was listless and off his game. And then I saw his girlfriend, Laura, approach him, fresh out of the wardrobe trailer, carrying some shirts on hangers.

Laura Flanagan was a slight young woman who today wore oversized aviators, a shirt off one shoulder, skinny jeans, and leopard-print spectators. She was in her early twenties, but she looked seventeen. The two of them had a brief, joyless discussion before she moved away and walked toward me, her head down, attempting to hide her emotions. I could see tears behind the amber lenses of her shades.

Lunch, scheduled six hours after call time, was in a church auditorium near the second location. Our caterer did a good job of feeding our army, but even a Parisian chef would have trouble pleasing this crew after several months of shooting and eating the same-tasting food, day in, day out.

We served ourselves cafeteria style, with two lines of people filling their plates on either side of a long table. Salad, bread, vegetables, pasta, beans and rice, chicken, beef, pork, fish, and dessert were usually on the menu, with some half-assed food event (Taco Day, Burger Day) thrown in on occasion. Sometimes we just couldn't face the catering grub and went off to nearby restaurants or fast-food joints, and sometimes we substituted naps for chow. The best that could be said about lunch was that the food was free, plentiful, and filling. It was also a needed break in our day.

Tables had been set up, and normally people sat with their friends, which generally meant the ones within their departments. The Teamsters were fed first, per their contracts, another source of Lazy Teamster jokes that went around from shoot to shoot.

What did Jesus say to the Teamsters?

Don't do anything until I get back.

What do Teamsters' kids do on weekends?

Stand around and watch the other kids play.

Teamsters were easy to ridicule, unless you needed one in a pinch, and then they came through. They were some of the most genial people on the crew when you got to know them, and also the toughest, along with our security staff, the gaffers, and the grips.

Some days I sat with Annette and her contingent, if they were around for lunch, and other days I sat with the hair and makeup folks, mostly women, the best-looking and most stylish people on set. I was just a man, no deeper than any other, and I liked the company of nice-looking females when I was breaking bread. But their table was full that day, so I sat with my boys, Van and Eagle, and a few other folks we liked: Kenny "G" Garson (picture car coordinator), Jerome Hilts (a camera dolly grip), and Victoria Lewis, our locations manager, who was normally out scouting but had stopped in for lunch.

Lomax was eating with Ellen, Bruce, and the lead actors at another table. Skylar had disappeared.

"When's the next script gonna drop?" said Kenny, looking across the table at me. He was fifty-five, with a gray Vandyke, short gray hair, a barrel chest, and a bearish belly. Kenny found us the cars that were featured on camera. If I was to have another job on a film crew, it would be his. It seemed to me that it would be fun. But he had his pressures like everyone else.

"Yeah, Vic," said Victoria. *"When?"*

Like all department heads, they were eager to get the next script as early as possible, so they could get a jump on their prep. It was counterproductive to give them the details I was aware of, because more often than not, scenes and locations changed. At night, Annette prodded me for the same information, but she had an advantage over them. I spilled for her.

"I don't know," I said, and then, by way of explanation, "Bruce is writing it."

"Ugh," said Victoria, a savvy local who knew the city and its players, and seemed to be able to get us in damn near every door. She also knew that Bruce Kaplan always wrote his scripts at quarter to midnight.

"Sorry," I said. "The good news is, we're going to beat out one-fourteen tomorrow, and then I can go off and start writing it. So if I have any intel on that one, I'll let you know."

"So the brain trust is about to meet," said Jerome, our grizzled dolly grip. Jerome was the senior member of the crew. While producers could work well into their sixties, most crew who worked on-their-feet jobs didn't make it past their forties. The work was just too taxing on the body, and the hours were

ridiculously long. Jerome was fifty-eight, an avid reader, curious about politics, with the weathered, leathery face of an old
sailor, the under bite of a Cro-Magnon, and the forearms of
Popeye. He was an intellectual and a bull.

"What do you guys do in that writers' room?" said Kenny,
with a twinkle in his eye. "Discuss, you know, character motivations? Do you talk about your feelings and stuff?"

Kenny, like much of the crew, thought a writer's job was
easy, which was not true, and less physically demanding than
the jobs of other crew members, which was. Crew liked to believe that writers were soft, which was one reason I did two
hundred push-ups and sit-ups in my room daily, without fail,
no matter what time I wrapped. It confused the grips to see a
guy in my profession who was also in shape. Plus, I was vain.
When I stripped off my shirt at night and walked toward Annette, waiting in my bed, I wanted her to want me.

"Yeah," I said, "we bounce idea balloons around the room.
And we wear togas and crowns of ivy, and we tickle each other
and laugh a lot, and then we eat grapes."

"What happens when you get sleepy?"

"We lie down on our sit-upons and take naps."

"You guys have the best job," said Kenny.

"I know."

"But you must get tired sitting in that chair all day. With
your name on it."

"It hurts my back a little. I think I need one that reclines.
Like a La-Z-Boy."

"If it was motorized, that would be my department," said
Kenny. "Maybe I can find you one with an engine in it."

"That's kind of you, man. That way I won't have to walk, either."

"I wish I was as smart as you, Vic."

"You don't have to be smart. Being a writer is easy. Anyone can do it. You should give it a try, Kenny."

"Nah," said Kenny. "I'm just a gearhead from Alabama. What do I know?"

"The brain trust," said Jerome, shaking his head sagely as he forked a mound of cheesecake into his mouth.

Gradually we all got up and prepared to make our way back out to the vans. I went to the dessert table on the way to snag an oatmeal raisin cookie and a toothpick. Brad Slaughter was there, staring at a slab of chocolate cake. He was still wearing his "gun," a feathery-light plastic replica Glock, in his shoulder holster, and he had his fake badge clipped to the waistband of his slacks. Brad wasn't the type to stay in character. He was simply absentminded.

"I better not," he said, patting his flat stomach. "I'm trying to watch my girlish figure."

"The cake's not that good, anyway," I said.

"I would have remorse afterwards. It would be like…"

"Banging your kid sister?"

Brad's eyes narrowed. "My little sister's dead, you bastard."

"I, uh…"

"I'm joking with you, man!" Brad smiled a perfect row of ultra-white capped teeth. At fifty, he was a handsome son-ofabitch, better looking now than when he had been in the ensemble of one of those teenage-rebel movies Coppola had made in his boy-erotica period.

"Don't do that to me, Brad."

"Banging your kid sister." He pointed his finger at me, pistol style. "That's why you're the writer."

"I do make my living with words."

"Let me ask you something. Why did you cut that line, 'I'm partial to fish'?"

"Meaghan felt it made her out to be a prostitute. She doesn't like that."

"Yeah? *Fuck* what that whore doesn't like."

Brad winked at me. His face was caked in makeup. It would play great on camera, but in person he looked like the victim of a drunken undertaker. Still, he had an aura about him, like nothing bad would touch him, ever, in his life. Not until death came to call. Which made me think: someday, this guy is going to make a stunning corpse.

According to plan, we were to have finished our third scene of the day before lunch, but Meaghan's actions had pushed us behind schedule. We still needed the close-ups on Brad, then the turnaround on Meaghan, which meant more mouth exercises, relighting, and three sizes on her to accommodate the peculiar standards of the TV screen. We'd need to get her "clean" (just Meaghan in the frame, medium and close) and "dirty" (looking at Meaghan over Brad's shoulder, which would partially be in the shot). To further complicate issues, Lillie noticed some matching issues with Brad (he was drinking his glass of water at different times on various takes, the kind of mistake that he usually did not make), so we lost some time there as well.

I visited Skylar after he'd finished setting up the lights for the turnaround. He was seated on the largest size apple box, which for some reason this crew called "the Schiraldi."

"Are you sure about those fills?" I said to Skylar. "I think you put them in the wrong spot."

It was a joke between us. I would tell him where to "put" the lights, and he'd reply with something like, "Do I tell you how to over-write your scripts?" But today he didn't even smile.

"What's wrong?" I said.

"Nothing," said Skylar. "I guess my head's somewhere else."

"Where is it?"

"I was thinking about my father."

"Your old man's good people." I had met him, and Skylar's mother, when they had visited set earlier in the shoot. I could tell that Skylar had been loved and carried no childhood scars. It was evident in the type of man he had become.

"I know he is. I just wonder what he'd think of me now."

"He's proud of you."

"If he *knew*, Victor."

"If he knew *what?*"

The second AD called me back to the Village. Lomax had a question.

"We're gonna talk later on," I said to Skylar, before I left.

When the last shot of the scene was done and the gate was checked, it was announced that Meaghan had wrapped for the day. She was halfheartedly clapped out by the crew, who were visibly relieved.

We moved on to the last location.

The final scene of day ten was a candlelit vigil on the steps outside a "deep urban" (read: ghetto) high school (EXT: HARRIET TUBMAN HIGH SCHOOL, THIRD DISTRICT—NIGHT) that the murdered teller had attended years earlier. She had been established as a standout high school athlete beloved by her classmates, so they and her former teachers had gathered to honor her and also protest the growing violence in the city. The network execs had asked for the scene in their script notes, to make our show more "socially relevant and responsible" (read: they were hoping for an Emmy nomination), and we had complied, though such a vigil for a student long since graduated wouldn't have occurred and didn't make much sense.

In the scene, the young, good-looking detectives working under Tanner (Tanner's Team) infiltrated the crowd, hoping to catch a glimpse of someone who didn't belong there, i.e., the killer. Two of the detectives were also staked out in a van, videotaping the event. The scene would employ many extras, one non-actor who actually had lines (a woman who gets up at the lectern and remembers her friend), effects, and a lot of coverage. To make things more complicated, Alan Lomax had asked for an overhead crane shot that would look down on the vigil from the roof of the school, then pan to the city at night (directors loved crane shots and usually asked for one every episode). Problem was, there was no stair access to the roof (it was a very old school), so the crane and camera equipment, as well as the necessary crew, had to be transported up to the roof via a Condor, a heavy-duty piece of equipment similar to a bucket truck, with an articulating, retractable 120-foot arm capped with a steel-mesh basket to accommodate people and gear. It was a complicated sequence and it was going to be a long night.

We needed to get the money shot first, as Lomax's pan of the city would look best at dusk, and we were losing light. The camera and crane had been taken up to the roof in pieces, and now humans were being lifted as well. I went over to the Condor as it came back down and landed in a grassy area beside the school building. Our key grip, Kevin Burns, was operating the Condor from a standing position in the basket, using a joystick to elevate and steer. I opened the gate and got into the basket, stepped into a nylon harness, buckled the straps and tightened them, and clipped myself to one of the rails. The first AD, who had followed me into the basket, did the same. I didn't like wearing the harness, but I had to follow the safety procedures.

"You girls ready?" said Kevin, a thickly built former stuntman from rural Mississippi whose bad knees had necessitated a career change. He kept old photos of himself in his wallet, shots of him doing dangerous "gags," him on fire and stuff like that. He lived in the past in more ways than one. The black guys on the crew said Kevin made Strom Thurmond seem like Rosa Parks.

The arm emerged from its cylinder, and we began to rise up in lurching, herky-jerky movements. I looked down at the crew working, setting up lights, standing around the trucks — the security guys and the Teamsters, the extras, all of them getting very small. I saw Annette, who had just arrived at the location, wearing one of her hats, staring up at me, her hands on her hips.

I raised my head and kept my eyes straight ahead on the horizon, a sailor's trick used to thwart seasickness. I had begun to sweat and was feeling a little bit nauseated. My knuckles were bloodless as my hands gripped the basket's rail.

"You okay?" said Kevin, looking over at me with a small smile.

"I think so."

"Don't like heights, huh?"

"Not really."

"Or carnival rides, either, I bet."

"Nope."

"You're white as a Klansman."

"You oughta know."

"Don't get anxious. It's safe."

"Okay."

"It's *pretty* safe."

At eighty feet from the ground, we finally came to the roofline. Kevin had to change direction, take the arm over the ledge, and drop us onto the top surface. The basket shook inordinately as he made the maneuver. When he landed on the roof, I quickly removed my harness and jumped out of the basket.

"Thanks for the ride, Kevin."

"Not a problem, sir. I'll try to make it less bumpy next time."

Kevin had ten years on me, but one of the peculiarities of the film business was that many crew members addressed producers as sir, irrespective of experience or age. I didn't like it, any more than I liked the silly chair with my name on it. But it was tradition.

I wondered if Kevin thought I was foolish for coming up here. He knew that I could have stayed on the ground, used the radios and monitors to communicate with the director, and still would have been able to do my job. I didn't have to ride the Condor.

I wanted to.

We got our shot as darkness fell. It was the last scripted scene of the episode, so the pan over the city would be a quasi-artistic ending before the fade to black and credits. Lomax tended to overshoot, but his eps had a distinct style. He, Eagle, and Van had made it work. The camera movement was elegant, and it landed on a sweet frame of the twinkling downtown skyline, a nice visual contrast to the ghetto neighborhood of the school. Tonight these guys were on their game.

The ride back down to earth was less unnerving. The fear of the unknown is always worse than the event itself, and I had already stared it down on the ascent.

Annette was waiting for me when I dropped out of the basket and hit the ground. She didn't look pleased. She was holding her iPad and was deliberately showing me its screen, which held a menu of photographs.

"Do you have a minute?" she said. "I need to know what you want at the restaurant."

"I'll have the filet, medium rare."

"I'm talking about the design of the restaurant interior in scene thirty-eight."

"Let's walk," I said, and she followed me away from the crowd, to the street running beside the school.

She lowered the iPad to her side. "I'm so frustrated with you. Why did you go up in the Condor?"

"It's my job to be with the director."

"Bullshit, Vic. You could have done everything you needed to do from the Village."

"Crew went up there."

"They *have* to. I hate when you do dangerous stuff just to do it."

"The Condor's safe."

"It's a machine. Machines break."

We stopped walking. Annette had her hand on one hip and she was tapping the toe of one boot on the ground, the way she did when she was annoyed with me.

"We'll talk about this later, Thumper."

"I'm not a rabbit." Annette's eyes relaxed. "Don't call me Thumper."

"Shake a tail feather, baby."

"You're mixing your animals up. I thought you were a good writer."

"I never said I was a good one. Look, I gotta get back to set. We both have work to do."

"You."

I leaned in toward her ear so she could feel my breath on her. "Are we?"

"Are we what?"

"Gonna talk about this later?"

Annette allowed me a smile. "Yes."

"I want to kiss you right now," I said. "You know that, don't you?"

"I want to kiss *you*."

"Think about it."

"The kiss?"

"Where you want it," I said.

She blushed and left me there.

We shot deep into the night. The candlelight vigil had many pieces, including van interiors, with dialogue. The surrounding streets and school exteriors needed to be lit and relit as we moved and turned around. On our thirteenth hour, food was brought in from catering, what was called "second meal," usually of the steak-and-cheese/Chinese/pizza variety, something that the health-minded among us avoided but sometimes could not. The aura on the set grew peaceful and relatively quiet, a result of fatigue and pride in doing an honest full day's work, mixed with the anticipation of the wrap. People hung around crafty, picking at snacks, or sat on apple boxes, or on their Zucas, and in between shots they talked about bands, bars, and restaurants, people they thought were hot, those who were not, and their plans for the night.

As we prepped a new setup, I broke away and walked toward my trailer, where I intended to freshen up and answer some email from my laptop. At the honey wagons, a nice name for a row of trucked-in latrines, I saw Skylar emerge from one of the heads and come down the three steps to the sidewalk.

"Hey, man," I said.

"Hey." Even in the darkness, I could see the trouble in his liquid brown eyes. He tried to walk past me, but I reached out and cupped his biceps.

"Hold up, Skylar."

"I need to get back and supervise those knuckleheads."

"They got it. Relax."

He pulled his arm out of my grip but he didn't move on. Our best boy, Lance, a skinny little snitch, walked by us and gave me a look.

When he was gone, Skylar looked down at the sidewalk.

"What's going on with you?" I said. "You haven't been right all day."

"Trouble," he said, and shook his head. He removed his ball cap and ran a hand through his longish hair.

"Anything you can talk about?"

"No. It's better if I don't involve anyone else."

"I'm guessing this has something to do with your other enterprise."

Skylar didn't reply, an answer in itself.

"Do you need money?" I said.

He looked at me directly for the first time. "Money got me into this."

"*What* are you into?"

"It doesn't matter. But, listen…"

"What?"

"I'm worried about Laura. She's just a little slip of nothin, man."

"Now you sound Texan, boy."

"Promise me you'll look after her."

"*You* look after her."

"Promise me."

"Okay, I promise. But Skylar, you can talk to me."

"It's too late," he said. "It's fucked."

I watched him walk away.

A couple of hours later, we finished. The martini shot, our last one of the day, was called by our first AD, and at Lomax's shout of "Cut!" and after the subsequent gate-check, we broke set.

"That's a wrap, everybody," shouted the AD.

I saw Skylar going around and thanking every single one of his crew, the way he did every night.

He didn't get in the van for the hotel. Van said that Skylar told him he was going out with his boys for a couple of beers.

I never spoke to Skylar again.

In the middle of the night I lay with Annette in the bed, both of us nude, drinking wine. We had started on the carpet, moving slowly, me between her strong legs, burying it, looking down into her eyes, green and alive in the flickering candlelight. We'd finished our lovemaking atop my sheets, now kicked to the floor.

My knees were rug-burned and raw, but I was satiated and relaxed. Come still dripped down my inner thigh, and there was a puddle of it on the mattress. My unit was languid in repose. Annette was up on one elbow, facing me, her beautiful, perfect breasts set before me, solid Ds, every boy's dream. She had a sip of red.

"You go," she said. "I'll guess the lines."

We were playing a game we liked.

"Okay," I said. "Tanner is about to leave the Homicide offices, angry and in a rush. He puts on his shoulder holster and shrugs himself into his jacket. One of his junior detectives says to him, *Where are you going, Lieutenant?* Tanner turns to the detective and says…"

"I'm gonna finish this."

I lifted the bottle of Merlot off the nightstand. "You?"

"Yeah," said Annette. "Give me some of that Strong Rodney."

I darkened her glass, then mine. We were halfway into our second bottle. It was three a.m., and we were a little tipsy.

"How about this?" I said. "Tanner's chased a perp, a child rapist he's been pursuing, to the roof of a building. Tanner's got his gun on him and he's ready to kill him in cold blood, but he can't pull the trigger. What's the dialogue, honey?"

"The rapist says, *Go ahead. You'd be doing me a favor.*"

"Then Tanner lowers his gun and says…"

"I can't. I'm not like you."

"What does the rapist say next?"

"We're more alike than you think we are. We're two sides of the same coin, Tanner."

"That's good. That variation there, with the coin. You're pretty smart."

"Just lucky."

"I'm the lucky one," I said, and reached out and touched her face.

She blinked slowly. "I worry about you."

" 'Cause I went up in the Condor?"

"Yes."

"*Don't* worry."

I brushed away the hair that had fallen over her eyes and kissed her lips.

"What was the purpose of that crane shot on the roof, any-way?" she said. "And then the pan to the city at dusk. It's a cop show, for crying out loud. Lomax was shooting for his reel, right?"

I nodded. "Guy thinks he's David fucking Lean."

Annette called me on my cell early in the morning, just as I came out of the shower. She told me that Skylar Branson was dead.

"What happened?"

She repeated what she knew, based on a conversation with Ellen Stern. Skylar had gone to Red's, a drinker's bar down by the river, after wrap with a couple of the guys on his crew. Red's, like all of the bars in this city, was open till four a.m. At some point, Skylar told one of his guys he had to take a leak. There was only one toilet in the men's room, and it was oc-cupied, so Skylar went outside to urinate between a fence and a nearby Dumpster. His guys heard the pop of gunshots and went out to investigate. They found Skylar, shot to death, ly-ing beside the Dumpster. One in the back of the head, three in his back. His wallet was on the ground, emptied of cash and credit cards. Police were calling his death a robbery/homi-cide.

"This city," said Annette.

I knew what she meant. Culturally, it was a vibrant, diverse town. It also had a high unemployment rate and a very high rate of crime. When we walked around at night, we put extra robbery money in our pockets, so as not to anger gunmen who were looking for more than a meager amount of cash. Violent shit happened here, randomly. People would say that Skylar's murder was bad luck. A case of wrong place, wrong time.

"You all right?" said Annette. When I didn't answer, she said, "Vic?"

"What about work?" I was scheduled for the writers' room; Ellen was supposed to cover set.

"Bruce and Ellen cancelled today's shoot. We'll be up again tomorrow. I've gotta go in."

"Me, too. I'll see you at the offices, honey. Thanks for the call."

I phoned Eagle first. It was the easiest call I'd make, and I was putting off the hard ones. I knew that Eagle, true to his Northern European temperament, would be the strongest and most stoic of Skylar's friends. And indeed, all he said was, "It is a tragedy."

"What are you going to do now?"

"I think I'll sleep."

Van Cummings was the tougher one to deal with. He was an emotional guy, the Jackson Browne of camera operators, unashamed to wear his heart on his sleeve. Van had been crying when he picked up my call.

"Why him?" he said. I pictured him right now, running a hand through his gray-blond hair, smoking a cigarette. "He was a sweet kid."

"I know it."

"Meet me somewhere, Victor."

"I can't. I have to go in to the writers' room today."

"Okay," said Van. "I'll be at the Low Bar, if you want to stop by after you get off."

He'd be on his favorite stool for the rest of the day, at the little bar near city hall. Drinking vodka and juice, going outside occasionally to smoke a little weed, then back in for more drink. He'd end up in his hotel bed with one of the crew members, the cute new camera assistant maybe, by late afternoon. That was how Van would deal with this. I had yet to figure out how I would reconcile Skylar's death.

The last call I made, the one I dreaded, was to Laura Flanagan. I was relieved when she didn't pick up. The call went to voice mail but I didn't leave one. Instead I texted her: "Be strong. If you need me, I'm here for you. I mean it, Vic."

I got dressed and took my rental car, a red Ford Focus, to work.

The production and writers' offices occupied a run-down building, built in the 1960s, off the Martin Luther King highway, which was, as it is in all American cities, on the blighted side of town. The space was unglamorous and spartan—cubicles for the production staff, offices for department heads and management. I had an office, which I rarely used, with a bare-top desk and an old couch that I was meant to sleep on but never once did. My window gave to a view of an empty lot where men sat on crates and drank beer in the afternoons, after their free breakfast. We were located near a homeless shelter and morning bread line.

The mood was dour when I arrived. In the production office, people were quietly talking amongst themselves or on their desk phones. My assistant, Lynn, a local woman with a law degree who was hoping to become a writer, got up from her desk and hugged me as I crossed into the wing of the writers and producers.

"I'm so sorry, Vic."

"It's rough. Is Ellen around?"

"She's in her office."

I knocked on Ellen Stern's open door and entered. Unlike my office, Ellen's was heavily decorated. Its walls were crowded with framed commendations and one-sheets of shows she'd produced, and her bookshelves were filled. She worked here for most of her day, while I rarely came in, so this was her abode. My home was the set.

She was typing on her laptop with one hand and eating an apple with the other. She looked at me over the rims of her reading glasses.

"I'm sorry about Skylar. It's awful."

"Yeah."

"We're going to have a meeting with everyone on set tomorrow, before crew call. Go over some general things about street awareness. Suggest they not walk alone at night, what neighborhoods to avoid, that sort of thing. Maybe if Skylar had been more cognizant..."

"You think that's what happened? That he was careless?"

"What do *you* think happened?"

"No idea, Ellen."

She placed her half-eaten apple on her desk and removed her glasses. "He was young. The young tend to think that nothing bad is ever going to happen to them. But this is a dangerous city. We're here because of the tax credits the state offers. The network mandated that we shoot here, and it's saving the production millions. We didn't have a choice. But while we're here I'm going to try and make sure that our people are safe."

She didn't know anything about Skylar's other life. Ellen sometimes criticized me for being too friendly with the crew and for not entirely committing to the side of the brass, but I was unconvinced that there had to be such a strict division between labor and management.

"That's a good idea," I said. "The safety meeting, I mean. Have you notified Skylar's family?"

"The police did. His parents are coming in from Galveston today. They're going to take his body home for burial, after the autopsy. We'll do a service of our own here, for the crew. Maybe in the park. We'll dedicate a tree to him, something like that."

"That would be nice."

"Are you going to be here all day?"

"In the writers' room," I said.

"I've spoken to the Homicide detectives. I told them everything I knew. Skylar was dating Laura in wardrobe, right?"

"Yes."

"I also told them you were one of his closest friends here. I hope you don't mind."

"Not at all."

"They'd like to speak with you later on today. Much later, I imagine. They've got a lot of work to do, interviews and the like. I think they're going to get into Skylar's room at the hotel as well."

If they got into his suite, they'd access his room safe. The contents of the safe would tell a story. They'd know.

"I'll be here," I said.

Ellen placed her glasses back on her face, and her eyes went to her laptop's screen. "They're waiting for you in the room. Bruce and the rest."

"Right."

Our conversation had been free of emotion. In this racket we were used to death. Because we worked together so closely, sometimes up to eighty hours a week, death showed itself to us with surprising frequency, and we became enamored of it. One of Ellen's partners on another show had died of a massive heart attack on set. A junkie actor on *Crucial Investigations*, a show I worked on for NBC, hung himself in his trailer the day he'd wrapped. We watched fellow crew members deteriorate, and continue to work, as they were dying of cancer. A dolly grip I knew, an alcoholic who had once pissed his pants while sleeping on my hotel-room couch, drank a quart of Listerine one night and did a Bill Holden, fell out of the shower while blackout drunk and hit his head on the edge of the bathtub. There were more casualties, too many to count. Skylar was the latest, a guy we'd remember and talk about less and less as the shoot progressed and we moved on to other jobs.

In my office, I took my notebook and pen out of my book bag, then headed for the room.

The writers' room was deliberately drab, with zero decor: two walls with mounted writing boards and windows with blinds kept drawn, so we wouldn't be distracted by the outside world. A long table, holding yellow legal pads and cups of pencils and pens, took up the bulk of the space. In the center of the table was an array of snacks, mostly of the healthy variety per Bruce's instructions, and bottled water. A coffee urn, constantly refreshed, had been set up at a nearby station, along with a cooler holding soft drinks, juices, and Gatorade.

Bruce Kaplan sat at the head of the table. At the other end of the table was Diego Rodriguez, our young script supervisor, who took the meeting's notes on his word processor, the only laptop allowed in the room, a rule that prevented us from surfing while at work. Diego, quiet and contemplative, was a sponge, and very smart. He would soon get a script assignment, and someday it was likely that, per his ambition, he would have his own show. Also at the table were our two staff writers, Randall Arrington and Fay Harmon. Randall, his hand in a bag of potato chips, did not look up as I entered. Fay's eyes met mine, and she gave me a kind nod. I nodded back and had a seat near Diego.

First order of business, as always, was lunch. A menu from a local restaurant went around the table, and we made our choices on one of the pads, placing our orders beside our names. While we did this, Bruce, rumpled and clearly unmoored, made a brief speech about Skylar's death and how deeply it resonated to management, as well as how we had to soldier on and proceed with our work. The others listened respectfully even as they chose between the Cobb salad and grilled shrimp over Caesar. They knew little of Skylar Branson except to recognize him by sight.

"Why would man fear that which is so inevitable?" said Randall, unprompted, speaking on death, quoting, no doubt, from Shakespeare or some other decomposed writer I had not read. Randall liked to do that. He knew it annoyed me, and he thought it made him seem intelligent.

"Let's get started on one-fourteen," said Bruce.

Scenes were discussed by character, then handwritten on the board by Diego, using a Sharpie. Often they were quickly erased. If they were deemed worthy of making it into the episode, the beats were transposed onto index cards. Lead characters (Tanner, Hart) got their own color card, as did supporting characters (Tanner's Team), and others who reoccurred in each ep. Criminals, too, if they had a multi-episode arc or we gave them POV. Then we put the scenes in order: day one, night one, day two, night two. Once thumbtacked up on the bulletin boards, the different-colored cards would tell us, graphically, whether or not our cast of characters was fully represented. The process, called "beating out" an episode, usually took a couple of days, depending upon the level of nonsense and useless discourse allowed in the room.

"I need to give something a little extra to Andre Robbins in this episode," said Bruce, speaking of a young actor in our cast. His agent had complained about Andre's paucity of lines and the stagnant nature of his arc. Robbins played Cobb McCord, a handsome, "impetuous" junior member of the squad.

"Trouble at home?" I said. "He *is* newly married."

"Maybe he can't get it up," said Randall, and I saw Fay give an almost imperceptible roll of her eyes.

"We played that already," I said. "With Detective Richards, earlier in the season. We solved his problem with a pill."

"Okay," said Randall. "How about this? He wakes up one day and...I'm just spitballing here, I haven't figured out the details yet...all a the sudden, he thinks he's gay. Doesn't know if he's a cocksman or a cock*sucker.* We could play it out for the rest of the season."

"They did that storyline with Bayliss on *Homicide*," said Diego.

"And it didn't work for them, either," I said.

"Randy," said Bruce, with great tolerance, "I don't think that's what the actor had in mind when he asked us to expand his role."

Bruce had brought Randall, his former college roommate, into the writers' room and given him a staff position. Randall had once been an advertising copywriter and he convinced Bruce that he could do it. But he wasn't a screenwriter, or any kind of writer at all, and had no desire to learn the craft. Consequently, Bruce had to rewrite most of his work. In Randall's mind, he was here to collect a paycheck, eat free food, and hit on the females in the office. He had a beach ball for a belly and wore thick-lens oval-rim glasses that made him look like a Japanese villain in a '40s war flick. Women found him repulsive, and so did men, but that message didn't reach him or stop his inappropriate behavior. Guys like him never seemed to get it; I often wondered if there were mirrors in his house. At any rate, Randall was Bruce's cross to bear.

"We've already established that McCord is a hothead," said Fay, a veteran scribe whose reserved and dignified personality had actually hindered her advancement in the industry. She was the best pure writer among us.

"That's right," said Bruce, leaning forward to hear her, as she was very soft-spoken.

"Playing on that," she said, "we could have him assault a suspect during an arrest. Maybe the suspect is already hand-cuffed or something, and McCord punches him in the face."

"Why does he have to punch him in the face?" said Randall, whose comments were nearly always off point. "He could sucker punch him in the gut or somethin instead."

"Go on, Fay," said Bruce, tiredly.

"I'm thinking, his actions could imperil the case against the suspect. McCord's brought up on brutality charges, and it also puts him in the doghouse with Tanner and Hart."

"Which he has to work himself out of," said Bruce, warming to it.

"Sets McCord up for some kind of redemption," I said. "You could sell that to the execs, Bruce." The cable suits loved that concept: redemption.

"I like it," said Bruce.

"It's something we could play into next season," I said.

"If there is a next season," said Bruce, rather mournfully. Our first two episodes had already run, and the numbers were not stellar, despite a lead-in from a popular show. "But I do like it."

We discussed the beats for the McCord arc and got them up on the board, then on cards. It was my episode, and I began to see the scenes, how I would write them, the dialogue, everything. That's how it worked for me. The movie had begun to play in my head.

Lunch came, and then the inevitable post-lunch ennui. We

drank more coffee and tried to get back up. A second wind lifted us, and we got more scenes on the board, and more cards on the bulletin board. Late in the day, my assistant knocked on the door and popped her head inside the room.

"Excuse me, Victor," said Lynn. "The police are here to see you."

I got up out of my chair.

Two Homicide dicks, one black and middle-aged, one white and getting there, were waiting for me in my office, both of them seated expansively on my couch. They were in suits and ties, wearing Glocks set in clip-on holsters and badges on neck chains, like they'd just stepped out of the props truck via the wardrobe trailer. The only thing that wouldn't have worked for our show was their grooming; our hair department head, Jana Kendros, would have given them better cuts and some product.

They stood as I entered. The office was crowded for three, and I imagined that was the way they wanted me: uncomfortable.

"Dennis Mahoney," said the white one, late thirties, a little overweight but not soft, with strawberry blond hair that screamed Gaelic, a nose brilliantly veined from drink, and cheeks cratered with the laughing reminder of an acned adolescence. He wore a Men's Wearhouse–grade suit with pleated slacks and a rep tie darkened with an oval of grease.

"Detective Gittens," said the black one. "Joe." His suit was a little more twenty-first century than his partner's. He wore a thick mustache, had a face dotted with raised moles, and deep brown, tired eyes. He was on the green side of fifty and wore no wedding ring.

Gittens was the sensible one, Mahoney the meat-eater.

All of this I noticed before I spoke to them. An eye for detail is helpful in my profession.

"Victor Ohanion," I said, and shook their hands.

"Ohanion," said Mahoney, brightly. "You must be Irish. Me, too."

"I'm Armenian," I said.

Mahoney's smile faded. I might as well have said I was an A-rab or, worse, a Muslim. I was raised Orthodox Christian but hadn't seen the inside of a church since I was an altar boy. I'd been wandering the wilderness for more than twenty years.

"Have a seat," I said, gesturing to the couch. They did, and I took the chair behind my desk.

Gittens wasted no time.

> GITTENS
>
> We understand that you were friends with Skylar Branson.

> OHANION
>
> That's right.

> GITTENS
>
> In the last few days, did Mr. Branson say anything to you that would indicate he was in some sort of trouble?

OHANION
(beat)
No.

GITTENS
Was he acting peculiar in any way?

OHANION
Not that I recall.

MAHONEY
One of your crew members said he saw
you two talking last night on set, and
that it looked contentious.

OHANION
That would've been Lance. He's a bit of a
drama queen. Likes to get into other people's business. The truth is, Skylar and I
were just talking.

MAHONEY
What were you talking about?

OHANION
Designer shoes and handbags. Menstrual
cramps. That sort of thing.

MAHONEY

You're a funny guy, Ohanion.

OHANION

I have moments.

GITTENS

For the record, where were you last
night at the time of Mr. Branson's
death?

OHANION

What time was that, exactly?

GITTENS

He was shot around three thirty a.m.

OHANION

I was in bed at my hotel. Sleeping.

GITTENS

You stay at the crew hotel?

OHANION

Correct.

GITTENS

Were you sleeping alone?

OHANION

Yes.

GITTENS

Do you have any idea why your friend
was killed?

OHANION

My understanding was that he was
robbed. Skylar didn't carry much cash
on him. Could be that the gunman
didn't like the small take, and shot him
out of anger. That's the way it is in this
town.

MAHONEY

Now you're going to tell us about our
town. How long have you lived here, that
you know so much?

OHANION

I've been here a few months.

MAHONEY

That long, huh? Bet you've done a few
ride-alongs, too.

OHANION

I went on one. I watched your jump-out

boys entrap some kid and put him in
bracelets.

MAHONEY looks at GITTENS, then back at OHANION.

> MAHONEY
> One ride-along. That makes you some
> kind of law enforcement expert?

> GITTENS
> (sarcastic)
> Give him a break, Dennis. The man
> *writes* about crime. He knows what he's
> talking about.
> (to OHANION)
> Looks like you make a good living at it,
> too. That's an expensive watch you got
> on your wrist.

OHANION makes no comment.

> MAHONEY
> I've watched your show. With all those
> pretty police and detectives. All the dirty
> ones, too. So many dirty police officers
> on our force. Who knew?

OHANION

It's a television show. Corrupt cops make good drama. We're not going for realism.

MAHONEY

Okay, then. Let's get real.

GITTENS leans forward.

GITTENS

Here's the thing, Mr. Ohanion. Maybe Mr. Branson was killed in the commission of a street robbery. Maybe. But we found some interesting items when we went through his hotel room. Do you know what I'm talking about?

OHANION

No, I don't.

GITTENS

There was a large amount of marijuana stashed in his room safe, along with a digital scale, distribution materials, and a ledger. It's safe to say that the pot wasn't for personal use.

OHANION folds his hands atop his desk and says nothing.

GITTENS

You don't seem surprised.

OHANION

People smoke marijuana. They like to get
outside their heads.

GITTENS

I'm talking about the fact that your
friend was a dealer.

OHANION

I don't know anything about that.

MAHONEY

I find that hard to believe.

OHANION

So?

OHANION looks MAHONEY over in a way that no man likes
to be looked at. MAHONEY'S jaw gets tight. It looks like he's
going to get up and go over the desk at OHANION.

GITTENS
(to MAHONEY, sotto voce)
Dennis.
(to OHANION)
You're protecting your friend's reputa-

tion. I get that. But it's not going to help
us find his killer.

OHANION

You said there was a ledger.

MAHONEY

A notebook. Initials, with dollar amounts
beside the initials, some crossed out,
some not. We've got a list of your crew
members, and we'll match the initials to
those names. Then we'll talk to those
people and see what we can find. You
don't want to cooperate, fine. We'll figure
it out on our own.
          (beat)
Branson had a girlfriend on the crew.
What was her name again?

OHANION

You know her name. It's Laura Flanagan. She works in the wardrobe department.

MAHONEY

Right.

OHANION turns to GITTENS, ignoring MAHONEY.

OHANION

Detective Gittens, despite what you
might think of Skylar, he was a good
guy. Hard worker, always looked out for
his crew. Do you know what I mean?

GITTENS

Sure.

OHANION

His parents are coming into town. I
wouldn't want this thing you found to de-
plete him in their minds.

GITTENS

I'm not an idiot. I have kids my own
self. We're not going to mention what we
found in his room to his folks, unless it's
absolutely necessary.

OHANION

Thank you.

MAHONEY stands.

MAHONEY

One more thing, Ohanion . . .

OHANION

Don't leave town?

MAHONEY walks from the room, red-faced. GITTENS places his business card on the desk, shoots OHANION a look, shakes his head, and exits.

ON OHANION, unmoved.

When I was a teenager, growing up in a multiethnic neighborhood just outside the city, my friends and I had an adversarial relationship with the law. Though all of us got high, none of us were into anything that had violence attached to it. Many of the guys I knew or ran with got busted at one time or another for marijuana possession, or low-level distribution, and paid a price. Some got put into the system and never recovered.

The cops in my hometown were devious about it. They hid in the woods, waiting for kids to light up. They arrested kids and turned them into snitches. The younger police on the drug squad posed as buyers and jacked kids up like that. The black and Hispanic kids suffered worse than the whites. They were pulled over more frequently in their cars, were handcuffed and sat down on the curb in the dead of winter, and were assigned disinterested public defenders when it came time to go to trial. They didn't have a chance.

Six months ago, I went back home to visit my mother. A curfew on teenagers had recently been enacted in that part of the county, and there had been some complaints that minority kids would be unfairly singled out. The chief of police wrote an editorial in the local newspaper defending the curfew, saying no particular race or ethnic group would be targeted, claiming that his young police officers were of an enlightened generation who didn't "see color." When I read that, I laughed out loud.

Gittens was all right; maybe Mahoney was, too. But it didn't matter to me. I was nearly forty years old, a long way from my youth, and still, because of what I'd experienced growing up, I didn't trust police. I wasn't about to talk to them about my friend.

That night, I drove downriver to a part of town that was once a low-income, borderline dangerous district and was now a burgeoning neighborhood of newly arrived college graduates, folk resurgents, visual artists, and film production crew who were trying to make a living year-round.

Laura Flanagan lived in an old narrow-and-deep house with two young women who worked as prop and wardrobe assistants on other productions. I parked my rental on the street near one of the city's ubiquitous neighborhood markets and walked to her house. Skylar's electrics and rigging gaffers were grouped on the front lawn, and there were many people, some from our crew and some I didn't recognize, standing on Laura's porch and seated on her front stoop. They were drinking beer, wine, and liquor, playing guitar and percussion instruments, and passing around weed. Marijuana wasn't legal in this city, but its use was tolerated. The police had bigger issues to contend with here, like murder, rape, and internal corruption.

It was an impromptu wake of sorts and I moved into the crowd. I took a pull off a bottle of Jack that was offered to me, then grabbed a beer from a cooler. I could see that people were getting twisted in the go-to-hell way that is common after an unexpected death. We had a six a.m. call in the morning. It would be a rough day for those who were going hard at it.

I found Laura inside her house, a typical artist's lair, illuminated by candles and Christmas lights. Fish netting had been strung from the ceiling, and magazine photos were taped to the walls. Marijuana and cigarette smoke hung heavy in the room, where Laura sat on her couch, talking to friends. She was wearing her aviators, a loose flannel shirt, skinny jeans, and checkerboard Vans.

Laura stood as I approached. She came into my arms unsteady and we embraced. I held her tightly and for a long while. Her tears were hot on my face as she pressed her cheek against mine.

"It's gonna be okay, Laura."

"You think so, Vic?" Her tone was odd.

"Sit with your friends. I'll talk to you in a little bit, when the crowd thins out."

She went back to the couch. Out in the front yard I joined up with Skylar's crew, who were standing around, quietly getting wasted. They were telling stories and sharing memories about their beloved boss. The talk went from Skylar to counterpunches and defensive stances, firearms they'd recently purchased at shows, and back to Skylar. They were gun enthusiasts to a man, and Skylar, a martial artist, had gotten them into a regular training regimen at a local dojo. Though they weren't the show-muscle type, and none had flat stomachs, all of them were work-strong and knew how to go with their hands. They'd be hard to hurt. I pitied anyone who looked at them the wrong way tonight.

After midnight, Laura and I sat down on the edge of her bed and talked. Her twin mattress lay on the floor, separated from a roommate's bed by a curtain strung across the room. It wasn't the ideal spot to converse, but it was the only place in the house where we could find some privacy. I wanted to get to her before she got too sloppy, and it didn't seem that any of the visitors would be leaving anytime soon.

"The detectives spoke to you today?" I said.

"Yes. They asked me if I knew anything about Skylar's marijuana operation. That's what they called it: an operation."

"They found his stash in his hotel room. His scale and the ledger book, too. They're going to match the crew list names with the initials in the ledger."

"Why?"

"They're going to talk to people on the crew who you and Skylar were selling weed to. They're trying to determine if Skylar's murder was a random robbery or if it had something to do with his side business."

"Oh."

"Someone will tell them you were selling it as well."

"I don't care about that."

"Just deny," I said, and strengthened my tone. "I spoke to Skylar before we wrapped last night. I know he was in some kind of trouble."

Laura looked away and dragged on her cigarette. "I can't talk about this right now."

"You *have* to."

She was just a few years out of high school. Grieving, of course, and also confused. She'd gotten into the sales thing with her lover as a lark, not for profit. Their "operation" simply provided them with free smoke. In her mind, she and Skylar were providing a service for the crew.

Thursday was payday, and on Friday the out-of-town workers were given their per diem. So, every week, on Thursday and Friday, Skylar and Laura sold weed to the crew. Eighths for fifty, quarters for a hundred, three-fifty for an ounce. It was common knowledge to damn near everyone, except for Bruce, Ellen, our few straitlaced coworkers, and the crew members who were commonly thought of as untrustworthy.

"Laura, if I'm going to help you, I need to know what's going on."

"Why would I need help?"

"Look at me," I said, and she did. "If Skylar's murder was connected to what was found in his safe, make no mistake, you're in danger, too."

Laura tapped ash on the thigh of her jeans, though there was a foil tray beside her on the bed. "What do you want to know?"

"Tell me what's been going on."

Laura hit her Marlboro and exhaled a stream of smoke into the room. "Skylar was all jammed up."

"I know he was in trouble."

She nodded. "He fronted a pound to someone, and that guy couldn't pay. Skylar owed the connect about five grand…"

"And?"

"He had most of the cash he needed to settle up, but he was short by twenty-five hundred. He put the legitimate cash together with some phony money."

"Phony money. Why?"

"He made a mistake, Vic."

"What the *fuck*."

"Counterfeit. It looked real. Our connect had sent a couple of guys to collect, and Skylar paid them off. When they figured out that some of the money wasn't right…" She shook her head.

"*What?* Say it, Laura."

"They threatened us. Skylar put them off. He'd sold one package, and he was hoping to off the last pound…the one that the detectives found in his safe. He planned to make it right. He was going to tell them that *he'd* been duped, and that he was good for the rest of the cash."

"He took too long."

"Yes." Laura's hand shook as she brought her cigarette to her lips.

"Who did Skylar front the pound to? Where would he get counterfeit money?" When Laura didn't answer, I said, "Was it people on our crew?"

"I can't tell you," she said. "Skylar wouldn't want me to. He didn't want to involve anyone else in this, including you. You know him. Skylar was honorable. He told me that he'd gotten us into this, and he'd get us out himself."

It sounded like him. I'd offered him money, but he'd declined. Pride and his notion of manhood had done him in. That was who he was.

"Tell me how this works," I said. "How you two brought the stuff into town."

"Normally it got FedExed in from California. We had an arrangement with a guy Skylar had met on a show in Los Angeles. We always paid him within a week, also by overnight mail. One time a package got seized in the process, and Skylar made good on it. So there wasn't any problem with this dude. But this time, when the problem did come up, Skylar was light on cash."

"If that was the deal, why'd the connect send in a couple of guys to collect the payment?"

"We'd bought three pounds on this go-round. Three pounds is about ten thousand dollars at wholesale. For that kind of money, he felt the need to send couriers."

"They worked for him?"

"I got the impression they were freelance. Local collection agents."

"You saw them?"

"They came here one night to meet with Skylar and pick up the money. Two white guys, brothers, in their twenties. I think they were twins. They were okay that night, on the surface. You know how someone can smile at you, but there's nothing friendly there? It was…"

"Laura. Do you know their names?"

"Wayne and Cody. That's what they said."

"And after they figured out the money was fake, what happened?"

"They told Skylar he had a day to make it right. Two days passed, and Skylar got killed."

"You have no proof it was them, do you?"

"No."

"Skylar could have been robbed and shot at random."

"I suppose so." I watched her take a last drag and crush out her smoke in the foil tray.

"You have a cell number for this Cody or Wayne?"

"I captured one, yeah."

"They phoned you?"

"Not since Skylar died."

"What did they say when they called you?"

"*Wayne* called me. It wasn't about business. He said he liked to look at me. And what he'd do to me if he got the chance. Shit like that."

"Give me Wayne's number," I said. Laura read it off her phone and I typed it into the notes app of mine. I stood up. "Hold on a minute and stay right here."

I left the house and walked outside. Skylar's crew had left, but there were still some people up on the porch. I went down to the yard and called Bernard, the night manager of my hotel. When you live in a hotel, the desk people, the bartenders, the housekeepers, and the valets become friends. Some become family. I got hold of Bernard and told him what I needed. He said he'd hook me up for the production rate.

Walking back into the house, I tried to get my head around the situation. I wondered who Skylar had fronted the pound to and where Skylar had gotten the counterfeit money. Back in Laura's bedroom, I found her where I'd left her. She'd lit another cigarette.

"Pack up some things," I said. "Enough to last a few days at least."

"Why?"

"You can't stay here. It's not safe."

"Where am I going?"

"To my hotel."

"I'm staying with you?"

"No."

"Annette, then."

"Why do you say that?"

"Everyone knows you two are together, Vic."

"Let's go."

It was almost three a.m. by the time I got Laura settled in her room. I went up to my suite, where I found Annette in my bed. Her breathing was deep and there was that clicking sound. I stripped naked and got under the covers and spooned myself against her. She was on her side and she reached back to touch my thigh. I knew she preferred to wake up in her own room. She had come here, unselfishly, for me. Annette was everything I'd wanted to find in a woman since my divorce. The physical and the emotional, all in one. I stroked her arm softly.

"I'm here," I said. "Go back to sleep."

I only had two and half hours before I had to get up for call. When I closed my eyes I saw Skylar, lying on a morgue slab, his skin gray and marbleized, his scalp removed, his once healthy body cut up and autopsied.

I was sick with grief and anger. I couldn't stop thinking about my friend.

We were shooting on the soundstages the next day, located in the warehouse space of a Sam's Club, now shuttered, in an industrial area outside the city limits. For budgetary reasons, we'd built sets there that we used with frequency: the Homicide offices, the ADA's office, the courtroom, Tanner's apartment, and others. We didn't have any moves on stage days, which was convenient, but the hours were typically long. Once inside the walls of the warehouse, where there were no windows, it was easy to lose track of time. Here, we typically worked fourteen- to sixteen-hour days.

I parked my four-banger rental and walked across a dirt-and-asbestos lot, past Teamsters who had shuttled in crew and brought the trucks, and our security people, a freelance outfit of fathers, tight friends, cousins, uncles, daughters, and sons, all of them black and local. Security was run by a man named Toomer who had built his business rapidly after the state's film production tax credit was enacted, and he now serviced the majority of the shows and features that came through town. His staff were all physically imposing, the women included, which was helpful in defusing a situation before it progressed into something violent. They had nicknames like Manimal, She Girl, Creep, and Seminole Joe, and they were family men and women who rode motorcycles on weekends, and owned homes, and barbecued, and tended to their lawns. Some had been straight-up gangsters. One of them, Barry, aka Black Barry, a very large man with a bulbous nose and ridiculous guns, said "Sir" to me but cut his eyes away as I passed.

In the warehouse, I got my sides and watched the first rehearsal, a three-page scene in the Homicide offices (INT: HOMICIDE BULL PEN, POLICE HQ—DAY) between Tanner and his team. Brad Slaughter was there, ready as usual, along with the multiethnic cast of young actors who played his detectives. It was six a.m., and they had all been in the hair and makeup trailer since four. Despite the early hour, they looked fresh and groomed. Our hair and makeup department was aces.

Watching the rehearsal, it was clear to me that I had overwritten the scene, and I noticed some spots where I could make some trims. It was a delicate thing to do. Actors, especially the ones who were trying to get noticed, didn't like to lose their lines. They were like the rest of the crew, always working on getting their next gig. As a courtesy, I conferred with Alan Lomax and told him what I thought we should do.

"I want to cut Alicia's line," I said. "What she's saying, about the suspect having priors? We've mentioned that twice before in this ep. The information has already been conveyed."

"It'll save me a little time in coverage," said Lomax. "You want to tell her or should I?"

"I'll do it," I said.

After the rehearsal, I caught up with Alicia Nichols, who played Detective Angie Antonelli (the "earthy" Italian-American detective on the squad), on the way to her trailer. She was an actress who always knew her lines, hit her marks, and was unfailingly polite to the staff, from production assistants on up. Alicia Nichols was well liked, but that didn't stop some of the male crew from calling her Alicia Nipples, or just Bullets, due to the fact that her bumps, long as fingertips, were visible through the fabric of her shirt and bra in every shot. In the old days, the network would have had to cover her up, but no more. Her "points" were considered a ratings booster.

"I'm sorry," I said. "I've gotta cut your only line."

"It wasn't a very good line, anyway, Victor," she said, and my face must have dropped, because she laughed and said, "I'm joking."

"Right," I said. She wasn't really joking. The line I'd written for her, *He's got a rap sheet as long as my arm,* was completely generic. Annette and I could have composed it while drunk in bed.

"You'll still be prominent in the shot."

"Don't worry about it."

"I'll make it up to you," I said, and I would. She was a nice kid, someone's daughter who was out here trying to make it like everyone else. I'd give her some choice lines in one-fourteen. A soliloquy about a dog she once owned as a kid, and how she'd had to put it down. Something heartwarming like that.

I went back to the set as the stand-ins arrived, the grips set up the sticks and removed walls to accommodate the camera, and the electrics brought in lights. Ellen was talking to Gandy, one of Skylar's people, informing him that he was being promoted to gaffer. Gandy was mature, in his forties, a good lighting man who could handle the mechanics of the job. But, through no fault of his own, he had an interior personality and would make a poor manager. By the end of the shoot, Ellen would bring in someone from out of town to fill Skylar's position. Gandy would be a stopgap measure for now.

Brandon, our tall, bearded prop master, rolled the cart into Village and began to unfold the chairs.

"Here you go, boss," he said, as he placed my chair beside me.

"How do you know that chair's mine?"

"It's got your name on it, sir." It was our usual routine, but he didn't smile or look my way.

I had been thinking about Brandon just a few hours earlier, when I was lying awake in bed.

"You got a few minutes to talk to me later on?" I said.

"Sure thing," he said.

He proceeded to unfold the director's chair, Lillie's, Ellen's, Eagle's, and the cast chairs for the lead and supporting actors. Brandon said nothing else and never once looked me in the eye.

The long day went slowly. Lunch, under a tent outside the warehouse, was a bit of a treat, as our caterer, Mike Perez, grilled filets and lobster tails (Surf and Turf Day) on a grate set over hot coals in halved oil drums. It was the last shooting day of the week, and the mood ordinarily would have been upbeat, but Skylar's death had thrown a cloud over the set. I sat with the hair and makeup department, pretended to study the family photographs on their phones; listened to the stories about their boyfriends, husbands, and children; and quietly ate my food. I looked around for Annette, but she was not in the tent. She had not been to the stages as of yet. I missed her.

We shot into the night. In the late hours, I had a minor bump in the road with an actress named Susan Pine, a lovely, petite young woman who played Constance Browning, written as an Ivy League–bred blonde who had ditched the plan to work for her father (he was, naturally, a buttoned-down, "cold and distant" industrialist, rich white men being the last allowable villains on television) after her

graduation from Harvard Business School. Instead she had
entered the police academy, where she thought she could
"make a difference."

In the scene as written, Constance was in the Homicide
offices, talking to Cobb McCord about a case, after hours.
She was sitting, of course, on the edge of his desk, and he
was seated in his chair, looking up at her with "male intent"
(apparently McCord had yet to wake up one morning and
"think" he was gay). McCord asked Constance if she'd like to
discuss the case over a beer at Hawk's, the squad's local water-
ing hole.

> CONSTANCE
> I don't like Hawk's. Their jukebox plays
> country.

> MCCORD
> How about Bennie's? They've got a
> rockin jukebox.

> CONSTANCE
> Too crowded.

> MCCORD
> Where do you want to go, then?

> CONSTANCE
> (amorously)
> I have beer at my place.

Susan didn't want to say that last line. We did many takes, and she said something different every time, but not those words. Lillie had tried to get her to do it, and so had Lomax, but to no avail.

"Will you go in?" said an exasperated Lomax, turning to me in the Village.

I walked onto the set and got up close to Susan, keeping my voice low, keeping our conversation private. The crew and Andre Robbins, the young actor who played McCord, instinctively stepped out of range.

"Uh-oh," said Susan. "They sent in the heavy artillery."

"What's the problem, Sue?"

"That line, 'I have beer at my place.' Why is she being so sexually aggressive with this guy? I mean, she's supposed to be repressed, isn't she? That's how you guys defined her in the bible. *The emotionally stunted daughter of a cool, distant father, Constance has trouble with romantic relationships,* blah blah blah. I just don't think I would say that."

"You're not saying it. Your *character* is saying it."

"Okay. I don't think my *caricature* would say that."

Despite my growing impatience, I smiled. She always called her character her "caricature," and she was correct. Her character was not a recognizable human being, but a type. Susan was a smart young woman with good instincts and a keen sense of humor. But I had to do my job.

"Well, we've done it several ways now, Sue. Do me a favor and give it to me the way it's written, so we can have a take or two that way as well."

"But if I say the line as written, that's the take you'll use when you cut it together. I know how you all do."

"True," I admitted.

"I don't want to say that line," said Susan Pine. "That's my position."

"So, in other words, that's the Sue Pine position."

"The Supine position," she said, crossing her arms and giving me a charitable smirk. "I've never heard *that* before."

"I'm quite the wit."

"I'm still not saying the line, Vic."

We stood there and tried to stare each other down. I knew she wasn't going to budge, and we had to get through the day. I gave in to move things along. Plus, she was right.

"Okay," I said. "I'll give that line to Andre. He'll say to you, 'I have beer at my place.' And then your caricature can fork him."

"Thank you."

"Let's get back to work."

"Vic?" She touched my arm. "How come you never asked *me* out for a beer?"

"I'm not supposed to fraternize with the talent," I said. "Matter of fact, I think it's in my contract. But thank you for that. You made my night, Sue."

The truth was, she wasn't my type. And anyway, I only had eyes for one woman.

I was spoken for.

Later, as were shooting the singles of the last scene, I went over to the prop truck, backed against one of the warehouse bays, and walked through its open gate. Brandon was inside, doing some paperwork back in the office, called the Gold

Room, probably because it held a safe. In the safe were real, operable guns.

I moved past bins and totes labeled with character names. Tanner's bin held his badge, cuffs, rings, watches, and his plastic Glock, while Hart's held her reading glasses, her favorite pens, and the jewelry she wore in every ep. There were entire bins devoted to sunglasses, and jewel cases of wedding bands and fake diamond rings. Steel shelves held multiple jugs of grape juice and apple juice, which doubled for red and white wine, and bottles of nonalcoholic beer to be poured into bottles of Bud and Heineken for our bar scenes. One drink cart, now folded and up against a wall, could service hundreds of extras. All of the non-effect illusions we sold to the public emanated from this relatively small truck. Brandon had a boss, who worked from the office, dealt with our EPs, and attended tone meetings, and he had an assistant and an on-set dresser as well. But he was the main man who placed the props in front of the camera from call to wrap.

"Sir."

"Brandon."

He had been seated at a desk, but stood to meet me. Behind him, on the wall, was a bulletin board showing cards of the current day's scenes, detailing the props that would be needed for each.

We shook hands.

"Just Vic tonight," I said. "Okay?"

"Sure. You want a drink?"

"No, I'm good."

The prop truck doubled as the unofficial bar for the crew

who were so inclined. Especially on stage days, when there were no moves, select crew members began to control-drink late in the day and continued to drink until wrap. I knew it, and it was understood that I knew and wouldn't rat anyone out. As long as everyone did their jobs and made sound decisions, I was good with it. We were all adults.

Brandon was tall, blue-eyed, and fully bearded. He looked like a dude who drives a windowless van from the woods and steps out of it with bong smoke and a teenaged girl trailing behind him. But he wasn't a stoner, or not much more of one than anyone else on the crew. He had a master's in English lit and was better read than I would ever be. Not that he was destined to be a professor or a writer. He was born and bred to do the job he had now.

How Brandon had gotten here was a common story in prop departments: it was a family business. His father had been a prop master for thirty years, and Brandon had grown up working on his old man's truck. Further, Brandon was mentally suited for the job. He had the kind of mind that could recall a watch worn by a day player four seasons back, or the exact type of weapon a tender kept hidden beneath the bar in an episode long since forgotten by the rest of our crew.

"Sit down," I said.

I took a chair and pulled it over to his desk. We stared at each other for a while. He looked away, then looked back at me.

"Well?" he said.

"I think you know what this is about. Let's not waste too much time on this, Brandon."

"You here as a producer?"

"I'm here as Skylar's friend. If you're straight with me, you and I don't have a problem."

"Ask me anything."

"You gave him some prop money, didn't you."

Brandon nodded.

"Why?"

"He was my friend, too," said Brandon. "He was in trouble, and I helped him out."

"That was pretty stupid."

"I know it was, and I told him so. But I couldn't change his mind, and I couldn't say no. I guess I should have been stronger."

"Laura told me that he had mixed the counterfeit with the real. How did he expect to pull it off?"

"He put real bills over fake, for starters. It's called a Jamaican roll."

I made a mental note of the term. "Okay, but…"

"Right. Whoever he was dealing with, they were gonna find out eventually. He said he only needed a couple of days. He'd tell them he was unaware the money was counterfeit, that he'd been tricked, too. Then he'd pay them in full, with actual money, soon as he got flush."

This checked out with what Laura had told me. I nodded and said, "But how did he expect to fool them from the get-go?"

"I do good work, Victor."

"*How* did you do it? Doesn't it say, right on the bills, *'for motion picture use only'*?"

"It's in the same small font as the type on a real bill, so

it's not too noticeable. But, yeah. There's the other kind that switches the president's face with the denomination; they put Ben Franklin's mug on a twenty, like that. I use the first kind."

"Prop money looks fine on camera, but when you hold it in your hand, you know it's not right."

"I age it. Some guys use nicotine spray. I use tea dye. Steep tea bags in water, then soak the prop money in it and let the money dry."

"Wardrobe does the same thing with clothing, don't they?"

"Same process. It adds a yellow-brown tone to the paper and it softens it up, makes it feel real."

"So at first glance, and touch, you can get away with it."

"Maybe."

"Until someone tries to spend it."

"I told Skylar that, too." Brandon fished a cigarette from the breast pocket of his Western-style shirt, but he didn't light it. "Do you know who he was dealing with?"

"A couple of collection guys. That's about it."

"The police talked to me. Apparently my initials were in Skylar's ledger book."

"Did you tell them about any of this? Did you talk about what kind of mess he was in?"

"I didn't tell them a thing."

"Neither did I."

We stared at each other again. This time, Brandon held my eyes.

"Skylar fronted a pound of weed to a guy on our crew," I said, "and the guy didn't pay him for it."

"Yeah. The guy rotted him."

Rotted. That was a new expression to me. I made note of that, too.

"Who was it?" I said.

"Barry in security," said Brandon, without hesitation.

"Black Barry?"

"Yes." He struck a match and lit his cigarette. He wasn't supposed to smoke on the truck, but he had been jonesing for it and I made no comment. His eyes had filled with tears.

"Don't be too hard on yourself, Brandon. You were just trying to get him out of a jam."

"I shouldn't be thinking of me, anyway. I'm here, alive and working. I'm going home to my wife and baby tonight. It's him who's dead."

"That's right."

"I wish I could do something."

"You can," I said. "You could lend me a gun."

"Fuck no, *sir.* You know I can't open that safe for you. I'd be looking at time if one of my guns had a body attached to it and got traced back to me."

"I'm not talking about a real gun. I'm talking about one of those fake-ass plastic guns you give Brad Slaughter."

"What would you do with it?"

"Will you give me one?"

He nodded slowly and dragged on his cigarette. "Vic?"

"What?"

"You think those guys murdered Skylar?"

"I don't know."

But I knew I was going to find out.

*   *   *

After we wrapped, Annette came up to my suite. I had lit some candles, put on some music, and opened a bottle of Rodney Strong. I was ready for her as she came through the door. She was dressed in sweats and had a large leather satchel swung over one shoulder.

"Hi," she said, and smiled sweetly.

"Hi." I kissed her, and nodded at her bag. "Are you staying for the weekend?"

"I need to use your bathroom. Pour me a glass of wine, handsome."

She closed the door behind her as I retrieved two short glasses from the kitchen cabinet. I poured Merlot for the two of us and waited. It seemed to me that she was taking a long time. Maybe I was anxious. We'd skipped a night of intimacy, which was unusual for us. Since we'd been together, we'd rarely gone a day without making love.

Annette emerged from the bathroom, shutting the light behind her. She'd changed her clothing. She was now wearing a low-cup black bra, lace black panties, garters, black fishnet stockings, and simple black evening shoes—ankle straps with small rhinestones across the bridge. She walked toward me, languorously, with a feline sway. Her breasts heaved bountifully in her bra, and her thigh muscles rippled as she moved.

I felt my heart beat in my chest. It was hard to breathe.

Annette came into my arms and we kissed.

"Goddamn, girl. *Thank* you."

"I want to talk to you," she whispered. She didn't look pleased.

"Later," I said.

We made out for a long while, standing there on the carpeted floor. I could have kissed her for hours. But somehow we moved into the Magic Room, along with the music, the wine, and the candles. Then I was between her, both of us in fluid motion, my hands entwined with hers above her head, her hair spread out on my pillow, our chests damp with sweat.

"Can I get on top?" she said.

"Yes."

I withdrew and turned over onto my back. She moved onto me quickly, like an animal to prey. Her heavy breasts, long free from restraint, bumped my chest. I had torn her panties off her in a moment of impatient lust, and she had kicked her evening shoes to the floor. Only her stockings and garters remained.

"I'm gonna fuck you, Victor."

"Get on it," I said.

But first she went down on me, hungrily licking my balls and shaft.

"I can feel your vein with my tongue," she said, lifting her head to smile at me. "And you've got that bend in the river."

My rod was throbbing and slightly bent below the head. An overzealous woman had scarred me in bed one night, long ago.

"Are you complaining?" I said.

"You know I like it."

"Stop talking, then."

"Don't you want me to talk to you?"

"Yes, I do. You know I do."

She laughed, steadied me, and slowly slid herself down upon me. I closed my eyes and heard her gasp. Her hips moved like the tides. With each of her downstrokes I thrust upward and put my cock deep inside her. She reached behind her, pushed my thighs apart, and tickled my balls.

"How's that feel?" she said, as she picked up the pace.

I looked up at her, riding me. Her eyes were alive in the candlelight, and her hair was tossed about her face. I found her spot and stroked it, but she pushed my hand away.

"I'll do that," she said.

She fingered herself. I watched her eyes go dreamy, and I reached out and brushed her cool lips.

"Pull on my tits," she said, and I pressed my thumbs and forefingers to her nipples and pinched them lightly.

"Harder, Vic," she said. They were tough as licorice, and I pulled on them, and she said, "Oh."

"What're you going to do next?" I said, knowing the answer.

"I'm gonna come all over your cock," she said, and I laughed.

She climaxed, it seemed, in slow motion. Afterward, she went down on me, artfully. I came like a horse, and she took it all in. When we kissed, I could taste my own release in her mouth.

We were as close as two people could be. I never wanted to leave that room. I wanted to be with her forever.

* * *

We were lying in bed, nude, looking at each other, talking mostly with our eyes, working on our second bottle of wine. A slow, beautiful song, Jim James singing with heavy reverb from another world to ours, was playing from my portable speaker. I was not wearing a watch but I knew it was very late. The moon had dropped, and its light pearled the room through my floor-to-ceiling windows.

"Can we talk?" said Annette.

"Go ahead."

"I'm worried about you, Vic."

"Skylar's death hit me kind of hard, I guess."

"I'm not talking about that. I found a gun in your bathroom while I was changing. In the vanity under the sink."

"Did you pick it up?"

"Yes."

"Then you know it's not real. It's light as a feather. There's no guts to it; the thing can't even shoot blanks."

"I know. It's a prop gun. So what? You must have it for a reason."

"I don't know why I have it, to tell you the truth. I only know that I wanted it."

"*I* know why. You're going to use it in some way on the guys who killed Skylar."

I told her what I'd found so far. I shared everything with her, including my fears. I'd never opened up to anyone in that way before, not my male friends, not even my wife. It had been one of the problems in my marriage, maybe the biggest problem. That, and our differing visions for the future. Claudia, an Army brat who'd moved around her whole childhood, wanted a house in a neighborhood, babies, membership at the local pool, a savings card for the grocery store, stability. I wanted none of those things. The more I left town to work on shows and the longer I was away, the less comfortable I'd become with the idea of staying in one place. We'd split up after five years. Claudia remarried, had children, and lived in a Colonial on an oak-lined street. I'd gotten what I'd wanted, too.

"What were you thinking?" said Annette. "A *gun?*"

"I don't have a plan."

"Talk to the police and tell them what you know."

"Not yet."

She shook her head in aggravation. "Why are you going up in the Condor?"

"I can't live my life inside my head all the time. I have to *do* something."

"'Where are you going, Lieutenant? To *finish* this.'"

"Funny," I said.

"Seriously, Victor. You should hear yourself. You sound like a character in one of your scripts."

Annette took a sip of wine and placed her glass on the dresser. She got up on one elbow and faced me. I was still on my back.

"Steve was a lot like you."

"Your husband," I said.

Unlike my marriage, hers had ended involuntarily. Her spouse had been a carpenter who worked on set construction for features. They'd met on a show in Wilmington, North Carolina, when Annette was an assistant in the art department on a Dino De Laurentiis production. Steve had never out-grown his fascination with the muscle car culture of his youth. He'd flipped his vehicle, broke his neck, and burned to death in a street race on a foggy two-lane ten years ago. I knew she'd loved him very much. There were many photographs of Steve in her hotel room. She loved him still.

Steve and Annette had not had children, and now, at forty-four, she knew her maternal ship had sailed. Like me, she had become a professional wanderer, a hotel dweller, without roots, a person with tired eyes who worked seventy-hour weeks. It was hardly a healthy atmosphere in which to raise a child.

Film and television productions were like circuses that arrived in town and brought excitement to the locals for a short period of time. We came and went, leaving the straights to their families, their backyard barbecues, their churches, their nine-to-fives. "We've got sawdust in our veins." I'd heard that expression muttered by my coworkers countless times.

"Steve was always talking about the experience," said Annette. "How he only felt alive when he was red-lining his car. He was selfish, Vic. I loved him, but I'll never forgive him for that. You're being selfish, too."

"I want to live."

"So did he. But he died horribly. It happened because he took a chance that he never should have taken. I couldn't go through that again. I *won't* go through it, Victor. Do you understand?"

There was no malice in her voice, or threat. She was simply telling me her truth.

"Yes. I understand."

But I didn't say I'd stop. I'd already begun to make plans.

We slept in. Near noon, Annette went down to the basement, where there was a bank of coin-operated washing machines and dryers, to start her weekly laundry. While she was gone, I called the one named Wayne from my room phone. I introduced myself by name and said I had been Skylar's coworker and friend. He said, "Who's Skylar?" I said I wanted to make him whole financially, in exchange for his promise that he and his partner, Cody, would leave Laura Flanagan alone. He said he had no idea what I was talking about. I told him that I didn't care; he didn't need to admit anything—I *knew*. I was willing to pay him off, but only on my terms. After some negotiation, he agreed to meet in the place that I insisted upon. He was cagey, but also greedy, and that made him stupid. His voice and word choice told me he was uneducated, inarticulate, and proud of it. Wayne gave me the location of the house where he and Cody "cribbed up." I told him I'd see him that night.

Annette returned carrying her empty laundry hamper on her hip. I told her I had some errands to run. It wasn't a lie, except by omission, and she read it. I moved to kiss her mouth, and she gave me her cheek.

"I'll call you later," I said.

"I know what you're doing," she said. "If you care about us, you'll stop."

She looked at me with disappointment and walked out of my room.

I left the hotel and dropped off my dirty clothing at a full-service laundry shop, then had a late breakfast at a Greek diner. Afterward, I drove out to a trailer park on the edge of town, where Kenny "G" Garson, our picture car coordinator, lived in a silver mobile home he towed from job to job. His Harley-Davidson edition F-150 was parked beside the Gulf Stream, under a stand of pines. As I went up the grated retractable steps of his trailer, I could hear Rush Limbaugh's voice coming loudly from a radio inside. Kenny listened to loops of Limbaugh repeats on the weekends.

I knocked on the frame of the screen. Kenny appeared and suggested we sit outside. It was only March, but the weather had turned warm and would stay that way through October. The city was on a river, but open water was hundreds of miles away. There were no gulf or ocean breezes here. When the winds came, they came in the form of a hurricane. In this part of the country, productions tended to wrap before the summer months, as the weather was unbearably hot and humid from May till September. We were due to finish in about four weeks.

Kenny directed me to a folding chair with a canvas back, not unlike my cast chair in the Village.

"Ain't got your name on it," said Kenny. "Is that all right?"

"I can manage."

He was wearing a T-shirt over shorts and sandals. His sunglasses were on a leash and hung over his barrel chest. We settled into our chairs.

"What can I do you for, Vic?"

"I need a car for the weekend."

He nodded toward my red Focus, parked in the shade on a filled spot of gravel and shells. "What's wrong with your rental?"

"It's got four cylinders."

"Ford turbocharges some of those fours now."

"They didn't juice that one. I need something with more horses."

"Why? You planning on robbin a bank?"

"Nothing that serious. Can you fix me up?"

"Sure. Short notice, though."

"I'll pay the penalty."

"Why not just go to Hertz?"

"I'd rather give you the money."

"Lookin out for ol' Kenny, huh."

"Why not?"

Kenny's eyes twinkled. He had the loveable local-boy look of Ed "Big Daddy" Roth. He had raised four boys who were now men, and was still married to his high school sweetheart, Jolene. They had a house on the Redneck Riviera, two blocks from the beach in Alabama, near the Florida line. Rumor was that Kenny had done time for vehicular theft as a young man and turned his passion for automobiles into a living. Ours was a business that allowed felons to reform, if they had skills. Kenny had a down-home way with people and the salesman's ability to pick someone's pocket with a smile. Plus, the man knew cars.

"So you want somethin fast."

"It should be roomy as well. I plan to have a big man riding along with me."

"That leaves out a rice burner."

"I would think."

Kenny, who'd lost an uncle at Guadalcanal, didn't care for Japanese cars. Though Kenny had been born after the war and had never known his uncle, he nevertheless had held a grudge. Also, like me, he was a union man. We went American when we could.

"I know a fella's got a clean black Marauder. Two thousand and four. Last year Mercury produced the ve-hicle."

"Is it fast?"

"It's a V-eight. A little on the heavy side, but it'll move ya. Got the heads and block of a Mach One Stang." Kenny brushed a hand through his short gray hair. "What are you gonna do with this car, Victor? Like the man in that movie said, 'I gots to know.'"

"I've got an appointment to talk with a couple of guys tonight. They might not like what I have to say. Could be I'll have to make a hasty retreat. It would give me immense peace of mind if I knew my ride could fly."

"Immense peace of mind." Kenny barked a laugh. "God, you're fancy. I wish I was as smart as you."

"How much for the car?"

"Say, three hundred. Five if you want a driver."

"You throwing your chauffeur's cap into the ring?"

"Hell, I ain't doin nothing all weekend but playin with my pecker."

"You better be sure."

"This has something to do with Skylar, right?"

I nodded.

"I liked that boy," said Kenny.

I paid him with per diem money and told him I'd be in touch.

Barry Mason lived in the Southern District, a neighborhood of mostly black, working-class residents that locals called the Dirty South. But it didn't look all that dirty to my eyes. The houses were relatively small ramblers and shotguns, neat and tidy, with largeish yards bordered by chain-link fences. Behind the fences were mixed-breed dogs with a touch of boxer or pit, and in the yards sat johnboats, children's toys, motorcycles, and tricked-out GMs, Caprice Classics, and Cutlasses with oversized tires and aftermarket rims. To me, the area said family, work, and play.

I went through a gate and stepped into his yard, where a black Buick Grand National was up on cinder blocks. Barry came out of his yellow sided rambler to meet me, along with two of his dogs, a pit-Lab mix and something smaller I couldn't identify. Both of them were the same shade of tan.

"They're all right," said Barry, as the large dog galloped toward me. "Nothin but yard dogs. Just let 'em smell you."

I stopped walking and allowed the big animal to sniff at my jeans. His ears were pinned back, so I knew I was good. The smaller one was meaner, kept her distance and glared.

"Buster, Sandy," said Barry. "Go."

The dogs went back into the house through the open door. I thought of Annette. *I told you Buster was a dog's name.*

Barry approached. He was wearing a Panavision-issue T-shirt, and as always, he'd cuffed up the sleeves. He didn't need to do that. His arms were as big as a pencil-pusher's thighs.

Barry was a mountainous man, six foot two, three hundred pounds, much of it muscle. He didn't need to showcase his guns to make an imprthree-ession. Folks would have stepped out of his way had he been wearing a dress and Buster Brown shoes. But certain kinds of men roll like that into adulthood. It all went back to where you came up. Where I was raised, we wore our tees the same way.

"Barry," I said, and shook his hand, big as a first baseman's mitt. "Thanks for seeing me."

"You want to come inside?"

"Will we be alone?"

"My wife and kids are in there, watchin the widescreen."

"Let's stay out here. I won't keep you long."

Barry went over to the Buick and leaned his big ass against the front quarter panel. I followed and stood before him. He already knew what this was about. I'd told him over the phone.

"Let's talk about Skylar," I said.

"Okay."

"He fronted you a pound of weed. Is that right?"

"Yeah." He looked me in the eye. Whatever he'd done, Barry was no liar. "Then something went down, and I couldn't pay him."

"Couldn't or wouldn't?"

"*Couldn't.* You coming to me today as a boss?"

"No. Just tell me what happened."

Barry shook his head, as if the action could erase the memory. "The get-high was for my nephew. He been trappin like a fool."

"Trapping?"

"Dealing that tree."

Trapping. I took note of the term.

"If your nephew's in the game, he must have his own connect. Why would you go to Skylar?"

"My nephew's man came up short, and my nephew, goes by Daymo, needed some product to fill his pipeline. Told me if I could get him some, he'd have the money for me right away."

"Why would you do that?"

"On account of he's my sister's kid. I ain't want him out there tryin to cop cold from gangstas he don't know. I was looking to control the situation. Protect him. I didn't think for a minute that my own blood would do me like that."

"What'd you do?"

"Had a man-to-boy talk with Daymo, is what I did. Put his nothin ass up against a wall. He promised to get me the money the next morning. But when the next morning came…"

"Skylar was dead."

Barry looked away.

"It wasn't a random robbery," I said. "Skylar paid the collectors off with cash mixed with prop money. They murdered him because of it. I'm pretty sure of that."

"They. Who the hell is *they?*"

The Wild Bunch, I thought. Walon Green. Greatest screenplay ever written.

"Two young white dudes. They go by Wayne and Cody. I need to confirm that it was them."

"And?"

"I aim to keep those assholes away from Laura Flanagan."

"That skinny little girl in wardrobe?"

"She and Skylar were together."

Barry crossed his arms. "I'm sorry, man. You *know* I been stressin behind this."

"You can help me make it right."

"How? I can't bring that boy back."

"No, but we can fuck the ones who did it. I could use you, Barry. You walk into a room, you make an impression."

"Say it plain."

"First thing, you need to get the money from your nephew, so I can pay off Skylar's connect. Absolve that debt for the girl."

"What else?" said Barry.

"I've got an appointment with Wayne and Cody."

"And when you get up with them? You fixin to do *what?*"

"Are you with me, or not?"

"When?" said Barry.

"Tonight."

I called Detective Joe Gittens when I got back to my room.

"The TV writer," he said, with amusement, after I identified myself.

"Making any progress on the Branson murder?"

"Only my boss gets to ask me that."

"I was just wondering…"

"What?"

"I'm curious. What kind of slugs were recovered from Skylar's body?"

Gittens said nothing.

"Nine millimeter?"

"Why would you need to know that, Ohanion? Is this for one of your scripts? Tanner's Team gonna put this one down?"

"What about the shell casings found at the crime scene?"

"You make me smile, man."

"Well?"

"Wasn't no casings," said Gittens. "Now, if you'll excuse me, today is my day off, and I plan to spend it with my family. Unless you've seen the light of day and plan to suddenly co-operate with this investigation, I gotta go."

"Sorry to bother you."

He hung up on me without another word.

I lay down and tried to take a nap, but I couldn't sleep. The late-afternoon sun was coming strong through my window, strobing the room as the trucks on the nearby interstate passed, blocking and unblocking the rays.

I got off the bed and went to my laptop, open on the desk. The beat sheets for episode 114 were beside it. Similar to our shooting schedule, I often wrote out of sequence, especially when I was looking to crack a script on page one and staring at a dreaded blank screen. I found a place where I could start, and began to type.

In the scene (INT: INTERROGATION ROOM, HOMICIDE OFFICES, POLICE HQ—NIGHT), Tanner is in "the box," interrogating a drug dealer, a man named Glover, who Tanner thinks has information on a murder.

TANNER

So this Dwayne Elliot, he went by Day, right?

GLOVER

That was his street name, yeah.

TANNER

Day was a dealer?

GLOVER

That boy was trappin like a mug.

TANNER

Trapping?

GLOVER

Sellin tree.

TANNER

Why was he killed?

GLOVER

He rotted his connect.

TANNER

What do you mean, he rotted him?

GLOVER

Day owed the man money and Day
wasn't in no hurry to settle up. If you in
the game, and you do someone dirt, you
got to pay a price.

TANNER

Who killed him, Glover?

GLOVER

I ain't no snitch, Tanner.

TANNER

You tell me, I promise you, no one will
know where it came from.

GLOVER

You asking me to trust you?

TANNER

I'm asking you to do something right.

ON GLOVER, conflicted.

I wrote the scene, and then two others. It was coming, and
I could hardly type fast enough. The faucet was fully on.

The light in the room dimmed. I'd been sitting at the desk
for a couple of hours. It was night.

I dressed in jeans, running shoes, and a shirt worn tails
out. I retrieved the prop gun from the bathroom, then stood
in front of the mirror and experimented with its placement.
I settled for the front dip, barrel down, with the grip angled
so I could pull it easily with my right hand. I practiced my
draw several times, then covered the gun with the tail of my
shirt. I stared at my reflection in the mirror. I looked like
me, but different. A man armed with a gun, even a fake gun,
is changed.

I called Annette on the house phone, but she didn't answer. I left a message and told her I was going out, and hoped to see her later that night. I grabbed my book bag, slung it over my shoulder, and took the elevator down to her floor. I knocked on her door and there was no response. Maybe she was in there. Maybe she'd been in her room when I'd phoned her, too.

I got my car from the valet and drove over to Barry's place. He was standing in his front yard, playing with his dogs, when I pulled over to the curb.

Kenny was standing next to a clean black Marauder, under the beams of his Gulf Stream spotlight, as we arrived at his trailer park. We met him at the Merc.

"Black Barry," said Kenny, and they bumped fists.

"Kenny G," said Barry.

I had no nickname that I knew of, so Kenny just nodded in my direction.

"She's a beauty," said Kenny, running his hand lovingly over the hood.

"Looks like a Crown Vic with extended pipes to me," said Barry, who was a GM man. There was a decal in the rear window of his Grand National of a kid wearing a Chevy shirt. The kid was pissing on a Ford.

"It's all in the details, Barry. Eighteen-inch wheels, five-spoke rims with the god's head right in the center. Blackouts, color-keyed grille..."

"I see all the window dressing. But does it move?"

"It's a true muscle sedan."

"Will it run with an Impala SS?"

"I wouldn't want to split the difference."

"Can we go?" I said. "I already rented the car, G. You don't need to sell me on it."

Kenny looked Barry over, then said to me, "I see now why you needed the extra room, Victor."

"To fit your belly under the wheel?" said Barry. "Mines is flat."

"If a basketball is flat," said Kenny. "I see you been lovin that chicken at Popeye's."

"And I see you ain't rubbed the red off your neck."

It went like that for a while, and continued as we got into the car. They were friends.

Kenny got in the driver's side, Barry in the shotgun bucket, and I climbed into the back, like the third wheel on a high school Friday night.

"Where to, sir?" said Kenny.

I gave him the address.

Wayne and Cody stayed on the east bank, over the river, in an area that looked more country than city, with unkempt homes and properties, some abandoned or foreclosed. The river bridge, lit majestically at night, loomed over this section of the parish. We drove down their dark street, which faced railroad tracks and a field featuring blown-in trash and one rusted-out car. The road dead-ended at a concrete barrier.

"Turn around and face the way we came in," I said.

"I ain't stupid," said Kenny, adding, *"Writers."*

He three-pointed the Marauder, curbed it, and faced it toward the open run of the street. We looked at the house and its driveway, where an old Toyota Supra with custom rims was parked.

Barry got out of the car and I followed.

I slung my book bag over my shoulder and leaned in Kenny's open window. This made him recoil.

"Thought you were about to kiss me," said Kenny.

"Keep it running, Boss Hog."

"I'll write down the tag number of that Nagasaki nut-bucket." He meant the Toyota.

"Good idea," I said.

Barry and I walked toward the house. It was a ramshackle one-story affair with tan asbestos shingles that were half on, half off. Plywood had been fixed in several of the windows.

"Is there a plan?" said Barry, wearing an electric-crew T-shirt, rolled at the sleeves. He looked like a horseman.

"Just be your badass self," I said, as we stepped onto an uneven planked porch.

I knocked on the front door. Soon it opened. A shirtless, barefoot man in his early twenties stood in the frame. He had a pencil-line beard, braces on his teeth, and dull eyes. On his upper chest was a Celtic cross tattoo, an appropriated symbol of "white pride." Similar tats were inked on his inner forearm. He was holding a cell phone in his hand.

A second young man, who looked just like the first, stood behind him. He too was thinly bearded, and wore a wifebeater, jeans, and black motorcycle boots.

"I'm Victor. This is Barry."

"Wayne," said the one who was standing behind his brother. When he spoke, I saw that his teeth were brace-free. "You ain't say you were bringin no one."

"I didn't say I was coming alone, either," I said. "Can we come in?"

I let Barry go ahead of me. As I entered, Cody closed the door behind me.

The house was as small as Laura Flanagan's but without any of the artistic touches. The furniture was cushiony, torn, and probably infested with bugs. The place smelled of garbage, nicotine, perspiration, and weed. It was stuffy and hot.

We all stood there in the living area. I inspected the two of them, obviously identical twins, six-footers and solidly built.

"Well?" I said.

"Have a seat," said Wayne.

"You all first," I said.

Cody shrugged and sat down on the couch. Barry had been waiting for that. He sat down next to Cody, closer than he needed to be. Wayne and Cody both had size, but seated next to Barry, Cody looked like a child.

Wayne and I remained standing. He was not far from me. Striking distance, if that's what he wanted.

                    WAYNE
        Is the money in that bag?

                    OHANION
        Let's talk first.

                    WAYNE
        'Bout what?

                    OHANION
Skylar Branson.

                    WAYNE
Told you over the phone, I don't know
anyone by that name.

                    OHANION
He was murdered outside Red's bar,
down by the river.

                    WAYNE
Oh, *that* guy. I read about him in the
newspaper.
                    (smiles)
Friend of yours?

                    OHANION
    Yes.

                    WAYNE
Too bad he got his self snipped.

Snipped. I took note of the term.
"Why do you think I'm here, Wayne?"
"You tell me," said Wayne. "You said you was fixin to give
me some money. Only a fool would turn that down."
"Laura Flanagan," I said.
"Who?"

"Don't act like you don't know her. I got your number from her phone. You *called* her, Wayne."

Wayne smiled. "Skinny little thing, right? Works on movies. Yeah, I met her in a club. So?"

"I want you to leave her alone."

Wayne smiled stupidly. "But she's my type. See, I'm into those itty-bitty gals. I fuck 'em to the bone, Victor. I like to see if I can break 'em. You know what I mean?"

When I said nothing, Wayne's silly grin faded.

"Let's just do the business you came for," said Wayne. "Give me the money and you can get gone."

I hitched up my jeans and parted the tail of my shirt, just a little, and brushed my thumb on the checkered plastic grip of the prop gun. I then let the tail fall back over the grip. Wayne's eyes widened slightly; he'd seen it—I'd *wanted* him to see it. I supposed that Barry and Cody had seen it, too.

"Leave her alone," I said, pointedly.

"The money," said Wayne.

I un-slung my book bag and dropped it at his feet. He picked the bag up, unzipped it, and reached inside.

"You," he said, sharply tossing the bag aside.

"Wayne?" said Cody.

"It's empty," said Wayne.

In the corner of my eye I saw Cody furtively touching a pad on his cell. Momentarily, a phone rang in the back bedroom.

"You stay right where you are, slick," said Wayne. "I gotta get that."

I knew where he was going and what he was about to do. I looked at Barry with apology. He looked back at me, both angry and juiced. But he was a professional, and kept up his end. Barry had draped his arm over the back of the couch, behind Cody's shoulder.

When Wayne returned there was a gun pressed against the leg of his jeans.

As he walked into the room, Barry moved quickly, clamping down on Cody's neck in a choke hold and pulling him across the couch.

Wayne pointed the gun at my chest.

"Looks like we got a problem," I said.

Wayne's head swiveled toward the couch, where Barry had Cody's neck in the channel-lock of his massive forearm. Cody was already losing color. He was beginning to kick his feet.

"Pull that piece out your dip and drop it," said Wayne, panic in his voice.

I did it slowly. It fell with barely a sound to the hardwood floor.

"It ain't even real," said Wayne, with wonder.

"Your brother's not gonna make it," I said. "You might get us, but Cody will be dead, too. Think fast, Wayne. You don't have much time."

My knees were weak, and I'd felt the blood drain from my face. I looked at the gun in his hand, a snub-nosed revolver. It was why I came, and all I needed.

"I'll kill him, Wayne," said Barry, with great calm. "He damn near gone already."

"*Don't* kill him," said Wayne.

"Break the cylinder on that gun and let the shells fall."

Wayne emptied the revolver. Barry released his grip on Cody's neck and pushed on his back. Cody rolled off the couch and struggled for breath. I moved forward and kicked the rounds out of Wayne's reach. They skittered across the floor.

Barry got up off the couch. I picked up my empty book bag and the prop gun.

"Fuck," said Wayne, to no one in particular.

"Leave the girl alone," I said.

Barry and I backed out of the house. We crossed the yard quickly and got into the Mercury. Wayne had not followed.

"Drive," I said to Kenny. "You can take it slow."

But Kenny slammed the console shifter into low and pinned the gas. The big Mercury lifted and growled as I was thrown back against the bench seat. Kenny left rubber on the street as we came out of a fishtail and finally straightened. He upshifted to drive and slowed as he neared the turn ahead. In the rearview I saw his eyes, bright and alive as a seventeen-year-old boy's.

Barry turned to me from the bucket. He was not pleased. "I oughta kick your monkey ass. Bringin a toy gun to a situation like that. You shoulda told me... *shit*, you could've got me killed."

"I needed Wayne to pull that revolver. I had to provoke him."

"You did *that*."

"I handled it," I said, defensively. "Told him to break that cylinder and let the shells fall. Right?"

"*I* said it. *I* told that cracker to unload his pistol. You was so scared, you couldn't say shit." Barry looked down at the crotch of my jeans and smiled. "Boy, you even pissed your *got*damn pants."

I looked down. There was a wet spot there.

Barry began to laugh, and Kenny joined him. They were laughing still as we passed through the tollbooth and rolled onto the river bridge.

I stared out the window at the shining lights strewn on the bridge suspenders, and through the rails at the black water below. The plastic pistol was still in my shaking hand.

I woke up in the bed of my suite alone the next morning. I had called Annette when I got home, but she was out or didn't pick up.

After I'd dressed, showered, and had breakfast, I phoned Detective Joe Gittens. He was not happy to hear from me. It was Sunday, and he was about to go to church.

"I've got something for you on the Branson murder," I said.

"Oh. You've *got* something."

"Do you have a pen?"

"For God's sakes."

"Listen carefully: twin brothers, two white boys who go by Wayne and Cody, were responsible for Skylar's death."

After a silence, he said, "You happen to have a last name on these twins?"

"No. But I have their address and the tag number of their vehicle."

I gave Gittens the information, along with the make and model of the car.

"I'm guessing they're renting the house. But you can find the landlord by going to the database search on properties. The owner can give you their full names."

"For real? I didn't know that."

"Sorry."

"Are you gonna tell me why I should do this?"

"You said there weren't any shell casings found at the crime scene. Okay, the weapon could have been an automatic, and the killer might have picked up the casings after they'd been ejected, but I doubt it. There wasn't time. That means the murder gun was a revolver."

"Okay…"

"I saw the gun, Detective. They still have it."

"Why *would* they?"

"Because they're stupid. Because it was their daddy's gun and it has sentimental value. I don't know. But I *saw* it. I'm not certain of the caliber, but I'd say it was a thirty-eight."

"*You'd* say. I don't suppose you're gonna tell me why you suspect them, or how you came to see this gun."

"No, sir. You're gonna need to treat this as an anonymous tip."

"You should have called the Crime Solvers line if you wanted to stay anonymous."

"I called you."

"I'm your man, huh."

"Yeah."

"Boy, do I feel special." More dead air filled the line. "It's not much to go on. Sure not enough to get me a warrant."

"You'll figure it out. Trust me, those are your guys."

I heard a female voice call Gittens by his Christian name.

"I gotta go," said Gittens. "My wife doesn't like to be late for service."

"Stay in touch."

"You don't have to worry about that, Ohanion. You and me are gonna talk again."

I worked on the script for episode 114 for the rest of the day. I skipped lunch and drank hotel coffee, and as the afternoon sun blasted through my windows, the page count mounted. Usually, it wasn't this uncomplicated, but now I had only to sit there at my desk and type. It was easy.

That night, I walked up to Gino's, a bar and grill that was a half block from my hotel. It was Steak Night. I ordered a New York strip, medium rare, a wedge salad with bacon and blue cheese dressing, and a glass of California red. I sat at the stick and ate my dinner alone.

When I returned to my room, the message light on my phone was blinking. Annette had called. She wanted to know if she could come upstairs.

We sat on my couch and drank Merlot, listened to music and talked. I told Annette to lie back. I removed her shoes and put her feet up on my lap and massaged them. This relaxed her completely. Soon we were making love there, and on the carpeted floor, and on the bed. We came powerfully, almost at the same time, atop the sheets.

Afterward we stayed in bed and drank more wine in the candlelight. She asked me what I'd done the night before, and I told her everything. I couldn't lie to her. I couldn't even stretch the truth.

"Are you mad at me?" I said.

"No. And I'm not surprised."

"Anyway, no one got hurt. It's over."

"Is it?"

"I think so," I said, but I knew she wasn't speaking of the event. She was telling me that she knew my nature.

"What was it like?" she said. "Was it a movie?"

"In a way. I don't even know what I said or didn't say when I went into that house. It's like I imagined half the shit that went down." I had a sip of wine and placed the short glass on the nightstand. "I was scared, Annette."

"I bet you liked that, too."

"Maybe. But Barry wasn't afraid."

"Barry's a gangster. You're just a guy."

"You think so?"

"Just a stupid guy."

There was no humor or affection in her tone.

We were combustible lovers, and we'd be together until the end of the shoot. But I'd lost her, I knew.

"Tonight was really beautiful," I said.

She turned into me. "It was perfect."

Call, as it always was on Mondays, was very early. I was up at four thirty a.m., due to be on set at six.

The long van ride to the first location was strange without Skylar. Gandy was with us, and though he was a good guy, we were still getting used to his taking our friend's place. Van Cummings made it more palatable by playing most of Danny O'Keefe's classic *Breezy Stories,* through a cable from his iPhone. Van had introduced the record to Skylar, and it had become one of his favorites. As "Portrait in Black Velvet" came forward, all of us listened with contemplation and regret.

We arrived on set and I received my sides. First scene up was in a bar that catered to females (INT: DOLLY DAGGER'S, DOWNTOWN—NIGHT) and had Meaghan O'Toole (as Mackenzie Hart) interviewing a "friend" of the victim who'd been murdered by the shoe fetishist. The network liked the idea of setting the scene in a gay bar where the women were attractive and could be shown in provocative outfits ("lipstick lesbians," it said, so artfully, in the script). At the same time, the suits were keenly aware that they had to portray the culture with sensitivity and correctness, if only because that was the way the country's winds were blowing.

Meaghan arrived on set wearing an outfit that was unusually feminine for her, probably because she wanted to avoid any suggestion that she herself was butch in any way. The truth was, no one knew or cared about her sexual proclivities. Most of us assumed she abstained, which had earned her many colorful nicknames—Corncob, Sahara, and the like. Or, as our rigging gaffer so indelicately put it, "That woman has cobwebs in her snatch."

Bar scenes required many extras, props, fake beer and wine, fake ice, and fake cigarettes, and they created matching issues with crossings and background. We were also shooting day-for-night. Everyone was working very hard. The scene was rehearsed, blocked, lit, and slated. We rolled the first take.

"More shmoke!" shouted Eagle to the effects guy, whose sole job was to work the smoke machine and blow it into the room. Scandi DPs loved smoke for some reason, and in the monitor the shot looked like a scene from *Backdraft* or something out of an Adrian Lyne film. But bars did get smoky, and the look of the master could be corrected in post.

I was more concerned with the acting and the tone of the scene. The day player cast as the "friend" was very good, too good in fact for Meaghan, who didn't care to be upstaged. Meaghan was very clever, and she turned her head in profile, even when she was supposed to be looking directly at her fellow actress, so that her face would be visible in every shot, thereby making herself the focal point of the scene, something we would not be able to fix in the editing room.

Lomax caught it and said to me, "Should we say something?"

"Let it go. Just get a couple of clean close-ups on the friend."

I didn't have it in me that day to pick a fight.

During lunch, served in the auditorium of a Masonic temple near set, Barry approached me at my table and asked if he could see me outside. Beside me was Kenny, who ate his fried chicken and pretended not to hear our conversation. I followed Barry out to the street, to a blind corner where he handed me a plain brown envelope.

"There's your money," he said. "My nephew coughed it up. Too late, but still."

"Forget about this," I said. "And thanks."

Barry said, "Right."

Indeed, neither he nor Kenny mentioned the incident at the house again.

*   *   *

An office PA came to set with a large FedEx envelope at my request late in the afternoon. I went to my trailer and wrote a note to Skylar's connect in California, telling him that this took care of the debt and that his business with Skylar was concluded. I added that I would consider any further contact from him or any of his agents a breach of etiquette, and if they did so, I would contact the law. I put the money in the envelope, used the Los Angeles address that Laura Flanagan had given me, and sent the package back to the office with the PA, with instructions to overnight it immediately.

Walking back to set, I saw Laura, sitting on the steps of the costume trailer, smoking a Marlboro. She pitched the smoke aside and stood to meet me as I approached.

"Victor."

"Hey."

"I'm glad I caught you. I'm leaving in a few days."

"Where you headed?"

"I took a job up in Brooklyn. A friend hooked me up. It's an HBO show; they shoot mostly at the Steiner Studios."

"A period thing, right?"

"Yeah, it's set in the twenties."

"That'll be fun for you. Creative. With the costumes, and all."

"I hope so. I should get out of here, don't you think?"

"It's best."

Laura slipped off her aviators and placed them atop her

head, so she could look me in the eyes. "Thank you for putting me up in the hotel, Vic. And for everything. You've been a good friend."

"Don't forget me on your rise to the top."

She laughed and hugged me spontaneously, then broke away. "Don't forget *me.*"

"I better get back," I said.

"See you."

She had a rough road ahead of her. The series she was going to was a meat grinder, eight months of sixteen-hour days. She was on the frail side, not a fighter, and quiet. In our business that was seen as a weakness.

I walked back to set.

The next day we shot out by a marina on the lake, which was wide as a bay, where in our story the father of one of our young police officers owned a shrimp boat. There were several scenes set on the boat in this script, and the plan was to knock them all out in one day. It was pleasant to work outside, and I was enjoying it, but halfway to lunch I got a call from Ellen on my cell, asking me to return to the writers' offices. Detective Joe Gittens wanted to speak with me in person.

Gittens was waiting for me in my office. He was on my couch, his legs spread wide, wearing a nice brown suit with thin chalk stripes. A fedora with a red-and-gold feather in the band was beside him.

"You look clean today," I said, shaking his hand before I took a seat behind my desk.

"I got all gussied up for you."

"Where's your partner? Getting a facial?"

"Dennis is just a little aggressive, is all. I left him in the office today."

"So what'd I do now?"

"Your tip paid off, Ohanion."

"Oh?"

"Couldn't get a search warrant on Wayne and Cody's house, so we waited for them to leave their place of residence. They were driving that Mexican-looking Toyota you described. 'Bout a mile from their place, they stopped at a red light…"

"Let me guess. The front tires of the Supra were over the white line of the intersection."

"How'd you know?"

"Police officers in my hometown used to pull kids up for that all the time. Then they'd toss the car."

Gittens snapped his fingers theatrically. "That's exactly what we did!"

"And you found what?"

"Marijuana and paraphernalia, of course. And, oh yeah, a gun."

"A revolver, I bet."

"S&W thirty-eight."

"You ran tests?"

"Gonna take a couple of days to do the ballistic fingerprinting. That's where we match the striations on the slugs to the barrel of the gun it came from."

"I know the process."

"Course you do. You're a crime writer."

"I'm betting it's a match."

"We'll see. But here's the thing. We already struck gold."

OHANION leans forward in anticipation.

> OHANION
>
> How's that?

> GITTENS
>
> The revolver had shaved numbers. And
> our boy Wayne, Drown's his last name,
> has prior convictions. Multiple priors, in
> fact. How would you put it in one of your
> scripts?

> OHANION
>
> He had a rap sheet as long as my arm.

> GITTENS
>
> Right. That's an automatic jolt. Wayne's
> going away for five years.

> OHANION
>
> And Cody?

> GITTENS
>
> Him, too. They did everything in pairs.
> Even their felonies. Now, if we do get a
> match on that weapon, they'll both be
> lookin at long time.

OHANION

You got lucky.

GITTENS

Routine traffic stop, came up gold. It happens.

OHANION

I guess you won't be needing any further assistance from me.

GITTENS

No, I don't think so.

OHANION

How'd Wayne and Cody take it?

GITTENS

Cody made some racially insensitive re-marks to me at the time of his arrest. It hurt my feelings, somewhat. Funny, all those Aryan Nations tattoos he's got, and he talks like a brother. I really think those two are a couple of confused indi-viduals.

OHANION

They probably had a disadvantaged up-bringing.

GITTENS
I feel for 'em. I do.

GITTENS stands, puts on his hat, shifts his shoulders in
the jacket of his suit.

GITTENS
(continued)
What do you think? Would you give me
a cameo? My wife thinks I look like
Richard Roundtree.

OHANION
Is your wife blind?

GITTENS
Funny.

OHANION
Maybe we can work you in.

GITTENS
Have your people get in touch with my
people. Hear?

GITTENS leaves the office.

ON OHANION.

A week later, Bruce Kaplan called me into his office. He and Ellen had been talking quietly, grimly all that morning. I'd been around long enough to know what was coming, and I wasn't surprised.

Behind his closed door, I sat before Bruce's desk. Memorabilia of his past successes and near successes crowded the room. He'd drawn the blinds, as a doctor does when he's about to give a patient bad news. Bruce looked heavy and tired.

"We've been cancelled, Victor. I'm sorry."

"It's nobody's fault. We did our best."

"The numbers weren't there. They're dropping in fact, week to week. The suits considered reconfiguring the cast, but ultimately they felt it best to pull the plug and move on."

"It's just business."

"We'll tell the crew after we wrap. I don't like to do that, but people will jump ship. There's only two weeks left on the shoot, and Ellen and I want to finish strong and under budget. It's a point of pride with us."

"The crew will find work. They always do."

"As will you," said Bruce, and he picked up my script for 114 off his desk. "This is really good. Did I tell you?"

"Yes, you did. Thank you."

Bruce opened the script to a page he had dog-eared. "*'My man got his self snipped.'* Snipped. Where did that come from?"

"It means murdered."

"And, *'he rotted him.'* That's some authentic shit."

"I've been keeping my ear to the street."

"It shows. I'm going to submit this one for a WGA award."

"Great," I said, with little enthusiasm.

"You'll be fine, Vic."

My agent had been fielding offers as of late. I'd find work, if I wanted it. Hundreds of cable channels, original content, streaming…there was always work for a whore like me.

"I don't have to tell you," said Bruce, "you need to keep the cancellation a secret."

"I understand," I said.

Soon as I left his office, I phoned Annette and told her that she needed to start looking for a new job.

The day after the wrap party, we had a service for Skylar Branson in the city's largest park. We met around a weeping cherry tree the production had planted in his name. His parents had flown back in from Galveston, and there was a woman in vestments who said some vague, nondenominational words about Skylar's spirit, and many crew members, some of whom I'd see on other productions, some I'd never see again. Annette was there, looking stylish in black with a touch of flair, and Laura, who'd returned for the day from Brooklyn and would leave that afternoon. Some local musicians, neo-folkies Skylar hung with, played a couple of traditional songs on acoustic instruments, and then the ceremony broke up. That's what's left of you, I thought. A tree.

I walked back to my rental car with Jerome Hilts, our dolly grip, who was wearing a clean polo shirt and cargo shorts for the occasion.

"What do you think, Victor? What's it all mean?"

"If I knew that, I wouldn't be writing television scripts. I'd be writing my manifesto."

"Nobody's gonna remember us."

"You're probably right."

"But we gotta keep working. I'm headed up to Baltimore, for a Netflix show. You?"

"Raleigh. I'll be running the writers' room for a Cinemax thing."

I was due there in a week. I hadn't even read the pilot. Something about a hit man in Nixon-era America. I would read the script and the bible on the flight back to Delaware, where I planned to visit my mother. I hadn't seen her for a long while.

"We're the circus," said Jerome. "We just pull up our tents and move from town to town."

"That's right." I squinted bitterly against the sun. "We've got sawdust in our veins."

The next morning, I stood outside my hotel and helped Annette load the last of her trunks into her Grand Cherokee. She was headed back to her home in Wilmington, North Carolina, where she and her husband had bought a house just before his death. But she would only be there for a few days.

"I guess that's it," she said, as she closed the hatchback and brushed an errant strand of hair away from her face. We'd been up all night making love, and still, she looked lovely. I ran my hand down her bare arm.

"You don't have to do this," I said.

"I took a job, Victor."

"In Hawaii. You might as well be going to China. I could get you on this thing I'm doing in Raleigh. I could talk to the EP."

"We went over this many times last night. *I took the job.* We'll see each other again."

"*When?*"

Annette put her hand behind my neck, pulled me into her, and kissed my mouth.

                    ANNETTE
          I love you, Victor.

                    OHANION
          I love *you.*

                    ANNETTE
          Don't be sad. Think of how lucky we
          were to have found each other.

                    OHANION
          I don't want you to leave me. How can
          you? You always said we were perfect.

                    ANNETTE
          Then we'll leave it perfect.

ANNETTE turns, gets into her Cherokee, and drives away.

ON OHANION, alone.

FADE OUT

ACKNOWLEDGMENTS

Many thanks to my longtime editor, Reagan Arthur, of Little, Brown, and my literary agent, Sloan Harris, of ICM. Thanks go out as well to James Grady, Otto Penzler, Johnny Temple, Dennis McMillan, and John Harvey, who were the original editors of several of these stories. This collection is dedicated to Charles C. Mish and Estelle Petrulakis. Charles Mish taught a class in crime fiction, which I took as an undergraduate at the University of Maryland in 1979. He turned me on to novels and convinced me that all good writing, regardless of subject, has worth. It is not an exaggeration to say that Mr. Mish changed the course of my life. Estelle Petrulakis taught Sunday school with my mother at St. Sophia Greek Orthodox Cathedral for more than twenty-five years and was an elementary school teacher in some of D.C.'s most impoverished neighborhoods. Mrs. Petrulakis gave me books throughout my childhood and always encouraged me to reach for something greater than I thought I could achieve. There is usually one teacher who makes a difference in a person's life. I had two.

ABOUT THE AUTHOR

George Pelecanos is the bestselling author of nineteen novels set in and around Washington, D.C. He is also an independent film producer, and a producer and Emmy-nominated writer on the HBO series *The Wire* and *Treme*. He lives in Maryland.